BEST FRIENDS

RUBY JEAN JENSEN

Published by Gayle J. Foster

CONTENTS

The weapon began to slip from my grasp, pulled away by the rushing flow of stormwater. With a gasp and a sudden burst of inspiration, I extended my senses—like I'd done on the Federation battlecruiser, and reached beyond the tips of my fingers to sever the tree root holding the weapon.

"Aha!" I pulled my weapon out of the water and held it aloft like a trophy. "I knew it!"

Staring up, I saw how a strand of nanobots had extended from i*nside* my cybernetic hand to brace the gun's barrel.

"Well, that's not what I expected."

Apparently, some of those nanobots on the battlecruiser had stowed away in my alien hardware. I loosened the strands and quickly stowed the weapon in a pocket of my jacket. Now that I was paying attention, I could feel the nanobots there, hiding just below the surface of my skin, lying around the metal bones of my cybernetic hand in a pocket that seemed to be made to contain them.

I waded up stairs cut into the sloped embankment to high ground and caught my breath. My mind raced to make sense of this discovery.

The presence of the nanobots no longer frightened me, but I wanted to see how much control I had over them.

I pulled my hand out and held my hand open, palm up. Picturing three elephants in my mind, I watched the nanobots form the creatures. I made them march around my hand in circles. I had them raise their trunks and trumpet. Releasing the image caused the shapes to splash down on my palm and reabsorb into my skin.

This demanded further exploration. For now, I was happy to have exerted control over my new ability.

Grinning and soaking wet, I tromped back to my apart-

NIGHT WHISPERS

"Barry. Barry."

"Barry, come play with us."

Barry woke abruptly. He threw his blanket back and rolled off the bed. The floor was cool beneath his bare feet. It made sounds in the dark. Splat, splat, splat.

"Hurry, hurry, Barry."

He had to be quiet, or his daddy would hear him. His daddy wouldn't want him to go outside at night.

Barry opened the door and went out onto the porch. He started running, into the forest toward the arrow of light, and Reid.

"Barry. Barry. Come on, Barry. Come help us."

Help us? What were they doing? Barry had thought they were going to play, but instead they were going toward the car.

Juno made a great bound toward the car, and the man who stood there.

No, no, no. Barry's heart cried out against the fear that was growing in him.

"We won't be your friends anymore if you won't play.

If you don't play with us, we'll kill you . . ."

First printing: November 1985 in the United States of America

Published by: Gayle J. Foster

Carrollton, Texas

Library of Congress Control Number: 2020902034

Cover art by: SelfPubBookCovers.com/ ANMDesigns

❀ Created with Vellum

PROLOGUE

THE CHILD TWITCHED in his sleep, his arms and legs tensed and began jerking spasmodically. His eyes, behind half-closed lids, rolled in terror.

Barry was dreaming, and the dream was becoming larger than himself, just as all the people in his world were larger. The woman in his dream had a face that bent toward him, and the face was becoming frighteningly familiar, with fat cheeks and a big nose and a mouth that was spread in a horrible grin. She pushed him into the corner by the mere power of her presence, and he cowered, growing smaller and smaller, shrinking inside his clothes. Then suddenly the clothes were gone, and her hands were larger than the room behind her, from which the walls came closing in, and the hands reached for him, and he was helpless and vulnerable and trembling with his fear.

He woke shaking, his cry for help never leaving his throat.

In the dark bedroom he began to slowly make out familiar objects. His dresser. His desk, with the bookends and the books on top of it. The white frames of pictures on the wall. The shelves with the books and the stuffed animals and toys.

There was no one else in the room. He could see by the faint light coming in the window that his door was closed.

He was sitting up in bed, his arms stiffened at his sides, his fists pressed into the mattress.

His eyes flicked over the familiar outlines of his room with horror remaining.

Aloud he said, "Juno. Reid," his breath gasping out the calls softly, desperately.

They appeared instantly. Juno on the floor with his pointed muzzle sticking up in a friendly greeting, his sharp ears sharper than ever, his long tail that was like a monkey's tail curling in tight loops behind him, and his whiskers that were like cat's whiskers twitching and testing the air. And by his side stood Reid, tall and strong, but with a face almost exactly like Barry's, most of the time, though sometimes it changed and became sharper, like Juno's.

Juno and Reid.

Reid and Juno.

Strong, oh so strong, and so fast and so clever they could do anything.

Barry's best friends. He had drawn them in his book, made them up on paper, with his pencil.

Barry looked up at Reid's face, into the blue eyes that knew everything and understood all that trembled in Barry's heart.

Barry thought of the dream, of Miss Beatrice, of her coming down upon him, so helpless in his corner.

Reid nodded. A smile lighted his face, just as the moon outside lighted the dark places of the earth, and with a salute he was gone, Juno gliding at his side.

They went through the wall, leaving behind only a golden flow of their strength.

Barry lay back upon the bed and closed his eyes.

THE WOMAN SAT AT HER DESK GOING THROUGH THE RECEIPTS. HER nursery school had made good money this past year, with the extra money garnered from the films and other secret affairs adding cash to the box in her safe. But where would she be next year?

She had a trial coming up that she had to fight, and even though she wasn't afraid she'd lose—for where, exactly, was all their evidence? Not many people would believe all those wild stories of those imaginative little kids. And most of the kids removed from having to talk about it at all left her pretty well assured that she wouldn't go to jail. Still, it would take her money. All her so-called legal money. And the other money would have to be hidden again, and again, probably.

She stirred in her chair, and looked at the clock. Past one. The night was growing quieter, the traffic gone now.

She got up and stretched her arms over her head, and turned. And caught a glimpse of movement just beyond the door to the hallway. Her heart leaped.

She lived alone, and had since the death of her mother three years ago. Her doors were bolted; and her windows locked. The house had been quiet for hours. If anyone had broken in she would have heard.

She held her breath and listened. After a few moments she went toward the hallway. Again the shadow, darting just out of sight. But this time a bare glimpse showed her it was low, long-bodied, dark. An impression, nothing more. But she drew back sharply.

An animal had gotten into her house! But how? And what?

A rat?

Oh God.

No way was she going to put up with a rat in her house.

With determined strides she took out into the hall, her trepidation of a few minutes earlier gone beneath her intention of ridding her house of one large rat. The hallway was clean and bare, with only the telephone table midway between the front door and the door to the bedrooms. There was no rat, and no place to hide if there had been one. It had escaped into another part of the house, no doubt.

She went into the short hall to the kitchen, a square hall from which doors led also to the dining room and the utility room. Both doors were shut, but the darkened kitchen, ahead of her, had a swinging door that was still moving.

She stopped, momentarily taken aback. Was the rat large enough to push through that door?

No matter. It was running from her, which meant it was afraid of her. It was only a few more feet to the kitchen drawer that held her household tools, the screwdriver, the pliers, the screws and nails and nuts and bolts that were occasionally needed, and the hammer.

She caught hold of the door on its inward swing, and held it, peering ahead into the shadowed kitchen. A street light shone in the west side, laying streaks of light among the shadows, illuminating only faintly.

She moved ahead, and caught a reflection of her face in a mirror that hung over the antique wash basin by the back door. Her heart thudded at sight of the bulbous nose and large cheeks, then she realized it was her own image. She let out a long, disgusted sigh.

Why was she so nervous? One rat, that's all it was. But come to think of it, where did the rat get in? There were no holes in her house . . . unless the plumber had left a hole behind the washing machine when he fixed the drain.

Of course, he must have.

That was the trouble with people these days. You couldn't depend on them for anything at all.

But then, she considered, the door to the utility room was closed, had been closed all day, and remained closed at all times. Except when she was carrying dirty clothes in, and clean clothes out.

Then it must have escaped when her arms were full of laundry. It must have run along beside her feet, darting swiftly as it had done in the hallway. She shuddered. Just knowing it had been there so near her was too much.

She reached around the edge of the doorway and felt for the light switch. It clicked softly, and the overhead light dispelled all the shadows in the room. No rat here. Yet it had been here, for it left the door swinging.

She crossed the room to the outer edge of the kitchen cabinet, her eyes searching back over her shoulders, first right, then left, and peering at the swinging door that now stood still.

She opened the drawer and took out the carpenter's claw hammer. She had killed mice with this hammer a few times, but never rats. She had killed a cat once with it, a dirty cat that came to her back door meowing for something. Food probably. Cats were beggars, notorious beggars. She had tossed its limp body into the garbage can, smiling. Let the alley cats and stray dogs discover *that*.

For one moment she took her eye off the room behind her, off the door to the rest of the house. And when she looked again the door was standing open, pulled back into the hall and held there by something.

She felt the skin on her cheeks pull. For a moment she didn't move, or breathe. Her hand held the hammer in a death grip.

Then she saw something on the floor of the hall.

It lay across the hall like a snake, slightly curled. As she stared it moved, as though writhing, slowly, back and forth.

She swallowed, then she cried out.

"What is it? Who's there?"

The door was suddenly released, and it swung into the kitchen and back again, slowly coming to rest in its closed position.

No rat . . . something else. *She had to get out of the house.*

She whirled, reaching out for the exterior door, and jerked back with a cry.

A tall young boy stood against the door smiling at her. He had a beautiful face with heaven-blue eyes and long, thick lashes. His skin was as soft and perfect as a baby's, and his blond hair looked like pale silk strands curling slightly, coming to rest on one side of his forehead. She didn't know him, and yet he looked familiar.

Barry Frederick!

An older brother of Barry Frederick?

"What do you want here?" she demanded. "Get out of my house! How did you get in my house? *Now you get out.* I'm going to call the police." She raised the hammer, poised to strike him should he move toward her. Her hand tightened on the hard rubber cap on the handle.

"You're not going to get by with this, you know — "

The smiling boy disappeared. All in an instant he was there and gone, and she stood blinking stupidly at the bald interior of the kitchen door.

She turned, slowly, looking around the kitchen. He had gone. How could he move so fast? He had to have gone on into the front of the house, because she was positive he had not opened the kitchen door.

She looked over her shoulder at the bolt on the door. It was still in place.

The police. She would call the police. Let them come and take care of her for a change, instead of harassing her.

She looked at the distance to the door to the hall, and calculated the distance on to the telephone. Well, what difference did it make? She'd have to go there anyway unless she—

There was a sudden, sharp pain in the back of her leg, and she stumbled to one side and looked down. A long-bodied pointed-nosed animal stood looking up at her, its prehensile tail slowly moving on the floor behind it, winding, unwinding. Baring its teeth it began stalking her, bright little eyes as steady as the eyes of a reptile.

"My Gott, my Gott," she cried, backing away, bending at her thick waist, swinging at its head with the hammer. It swished through the air, back and forth, back and forth, holding at bay the unidentifiable animal.

She backed into the corner, swinging the hammer in front of her.

"You come back here, you juvenile delinquent! Wherever you are, you come back here, and take your mad animal off me! Come back here, I say."

The animal leaped, springing easily up at her face by using its tail against the floor, and she knew she hadn't kept it at bay with her hammer. She put her hands up, and just before they covered her eyes, she saw the boy again.

He came through the wall, smiling, smiling.

Her heart exploded, rushing blood ferociously into her brain, draining it away through broken arteries.

As she sank to the floor she saw that she was alone in her house, after all.

CHAPTER 1

"Mister Frederick."

Ramon stood up, adjusted his jacket, ran his hand down over his tie. The nurse stood in the doorway smiling, waiting. She was motherly plump, dark-haired, round cheeked, pleasant and safe looking; but so had been Beatrice of Beatrice's Nursery School.

He shouldn't do this, he thought, censuring himself. He must not compare every woman he looked at now with the woman who might have molested and horribly abused his son.

Somewhere back in the rooms behind the nurse Barry had spent the past hour going through whatever kind of rituals and tests psychologists and psychiatrists put a three year old through in order to learn the measure of his mental trauma to incidents that were only guessed at. It had been one of the longest hours Ramon had ever waited in his life. Part of him wanted to go in and watch every movement of the strangers with his little son, and another part just wanted to take the kid and run.

"Come this way please," the smiling nurse said. "Doctor Coleman is ready to see you."

"Is Barry—my son—?"

"He's in the playroom right now. He'll wait for you there."

She led the way down a corridor from which dark doors were closed, turned a corner into another corridor and went to the room at the end. Still smiling, she held the door until Ramon had passed through, then she closed it softly behind him.

A tall, thin man came around the end of a large desk and shook Ramon's hand.

"Mr. Frederick, I'm Doctor Coleman. Please be seated."

"Thank you." Ramon sat ill-at-ease on a straight chair in front of the desk, choosing it over a deep, brown leather armchair. But when he sat down he found there was no place to put his hands. He gave the doctor a one-sided grin. "I'm not usually this nervous."

"I understand. It would be hoped that what the parents go through in cases like this is worse than what their children suffer, but of course there's no real way to know. The individual reacts in different ways, even though some things seem quite predictable."

"Cases like this? I thought our problem was unique."

"Everyone thinks that. That's why our group therapy is so successful, for the parents especially. You don't feel so alone." Doctor Coleman leaned back in his chair. It squeaked a small three-note tune as he rocked. "We can't say for certain if there will be, or is, any deep damage in Barry's case. It's impossible to tell at this time. With a child the age of your son, we hope there are no permanent scars. Don't let me alarm you, Mr. Frederick. He does not seem unduly traumatized. But he may be withholding. I would prefer to leave him alone for the summer, rather than try to dig too deeply into his thoughts. He does seem slightly wary, distrustful. Especially of women. He doesn't talk much, and could well be holding something in. But let him have a good, safe summer, in an environmental change, if possible. Does he have grandparents he can visit? On a farm, perhaps?"

"No. He has my father, but he's still in the service and is stationed in Germany. His mother's parents both died fairly young. And, as you probably know, his mother is dead."

Doctor Coleman glanced down at the open file on his desk. "Yes. That's too bad. He has a sister and a brother?"

"Yes, Becky is thirteen, and David is eleven."

"Is there a mother figure in his life?"

"Not really. We have a housekeeper who comes for a few hours each day. She's been good, but I can't say she's a mother figure. She's only been with us since Marlene died, and Barry has spent his days since he was two and a half in the Beatrice Nursery where, obviously, I thought he was safe."

"Yes, of course."

"I read in the paper this morning that the woman died a few days ago."

"Yes, I read of it too. A stroke, I believe. It does eliminate any chance of Barry being called for her trial, and questioned."

"I wouldn't have allowed it."

"Is there any way you can get him out of town for the summer? Away from home, from all the familiar sights and associations?"

"If I had someone to take care of him, someone I trust, I could send my kids up to the lodge this summer. My sister and I inherited it from our mother's people. It's on the lake at Big Bear."

"That sounds ideal."

"I could go up on weekends, but I can't afford to leave my job for the summer."

"Not many of us can, Mr. Frederick. Let me see . . ."

The doctor rocked a moment, looking at the wall above Ramon's head.

"Let me see . . . I know a young woman who might work out very well for you. Her name is Shannon Bernard, and she's gone back to school after losing her husband and two-year old son in a car accident last year. She isn't well off, she has to take a summer job, and she was a patient after losing her husband and child, so I can recommend her highly." Doctor Coleman sat forward in his chair and rested his elbows on the desk, a possible sign of dismissal. "I'll call her this evening. Let him have a happy, carefree summer, and bring him back to see us in the fall. I think we'll have a different boy by that time."

Ramon edged forward on his chair, preparing to leave.

"Just how long has Barry's mother been dead, Mr. Frederick?" Doctor Coleman asked, picking up a pen on his desk and beginning to make notations on the open file in front of him.

"Since three days after his birth. It was one of those things that is never supposed to happen anymore. She hemorrhaged, and they couldn't stop it or give her enough transfusions to keep her alive."

"That's too bad."

"Yes. My older children were hit hard by her death. They were ten and eight then."

"But they've adjusted well?"

"They seem to be happy kids now."

"How did you handle the care for the baby? Did you have a permanent sitter?"

"Not really. For his first two years I took him to a babysitting service where different women worked. Of course there was Mrs. Ashley, our housekeeper, but she only came in afternoons, five days a week. Then her husband was ill for several months before he died, and she just came to clean three afternoons a week during that time. She's back five days a week now, full days, but she doesn't take care of Barry except a few hours now and then."

"Well, if you can get Mrs. Bernard to take Barry to the mountains for the summer, it might be the answer. The close relationship might allow Barry to learn to trust women again."

This time the doctor stood up, and reached across his desk to shake Ramon's hand again. At the door he pointed Ramon in the direction of the playroom.

Ramon followed arrows down a corridor to the playroom at the end. The room was a bright contrast to the browns and beiges of the doctor's office and the front waiting room. Three walls of the playroom were papered in a yellow nursery rhyme print, with wood hangings depicting the cow jumping over the moon, the three little pigs and a wolf with a sweet smile on his comical face. In this world even the wolves were kind. The evils lay in the real world, with devils lurking in the minds and lives of the disturbed children who played here.

There were four kids in the room, ranging in age from a toddler at her mother's knees to a boy about eight years old. The boy and a girl were playing in the center of the room at a small table where they were putting a wooden puzzle together. Barry sat apart from all of them, watching in silence.

Ramon stood for a moment looking at his son. Beautiful, fair-haired Barry, a little tall and slender for his age, his pale-skinned face a mask that hid whatever he felt. Ramon himself had never felt so helpless as when he looked at this little boy. He had been reduced from a capable, successful man who held together a motherless family, a man who managed a department of hundreds of people in his job, to—whatever the hell he was now. He knew his job well enough that it still ran smoothly, and his relationship with his kids hadn't seemed to change, yet he felt as though part of his life had been shattered, that it was no longer under his control. He had thought he had everything under control, and then with no warning the nursery school where he had felt Barry was safe was closed down. In the newspaper he learned why. Several parents had been complaining, and finally the proof was irrefutable. Children there were being exploited sexually. Abused. Intimidated. Threatened. Terrified.

At first his main hope was that Barry had been one of the lucky ones, that somehow the woman accused had allowed him to come and go without harming him. Barry was, he told himself, just a naturally quiet child, having gotten more quiet because he was getting older.

But this trip to the psychiatrist dispelled that hope. Damage had been done to his child.

Anger boiled within him, and released a sudden sense of satisfaction that the woman was dead; followed by a feeling of guilt for having wished death on another person. Fighting for equal time was the wish that she could have been tried and sentenced.

If his own feelings were so mixed, what were Barry's? And how should he be treated now? The psychologist, whom he had seen for a few minutes after he had first arrived at the mental health clinic, had assured him that Barry would be more at ease if he were treated just as always by his father and siblings.

Ramon drew a long breath, and managed a smile.

Barry looked up and saw him, but the expression on his face hardly changed.

Where was the little boy who had come running to meet him?

He stooped to pick up Barry, then changed his mind and took his hand instead.

"Okay, son, we can go home now."

Barry said nothing. Like a meek puppy, he allowed his father to lead him from the playroom.

Ramon sent forth a quick and urgent prayer: send someone good, Lord, to take care of my son, to help rebuild his faith in people.

SHANNON'S FIRST, SECOND, AND THIRD THOUGHTS, AFTER HEARING about the Frederick case, was to say no. No, I can't possibly. If Kelly had lived, he would now be three. The same age as the Frederick child, Barry.

Any other job would be better, she thought as she looked at the telephone number she had written down on her note pad. Waitressing. Especially cocktail waitressing, which was said to pay extremely well in tips. But she wasn't the cocktail waitress type, which had to have a better sense of humor than she had, and a liking for night in place of day. Or so, at least, it seemed to her. She didn't like bars or clubs even for entertainment.

Still, it wouldn't hurt to talk to Ramon Frederick. And, her interest in school was turning toward child psychology. The poor little tykes didn't stand much of a chance unless they were blessed with good people around them.

She found herself dialing.

After the fourth ring a male voice answered. It was, she assumed, the father, Ramon. Instructions, which were also written on her note pad, said to call after six.

"Mr. Frederick? This is Shannon Bernard. I received a call from Doctor Coleman's office that you wanted someone dependable to stay with your three-year old son, Barry, for the summer. If you haven't found someone, I'd like to talk to you about it."

"Thank you for calling, Mrs. Bernard. I haven't found anyone. When would you . . . could you come over to my house?"

"Yes. I'd like to meet Barry if I could."

"Would this evening be convenient?"

She asked for directions, and received them. Although they lived in separate suburbs, they were joined. She would be able to make the drive in fifteen or twenty minutes.

The evening air was cool, and she drove slowly, with her windows open. Her car was small and clunky, now six years old, but she had faith it would last her another year or two when school might be behind her, and a financially better future at least not so far away.

She drove from her own apartment complex address to an upper middle-class neighborhood. The Frederick house was Spanish stucco, settled back in the rich greenery of a well-landscaped yard. As she drove into the half-moon drive that curved by the double front doors she decided that Frederick was not, at least, as poor as she, and she would probably get paid. She smiled at her private joke, knowing deep down that it had nothing to do with her reluctance to come looking for this job.

The door opened before she reached it, and the man who stepped into view looked even more desperate than she felt. He was wearing a pullover knit shirt on the outside of blue, knee-length shorts. His dark hair was slightly tousled, as though he had been exercising, or running. As she glanced over him she saw him raise a hand and smooth back his hair. Then, with a further nervous gesture, he rubbed his slightly raspy chin, and reached down to tug at his shirt. "Mrs. Bernard?"

"Yes."

The man put out his hand, then drew it back and wiped its palm on his shorts before he extended it again. His grip was almost painfully strong on her small and supple hand.

"I was out playing a game of basketball with my son. Saw your car enter, and had to run to get here."

"You were playing ball with—?"

"Oh, not Barry. He's only three. My older son, David. I have a girl, Becky, who's thirteen, and a son eleven. That's David. Won't you come in?"

They entered a carpeted hallway, and went on into a den on the right.

"You'll want to meet Barry and the kids. Sit down, please, and I'll go get them. If you think you can stand them for the summer, we'll talk later."

Shannon watched him go. She sat on the end of a sofa and looked around at a slightly untidy room that was filled with comfortable chairs, a couple of desks, and books. One of the desks was small, the other large. His and hers? He was a widower, she had been told, but that was all she knew about it.

After a few minutes she heard them coming along the hall, the chatter of a young female voice interspersed at times with a young male voice. It was not the voice of a three-year old. He was silent.

The girl entered the room first, her light brown eyes alive with curiosity. She was slightly over five feet tall, and beginning to mature. Her small breasts poked with plant-like aggressiveness into the soft jersey of her bikini top. She had been swimming, and her hair hung in rich dark strands over her shoulders. The boy, David, was a couple of inches shorter, with darker eyes, and hair streaked by the sun. Both of them had pretty faces, features even and attractive, small noses, full lips.

The little boy came behind them, led by his father. He stared in round-eyed timidity at Shannon. Ramon bent slightly over him, one hand at his back urging him forward. The boy stood unyielding, staring at Shannon.

"Kids, Becky, David, Barry, this is Mrs. Bernard. Barry, would you like to shake hands with Mrs. Bernard?"

"No," Barry said firmly.

He was a fairer child than his brother and sister, but it might have been his age, the remnants of babyhood in his hair and his skin and eyes. Shannon's fear of him, that something about him would remind her too sharply of her own dead Kelly, left her. Kelly had been a baby yet, and this child was a little boy. In appearance he had almost left babyhood behind.

Instinct warned Shannon against putting her hand out to him. Instead, she shook hands with Becky and David.

David asked, "Are you going up to Big Bear with us for the summer?"

Shannon smiled at him, liking instantly this bright-eyed friendly boy. "I don't know yet. Would you like me to?"

"Oh yes," Becky said, as David nodded.

"If you don't," David said, "we might not get to go, except for Dad's vacation and the weekends. If you go, we can stay all summer. And it's— "

"Really great up there," Becky said, finishing his sentence as though impatience with his slower speech had gotten to her. David kept smiling, without so much as a glance at Becky, as though he were used to having his sentences finished.

"Have you ever been there?" David asked.

"Yes, a few times."

"Don't you just love it?" Becky asked. "I could live there year round."

"The snow would be great, too," David said. "We could sled and ski."

Becky added, "Sometimes. But Dad says we have to stay down here," she wrinkled her nose and cast a sideways glance up at him, "because of his job, and our house. Of course we could get rid of the house, but his job is here. We can't afford to move permanently."

"Not yet," David said, "but we might spend more time there. We own a—"

"Lodge," said Becky. "Along with our Aunt Lynn. Dad and Aunt Lynn inherited it when our grandma died." For the first time the light and smiles left the faces of both older children.

From the corner of her eye, Shannon caught a glimpse of a long shadow moving just inside the door, yet Ramon Frederick and his three children, all standing, were stationary.

She glanced over to the open door, but no one else had entered. The shadow was gone.

Barry, still standing next to his father, still staring at her, looked somehow different from her first impression of him. In his solemnity and silence, he had drifted to the back of her mind, the livelier children becoming dominant, and yet now, though he stood halfway back between them and the door, there was something about him that drew Shannon's attention.

She saw the shadow on the floor behind him, thrown by the table lamps on the desk and at the end of the couch in the growing dusk of the room. The shadow there was almost as long as the shadow of his father, and it wavered slightly, as though the child moved when he did not.

A trick of the light, Shannon told herself.

"Would you like me to go with you to Big Bear Lake?" she asked the little boy as gently as she could, refraining a desire to reach toward him.

His gaze faltered. He glanced swiftly at his brother and sister, then he looked over her shoulder. His eyes, coming back to meet hers, held a subtly different light, as though part of his fear of her had in some way melted.

Becky bent over him, her hands on his thin little shoulders. "Of course you would, wouldn't you, Barry?"

The girl looked up smiling at Shannon, volunteer spokesperson for both her brothers. "Of course he would," she said. "He'd like that a lot."

CHAPTER 2

SHANNON DROVE HOME SLOWLY, the heavy traffic of earlier evening gone. Driving helped her to think, to solve a problem an easier way than she sometimes did by walking the floors from wall to wall. She chose back streets, neighborhoods that were quiet, where lights had been turned on in dining rooms and kitchens and the families had gone in to eat. Occasionally she passed a lone biker, still out in the twilight, peddling quickly and easily along.

Her heart was beating faster than normal, adrenalin spurring her on with its warning that danger was near. What kind of danger? She could find no concrete answer to this question, as she frowned into the quickening night and the street lamps that were beginning to glow with their greenish lights. But down deep in her heart a voice was shouting, "I can't take this job! I'd be better off waiting tables this summer."

Was it because of the family? No. It was a nice family, the children friendly and well-adjusted, so it seemed, with the exception of the one for whom she would be responsible. And he was just a little boy, a very little boy, and her heart yielded at the thought of him.

Yet it was the child himself who was holding her back.

She reached her apartment, parked her car and glanced over her shoulder at the dark spots in the roofed area that provided parking areas for dozens more cars and provided hiding places also for an occasional mugger. One of her friends, a woman who lived in a nearby apartment, had been attacked in the garage area just a month ago. The assailant had gotten away with her purse, with all its credit cards and a few dollars cash, leaving her with only her keys, which she'd had in her hand. Instead of going into her own apartment she had come to Shannon's, where Shannon fed her hot tea and tried to calm her down. The police had never found the man, or woman, who had stolen Edie's purse.

Shannon hurried around the corner of the apartment building and reached a lighted flight of steps. Her high heels clicked loudly on the balcony, and Shannon found herself looking behind to see if she were being followed. She had an uneasy feeling of being not alone, and, she realized now, she'd been feeling that way ever since she'd left the Frederick home. It was as though her heart was pounding in fear of whatever followed her, something her five senses were not yet aware of.

She saw with relief that two people were coming along the balcony from the opposite direction. Whether she knew them or not, their presence gave her comfort. She met the first one, a man only vaguely familiar. He nodded and smiled and paused to unlock his door. Shannon went on, and as she drew nearer to the second figure she saw it was Edie. She was carrying something in both arms, a sack of groceries that looked bulky and heavy, and in the other a satchel of books.

"Let me help you," Shannon said, and took the brown sack from Edie's arms.

"You came up from the dark parking lot?" Edie inquired, her short eyebrows raised and making her eyes look more round than normal. She was a small woman, slightly plump, several inches shorter than Shannon. She always wore low heeled shoes, skirts and blouses, and almost no makeup. She worked in a health food store just a few blocks away. "I don't go near that parking lot at night anymore. I've decided that walking will hurt me less."

"You've walked all the way from the market?"

"And the library. But altogether it's just eight blocks, and at least they're brightly lighted. I wonder if it would do any good to talk to the landlord about putting more lights in the parking areas?"

"I don't think it would help. Each stall is already lighted. Hiding places can be found anywhere I guess."

Shannon carried Edie's sack of groceries to the kitchen cabinet. She knew Edie's apartment as well as her own because they were precisely alike, even to the ivory paint on the walls and the gold carpeting. The only differences were in their choice of house plants, for even the furniture was similar. Neither of them had kept anything from their marriages. Edie, divorced three years ago, had simply moved out of their house, taking only her clothes. If, she told Shannon, he wanted another woman, then she didn't want anything he had given her, or they had purchased together. It wasn't worth it. She took her hurt, her pride, and left.

Shannon had been forced to sell all she and James had accumulated in their five-year marriage in order to finance herself toward a life without him. She had needed nothing but a place to stay while she continued an education that had been postponed when she married. From the lovely little house they had bought and lived in she took only the most personal items: picture albums, cards given her on Mother's Day, little presents Kelly and James had chosen for her, and clothes. She had given away all of Kelly's clothes except two items, one for each year of his life. When she left the home she had loved, she carried with her only a set of luggage and one trunk. The next time she moved she would probably have to abandon the trunk and take only what she herself could handle. Since she had lived in this apartment just a year now, she had acquired a geranium and a coleus, both of them forced on her by Edie. "They'll make you feel less lonely," Edie had said, but it had taken a long time before Shannon began to see the plants as living things that responded to tender care. The geranium now was a cheerful red adornment to her kitchen cabinet, placed where it got sufficient sunshine, and the coleus was just as colorful in its way on the window sill behind the couch.

"Won't you stay awhile?" Edie asked. "We can have something to eat and drink, if you'd like."

"I'm not hungry, but . . ." Shannon looked out the door to the narrow balcony. A breeze had risen, and shadows ebbed and receded, probably from one of the trees down in the small park in the center of the apartment complex, but Shannon drew back from it nevertheless, and closed the door. "I'd like to stay awhile, if it won't keep you from eating your dinner." Edie made a vague motion with her hands. "No hurry. I'll put in a TV dinner later, and eat it while I watch the movie on CBS. Would you like to watch it with me?"

"No thanks. I really can't stay that long." She accepted a glass of Coke that Edie handed her, and sat down on the couch. On the window sill behind Edie's couch was an entire indoor garden, ranging from cactus to herbs. Sometimes dust collected among the varying sizes of pots and containers, but it was Edie's dust, and Shannon didn't let it bother her.

"I interviewed for a summer job this afternoon," she told Edie, and sipped her Coke. It stung her lips delightfully. Now that she was here, closed in, and with someone she'd known almost a year, the job didn't look so difficult.

"Oh yeah? Tell me about it," Edie sat down in her favorite chair. In it she could sprawl. Beside it was a table that held her books, her lamp, and the remote control device to her television. From all appearances, Edie was comfortable with her life.

"It's child care, really. They—or rather he, there's only a father—wants someone dependable to stay with his three-year old son this summer. There are two older children, and a housekeeper."

Edie raised her eyebrows. "Can't they take care of him?"

"Apparently not as totally as the father feels is needed. Well, actually, Edie, this little child is one of the children from that notorious nursery school. They don't know how abused he was, if at all. He's somewhat withdrawn."

"Oh, the poor baby." Edie leaned forward, her face twisted in sympathy, her heart feeling as though it were bleeding. Of all regrets in her past life, the major one was that in her nine years of marriage she had not had a baby. Even though Shannon had lost hers in an accident, there were times when Edie felt Shannon was fortunate for having had a child for two years. While she, lonely arms with no promise of fulfillment, dreamed nightly of being a mother.

Shannon was saying, "They have a lodge up in the mountains, and it's there I'm supposed to take the child—Barry is his name. We're to spend three months there, or until school starts. And the father will come up on weekends."

"And you're reluctant? Why, that's a vacation and a half, Shannon! The mountain air, the peace and beauty, and children. I have a feeling you're hesitating. I don't know why."

"You're right, I am hesitating. And I really don't know why either."

Edie settled back into the chair and tried to look at it from Shannon's side. But all she saw was a young woman with long blonde hair who didn't realize how good she looked no matter what she wore, whether it be jeans, suit or an old robe, and whose eyes were still looking at a world that did not hold the ones she had loved so dearly.

"Is it because of Kelly?" she asked softly.

"Yes, I think so. Kelly would have been Barry's age now. It hurts to look at a little boy sometimes."

"But this one needs you."

"Not me, specifically."

"Then who? Just anyone trustworthy, I suppose."

"Well, they do have the housekeeper, who would be there twenty-four hours a day. And the sister, Becky, is thirteen."

"But for some reason you were asked to take the job."

"It was my doctor. The psychiatrist who helped me through the worst of the days after the accident, Doctor Coleman. Ramon Frederick took Barry to his clinic, and Doctor Coleman called me and said he had recommended me."

"Then he must feel it would benefit you too."

"Yes, I guess he does."

"You are going to take it, aren't you? The poor baby needs someone he can trust."

Shannon stared into her Coke. The sharp anxiety she had felt, the feeling that something was behind her, watching her, standing just out of her vision, was gone and replaced now by a dull dread. But the dread was part of her life so much of the time. Dread of facing a new day. Dread of going back again to the lonely apartment that was not and never could be a home.

"Well," Shannon said, "I'm going to spend the afternoons for the next week at the Frederick house getting acquainted. Maybe at the end of that time I'll know for sure whether I can take the job. The child seems shy at this point. The other two were eager to accept me. But . . . we'll see."

Shannon said good night after a few more minutes and went out onto the balcony. The minute Edie's door closed behind her, Shannon felt the anxiety come back. She found herself looking toward the stairs at the end of the balcony, and decided that her nervousness was caused by Edie's experience there. She turned her back to the lurking danger and hurried on toward her own apartment three doors down. Behind the drawn draperies of one apartment she could hear a television, but the apartment next to her own was dark.

She got her keys out of her purse and fumbled nervously at the lock. Someone was coming along the balcony, she felt sure, yet there were no footsteps. The door opened, and she looked over her shoulder and saw the balcony was empty in both directions, and only the shadows played, dancing, pushed by the breeze.

SHANNON DREAMED THAT NIGHT OF KELLY. THEY WERE WALKING along a road that was edged by tall pines, a narrow road that curled through the forest reaching on and on. She felt his hand in hers, warm and small and trusting. She heard his voice chattering away happily. She looked down at him and saw upraised toward her a face that did not belong to her son. It was the face of Barry Frederick.

The shock woke her, and she lay staring into the darkness of her room. A pencil of light made its way between her draperies, and drew its way brightly across the rug, and across her bed, ending at last halfway up the wall. Shannon sat up, aware of the contrasting darkness in her room as never before. She reached for her bedside lamp and turned it on, then she snuggled down into her soft blanket and turned her back to the light.

She slept the rest of the night with her light on.

As she took her shower the next morning she realized she had made a decision. Although she would rather that it was fall again, with school in progress, with books and classes and so much to do she had no time to think, she knew she would take this summer job that Ramon Frederick had offered her. Uneasily she looked forward to the months passing quickly, and releasing her from something she didn't really want.

But why, she asked herself, did the prospect of a summer with Barry Frederick make her so nervous? Was it because she felt he might need more specialized care than she could give him?

With that thought in mind, she called Dr. Coleman's office and asked if she could see him, and explained it was only for information concerning his young patient, Barry Frederick. After a reasonable hold, a nurse told her to come on in, the doctor would see her at eleven-thirty.

After waiting ten minutes, she was ushered in between patients. She hadn't seen the doctor in several months, but it was like meeting someone who was more than a friend. He had extended to her an almost God-like understanding when she had thought she couldn't face life alone, and convinced her that she could.

"I was wondering, Doctor Coleman, why you recommended me to take care of Barry?"

"Students usually have a summer to fill, and you did go back to school, didn't you?"

"Yes, I did."

"I hope that you did agree to spend your summer with Barry?"

"Mr. Frederick and I agreed to a week's trial to see if it would work out. I'm not sure the little boy needs anyone beyond the housekeeper and his brother and sister during the day, and of course his dad is there in the evening."

"But we felt a change in environment is needed for Barry at this time, and the mountains would be ideal. I think it would work out well for you too."

"I'd like to know if there's anything special I should know regarding Barry? I'm not sure I feel qualified to take care of him, certainly not to adding any special therapy."

"Just treat him the way you would your own child, except let him approach you first, physically. Reach out to him, make friends with him, let him know he can trust you. Talk to him, but not about his experiences. He's very reticent about anything to do with the nursery school. In fact, he clams up tightly. We suspect there's a lot of fear, or some kind of strong emotion there. But what we're trying to do is get him to simply put the past behind, forget it, and learn to trust a woman again. I know of no one who is available to spend the summer with him who qualifies more than you. That's why I recommended you."

So it was partly a matter of availability. Shannon felt somewhat better. The doctor knew she had gone back to school, and that her summers were probably a matter of a job here and a job there, whatever she could get. At least there wasn't any special therapy intended, such as trying to fill Kelly's place with another little boy. And taking care of that other little boy didn't involve a lot of complicated adjustments or specialized knowledge on her behalf. Perhaps she was qualified after all.

The doctor walked her to the door with his arm across her shoulder. "Just relax, take some good books along, read, swim, hike, but keep him in sight. Let him do his own thing, but keep an eye on him. Encourage him to like you, but don't push yourself on him. Of course that's superfluous advice. I know you won't. I fully trust you with him, Shannon. Somehow, I saw the two of you together. It seemed a natural. I hope I wasn't wrong."

"I hope so too," Shannon said, and smiled, returning his smile. "I'll do my best."

When she drove away from the clinic complex, out the curving driveway, past the flower gardens and stands of trees, she was able for the first time to see the beauty of the landscaping with a light heart. Suddenly she felt good. The summer could be great, she would see to it personally. Her assignment was an easy one.

The doctor had faith it would work out well, and she had put her faith in the doctor more than a year ago.

As Shannon drove to Barry's house after lunch she wondered what his daily habits and schedules were. Did he take a nap? At one-fifteen in the afternoon he should be asleep, curled on his bed with his teddy bear.

She found him instead in the middle of a sandbox in the back yard. He had a red plastic pail, two plastic shovels, one red and one yellow, the yellow one looking as though it had been chewed by someone's pup. In the sandbox also was a toy dump truck. Barry was busily shoveling sand into the bed of the truck.

"Hello Barry," Shannon said.

He glanced up at her and it seemed to Shannon that his eyes flickered, as though in surprise, or perhaps fear. But whatever emotion lay behind his clear, sparkling eyes was concealed quickly. Without speaking, he pressed a lever on the side of the truck and watched the bed rise slowly and dump its load of sand back into the box.

Becky and David had come dripping out of the swimming pool to stand beside her. The housekeeper, who had shown her into the back yard, stood with her arms folded across her chest, watching.

Becky said, "He doesn't speak sometimes, but he's glad you're here. Did you bring your swim suit along?"

"No, I didn't. If Barry doesn't mind I'd like to sit here on the grass and watch him play for awhile."

"He doesn't mind," Becky said. "But can we bring you a chair from the patio?"

"Thank you, but that's not necessary." Shannon bent forward with her hands on her knees. "Do you mind if I watch you play, Barry?"

Barry's eyes met hers again briefly. After a hesitation he shook his head.

Shannon sat down yogi style, her legs crossed. She felt vaguely uncomfortable as she tried to relax. The two other children returned to their play in the swimming pool, and the housekeeper disappeared back into the house. Barry turned, pushed his truck through the hub-deep sand, and began shoveling on the far side of the ten-by-ten sandbox.

He had effectively put her behind him.

THE FIRST THREE DAYS WERE THE MOST AWKWARD. SHE WAS A SUBJECT of curiosity to the older children, who interrupted their play frequently to come and talk to her; and the housekeeper seemed to feel that refreshments and encouragements were in order at specified times until Shannon had assured her at least twice a day that she was not to be treated as a guest.

Barry, Shannon discovered, did not take naps. After the second day, Shannon gave up trying to talk him into the bedroom. He simply looked at her from his big eyes, as though listening intently, but then he walked away, in a direction opposite to his bedroom.

"He hasn't napped since he was two," Becky offered.

"Sometimes," David added, "he wakes up at two or three o'clock in the morning and comes into my bedroom. I let him sleep with me sometimes, but he kicks a lot, and he turns sideways in the bed."

Shannon tried another tack. "Would you let me read you a story, Barry?"

"All right," he said. "I've got my storybooks in my bedroom."

It was the longest sentence he had spoken to her, and Shannon felt a lift in her heart. At last she had chosen the right approach.

He dropped the ball he was carrying around and ran into the house and along the hall to his bedroom.

Shannon followed him into a bedroom that had almost everything a child could want. Shelves on the wall held stuffed animals, a variety of toys, and dozens of books. Barry climbed onto a stool and reached up, as if he knew precisely what book he wanted. He brought it down and handed it to her.

Shannon saw it was a plain book, about ten by twelve inches, with mostly blank pages. On the blue cover someone had printed in red ink, "Barry's Book." At first Shannon thought all the pages were blank, and then she found, on the beginning pages, the drawings of a child.

Barry stood silently looking up at her, and a glance at his face showed her he waited in anticipation, and she started to ask if he had made the drawings. But then she saw that they were too carefully done, too graphic to be drawn by a three-year old child. Unless that child were unusually talented. She hesitated, and looked more carefully. On page one was a husky boy with muscled arms and large hands. The head was shaped well, but the face was blank. At the bottom of the page was printed in neat capital letters the name "REID." Of course Barry had not done that. Perhaps his father? Or David or Becky?

On page two was an animal. It had a pointed muzzle with long whiskers, a tail that looped over its back like a rope, and slitted black eyes that had a strangely even, evil look. Printed beneath it was the name "JUNO."

Barry still looked up at her, his lips parted, as if he waited, eagerly, for her reaction.

"Barry, these are very good drawings, did you draw them?"

Suddenly he was running out of the room. His steps faded away, quick and muffled in the hall carpet.

Well, she thought, so much for tricking him into a nap.

She stood indecisively in the middle of his room, the book in her hands. She had offered to read to him, and instead of taking down a story book he had chosen this one. Because he wanted her to see his drawings, obviously, but then he refused to talk about them.

She found her attention caught again by the animal named Juno. The uncertain lines of its body indicated that Barry himself had probably done the drawing, but the face was very well done. Shannon shuddered. It seemed a nightmarish creature, too horrible to have come from the imagination of a child so young.

Shannon turned the page and found it filled with circular scribbles. Almost lost among the swirls were bits of faces, eyes, noses, ears, horns, or something curled and sharp that resembled horns. Shannon frowned uneasily. She had a sensation that something was being assembled on that page from the depths of hell itself.

The rest of the pages were blank.

She closed the book. She would take it out with her, find Barry, and try to discuss the drawings.

To her left, almost hidden in the fold of bedspread near the corner of the room, something had moved. It was dark and fleeting, and disappeared in an instant beneath the bed.

A cat?

In the days since her arrival, Shannon had not seen a pet on the premises, but that didn't mean one did not live here. It was quite natural, in fact, that the children would have a pet.

The bedspread fell to the floor all around the three sides of the bed that weren't against the wall. It was a gaily decorated spread of geometric design, in blue, red and yellow.

She started from the room when suddenly she was aware that someone was standing in the shadowed corner by the bed. She turned sharply, and felt a shock of surprise to see that no one was there at all. Yet even as she stared at the empty corner, a sense of being observed by something that was there, and yet not there, began to bear down upon her. She felt an uneasiness grow, as if the room itself were taking on characteristics that were unreal and terrifying.

She stared, and found herself backing toward the door to the hallway and whatever safety she would find there.

When she reached the hall she drew a long breath, feeling as though it were the first breath she had taken in much too long, that she was smothered and in need of air. She wanted to turn and flee, but she couldn't take her eyes off the door to the bedroom. She stood a long moment longer, looking through the rectangle of the door, but all she could see was the shag carpet, one corner of the foot of the bed, and a space of shelving with a blue teddy bear about to tip over. Nothing moved, no sound invaded the silence.

What's the matter with me, am I going crazy?

With deliberate care, she turned her back on the threatening doorway and walked with all the dignity she could muster along the hall, while every nerve in her body cried out for her to run, run, run.

Rim out of the house and away, forever, back to her own world, where her fears had at least some basis in reality.

She went instead through the back rooms to the kitchen, and as she came into the cheerful brightness of that room, and the company of Edna Ashley, the strange sensations of terror dropped away.

Edna looked up from some final cleaning work at the sink, and looked again.

"Is something the matter?" she asked.

Shannon tried to smile, and succeeded. "Nothing, really. I think I just almost met the family cat, and it startled me."

Edna gave Shannon an even more thorough look. "Family cat? There's no cat." She folded the small towel she'd been wiping the sink with and laid it neatly on the counter. "You musta seen its ghost. There was a cat, but it died of old age a few months ago. Mr. Frederick had to take it to the vet to have it put to sleep, the poor creature got to where it couldn't lift its hind quarters. You know how so many animals are affected that way. I think it's the kidneys that fail. I know it was that way with one of our old dogs. It's sad. But at least with elderly, terminally ill animals they can be humanely put to sleep, while with us humans it's not to be. We have to tough it out, we do. Makes a body wonder why. But the old cat, it died about six months ago, and it was hard on the family. They mourned that old Tom just like he was one of them."

"Could it be that one of the children brought in a stray to take its place?"

"No, there's no cat in this house. I've been all over it today, stem to stern, made up four beds, dusted a little here and there and vacuumed where it was needed. If there'd been a cat I'd a seen it. Of course," she added as she poured herself a cup of coffee, "with kids you can never be sure. Would you like a cup of coffee?"

"No, thank you. I think I'll check Barry's room just to be sure."

SHANNON WENT BACK THROUGH THE HALL TO THE BEDROOM AND remembering her irrational fear paused at the door. But the room looked quiet and neat and entirely innocuous, and she began to feel embarrassed at her earlier reaction.

She crossed the threshold and glanced around at all corners of the room. There was no sensation of anything there at all, not now, and she wondered at her earlier feelings. She shrugged it off, and returned the book to the shelf. Perhaps, she told herself, it would be better to wait until another time to discuss the book and his drawings. She would be sure to take it along when they went to the mountains next week.

She realized she had just made a final decision. She would be spending the summer with little Barry. So far, it had gone fairly well. There had been no discordant incidents worse than the one today.

She got down on her knees and lifted the edge of the bedspread. It was dark and crowded in space under the bed, the box springs no more than six inches off the floor. And there was no cat there. Not even a misplaced stuffed animal or other toy.

Nor was there anything in the corners.

The room was cool and shadowy and quiet and peaceful.

But when she left it, her feeling of being closely watched returned, and she hurried out with a sensation of coldness racing up her spine into her hair.

ON FRIDAY, WITH RAMON'S PERMISSION, SHANNON DROVE THE children, and Mrs. Ashley, to a small park not far from her apartment where she knew there was a collection of animals. She hoped that Barry, in his enthusiasm for looking at the water fowl on the small lake, and the monkeys that had the run of the tiny island in its center, would allow her to hold his hand. But when she reached down and took it, he let his hand relax in hers for only a moment before he twisted it away.

She wasn't prepared for the lurch of her heart. She hadn't touched a child's hand since Kelly died, and the small, nearly boneless feel of Barry's hand was so much like Kelly's that she wasn't sorry when Barry pulled away. He stood at the edge of the pond and gazed wide-eyed at the monkeys, and Shannon looked down at him, glad that she had thought of this outing.

Edna Ashley was saying, "Funny little creatures, ain't they? So human with their hands and all, and the way they watch us makes one wonder who's entertaining who."

"It works both ways I guess," Shannon said.

Becky said, "Is it all right if I go over to the concession stand? I'd like to have a drink of something."

"Of course, go on," Shannon said. "Just don't get lost from us."

"I'll watch out for you. Do you want me to bring you something, Barry?"

Barry shook his head.

David said, "Bring me a frosty."

"Bring it yourself," Becky said. "I plan to do other things than wait on you."

"Like what?"

"Oh, I don't know," Becky shrugged. "Look around."

David made a sound of disgust. "Look for boys, I know."

With another shrug, Becky walked off, her head swiveling to take in the groups of people, and taking time to carefully inspect any that contained young people her own age. Amused, Shannon watched her a moment. She was a darling looking girl, Shannon thought, with a cute figure and a pretty face. She looked especially good in the matching shorts and halter she was wearing today. On her slim, small feet she was wearing sandals with long laces that tied around her ankles.

That she had entered the boy-crazy stage was beginning to be obvious. Shannon felt a momentary qualm about being responsible for her at the lake. Of course nothing had been said about her responsibility extending beyond Barry, but it was pretty obvious that the only adults there with the children would be herself and Edna. Of course if the aunt came also, she would probably take the responsibility of the older children.

Barry stepped backwards several feet from the lake as a large white goose came along and gave him particular attention. As he backed away, Shannon heard him giggle. He was pleased at the attention of the goose, yet a bit wary too. Shannon watched them closely, knowing that geese could bite. But the goose was eyeing the child with mere curiosity, its head drawn back, its neck a graceful arch, rather than extended in aggression.

"Shannon!" a familiar voice called.

Shannon turned, and saw Edie coming across the grass toward her.

"Hi, Edie. Do you have the afternoon off?"

"Yes, and I just finished having a little picnic all my own. I often bring my lunch here to eat. If I'd known you were going to be here, we would have planned a picnic together."

"That would have been a great idea. But we came after lunch. I don't go over to the Frederick home until after lunch, you know. I'd like you to meet Mrs. Ashley, Edie. She's the housekeeper for the Frederick family. Edie Conroy," she added to Edna.

The two women spoke and exchanged the usual words of greeting, then Edie's eyes went to Barry. He was standing still about two feet in front of the goose, with his hands clasped behind his back, his chin tucked down, and a little grin on his face.

"Oh what a darling child," Edie exclaimed softly. "Is this the little boy you're taking care of?"

"Yes, that's Barry."

Edie crossed the few feet of neatly mown grass to the little boy and bent down, her arms going out to clasp him to her. Murmuring endearments to him she started to lift him.

A look of absolute terror flashed across his face. He stared at her and put his hand out, pushing at her face, the palm of his hand on her chin, his fingers spread as though he couldn't bear to touch her. His face twisted, crumpled, and he began to wail softly, a terror-filled cry that was forlorn and tearing.

Edie looked dismayed, her own face crumpling almost to tears. She released him immediately. "Oh, I'm so sorry—I didn't mean to scare him."

Barry was stumbling backward, staring up at her; the soft cry still coming from him in gasps and sobs. Shannon rushed toward him, thinking only to comfort, but her movement caused him to whirl instead and run blindly. He bumped into a woman and fell to his knees, and when the woman reached down to help him, he screamed and rolled away. He at last clambered to his feet and went running instinctively, dodging groups of people and individuals who had stopped to stare at him. Then David too was running, calling out to him, and Barry turned and collapsed against him, his face buried in David's arms.

Edie's face was as white as her blouse. "Oh, I'm so sorry," she said again. "I just didn't mean to scare him."

Shannon put her hand comfortingly on Edie's arm. "It's all right. He'll be all right, I'm sure. I'll see you later this evening."

Shannon went over to David and Barry and bent down by them. Barry was weeping, but silently now. He looked at Shannon with tear-filled eyes, and she took a tissue from her purse and gently pressed it to the tears on his cheek. Safe in David's arms, he didn't turn his face away from her.

"She meant you no harm, dear," Shannon said. "She's very fond of little children. She was not going to harm you. Now," Shannon forced a smile. "Would you like to go over to the concession stand for an ice cream cone? Maybe we could buy some peanuts there and you could feed them to that nice friendly goose. She'd like that very much, don't you agree, David?"

"I'll bet she would, Barry. And I'll eat an ice cream cone with you."

Barry stood back, on his own, without the support of David's arms. Then he looked up at Shannon. "Would you eat one too?"

"Yes, yes of course I will, if you want me to, and so will Mrs. Ashley, I'll bet."

Barry smiled, and the final tear sparkled for a moment on his cheek before it rolled away. He nodded.

"And we'll get some peanuts for the goose." He put his hand in David's and led the way toward the concession stand.

A near catastrophe had been diverted to surprising success, Shannon thought as she joined the small group for ice cream. Although Barry had run from her too, he had in the end wanted her along.

It was a decided achievement.

She waved goodbye to Edie, hoping that her smile of assurance was enough, at least until she could explain that Barry was fearful of all women, and that his rejection of Edie should not be taken personally.

EDIE DROVE AWAY FROM THE PARK IN A DEPRESSED FRAME OF MIND. She felt like a fool. Why was it, she wondered, that a child could so easily make one feel like a fool? It was not the first time that had happened to her. She ought to learn, she thought, to mind her own business. It was almost like the time she had picked up her little niece and the infant started to scream as if she had stuck a pin in her.

Face it, kids just didn't like her.

And for that matter, neither did dogs especially. Nor cats. Let her go to a friend's house where there were a lot of friendly cats and dogs, and they never bothered her, the cats never rubbed on her legs nor leaped onto her lap. Well, not often anyway. Face it, Edie told her self. She was a klutz, a jinx of some kind.

To appease herself she went shopping, but none of the outfits she tried on looked good on her. She finally decided she was just too down on herself this afternoon, and needed instead to go back to her apartment where at least she would be surrounded by the healthy bodies of her plants. She might not be very successful in the animal or people world, but plants were different.

She realized as she left the last store that it had gotten later than she thought. The sun was a huge red ball in the west and the street lights were already coming on.

She drove to her apartment carport quickly, dreading to face the shadows she knew she would find there between the parked cars. She thought of parking her car elsewhere, but that would mean on the street where the meters were, or several blocks away in a strange neighborhood. It was better to brave the parking area at home. What chance was there that she would run into another mugger at the same place? Not much, really. Besides, it was still early. Tenants would still be driving in, after a day's work, or going out for the evening. She probably wouldn't be alone in the garage for very long.

She drove in to her apartment slot and sat for a moment with the engine idling. The tenant on her right had not arrived yet, and the overhead light shone down upon an oily spot in the concrete floor. To her left a car was parked, and beyond that were three more before there was another empty slot.

She got out of her car, put her shoulder strap over her arm and hugged the purse against her side. Looking over her shoulders in both directions, she locked her car and closed the door as quietly as she could. The open-sided garage looked absolutely empty except for the parked cars, three rows of them beneath the roof. The roof was supported by steel posts in two rows down the middle, and on three sides. The fourth side was connected to the apartment buildings. Stairways went up to second floor balconies at both sides. Her stairway was the one on the left of the building.

She swiveled her head slowly all around, turning as needed to make sure there was no one in sight. Assured she was alone, she began to walk rapidly toward her flight of stairs. The mugger had come at her unexpectedly from behind a parked car. She had not been afraid before that. But now she felt uneasy every time she passed a parked car, even if it were out in daylight and in a safe area. She tried now to tell herself that her feeling of imminent danger was because of her past experience, that it had nothing to do with the present.

She angled across the carport toward the stairs, and then she noticed that a boy and his dog had entered the carport. They were only a few cars away. Strange, that she had not seen them before. Their presence gave her a feeling of safety. If a young boy and his dog would be walking so casually through the carport, probably taking a shortcut, then what had she to fear?

She turned her head and was walking on toward the stairs when suddenly it struck her that the animal with the boy was not a dog.

Startled by the thought she stopped, turned, and stared. And found herself looking into a familiar face . . . vaguely familiar . . . newly familiar. The little boy in the park! Yet this boy was older, perhaps fourteen years old, and the look on his face was becoming chillingly visible as he drew nearer to her. Although his features were handsome, molded in perfection as to the face of a baby, an unworldly evil was stamped in the light of his eyes, the curve of his mouth. She noticed then he had the body of a weight lifter, with biceps that bulged and large hands that hung ready at his sides like weapons. The animal that walked beside him watched her with black and glistening eyes, and coiled upon its back was a tail that quivered with eagerness, its tip vibrating like the tail of a rattler.

With a cry of horror gurgling in her throat she whirled to run, and from the corner of her eye she saw the tail of the animal uncoil with lightning speed and whip forward. It caught her around the ankles, tying them helplessly together, jerking her feet out from under her.

She fell, her head crashing into the concrete floor of the carport.

CHAPTER 3

"Barry. Barry."

The sound carried like a soft cry of the wind, Reid's voice calling from somewhere. Barry looked around for him as he got out of the station wagon in the driveway of his home, as he followed David and Becky and Mrs. Ashley toward the gate to the back yard and the patio doors; he looked for him in the bushes beside the house and in the branches of the tree, but this was one of the days he chose to be invisible.

Becky said, in a querulous voice, breaking a silence she had maintained all the way home, "Just when I begin to have some fun, then something weird has to happen and we have to leave."

David said, "You weren't doing anything but walking around."

"Well, does it ever occur to you that I might like to walk around? And what happened to him, anyway? Did the goose bite him? I don't know why I couldn't have stayed a little longer. I saw some kids there that I think I know. I could have come home with them."

Shannon said, "Becky, I'm sorry your afternoon was ruined. But it's getting late anyway." She stopped at the gate, hesitated, then added, "I'll be getting in touch with Mr. Frederick this evening. I guess we're all ready to go to the lodge on Monday?"

Becky's face brightened considerably. "Oh that's right. I have so many things to pack this weekend."

"Just remember," David said as he went through the gate into the back yard. "The station wagon will only hold so much. You can't take everything, like you usually do."

"I have to have something to wear! Of course I could buy more if I needed it."

"Barry. Barry."

"We'll see you Monday morning?" Mrs. Ashley asked. "I'll be here bright and early and ready to go. I won't need to take a lot along, and if I need more my sister can bring it up. She'd like an excuse to drive up into the mountains anyway, she and her husband, John."

"Yes, I'll be here Monday morning. Have a good weekend everyone. Goodbye, Barry."

He didn't answer her, nor look around at her as she was leaving. He went on into the back yard looking for Reid and Juno. Sometimes they hid and jumped out at him, and just remembering made him tighten his arms against his body in protection against the surprise. They wouldn't hurt him. He knew they wouldn't hurt him, but the surprise of having them appear in front of him suddenly made him feel like drawing all up into a little knot. Like *she* had made him feel.

"Barry. Barry."

It was a thin, wavery voice, a strange voice that didn't fit Reid's strong looks. And hearing it, dislocated in the air, coming at him from no certain direction, made Barry feel scared sometimes. And then angry. He stood by the edge of the pool and looked into the shadows behind the garage where a lot of shrubbery made dark hiding places.

"Come out! Come out now!" he demanded, his fists knotted at his sides half in fear and half in anger. Not even Reid and Juno could make the dark places safe all the time.

He waited for movement and there was none. He waited for sound, and all he heard were the voices of David and Becky and Mrs. Ashley as they went into the house. He heard the glass door slide open, and the screen slide shut. He heard Mrs. Ashley talking about things at the park, and at the mall where they had gone later, and about supper. She was going to make a casserole and put it in the oven to bake, and she would set the timer for one hour, and Becky was supposed to take it out then. Daddy would come home and the casserole would be ready for supper. Until then they would stay alone. But only for an hour.

Barry called out softly into the dark bushes, “Reid? Juno?”

Becky said, her voice carrying clearly through the evening air from the open door of the kitchen, “Why is it I’m the one who always has to take out the dinner? Why not David?”

“My, but we are peevish this evening, aren’t we?”Mrs. Ashley said. “Perhaps David would take it out this evening, then, if you’re so set against it.”

“I’ve got to go throw some ball with Wally. I promised him.”

“You’ll be back by dark, you’ll have to be, or your dad will be out after you,” Mrs. Ashley said. “You can be back in time to take the casserole out and set the table for your supper. Becky’s right. Boys should take some responsibility in the home.”

“So I’ll set the table. What’s she going to be doing? I’ve got to go, if I have to be back in an hour—”

David’s voice faded as he went on through the house.

Barry sat down on his heels, safely back from the dark places beneath the shrubs where in bright daylight he often played. He peered into the shadows. He saw his red dump truck and two of his smaller cars. He saw the pile of dirt he had made for a hill, and the roads he’d made going up that hill. But he didn’t see Reid or Juno. He drew back and looked around the broad expanse of the yard, from corner to corner in the surrounding brick wall, from clumps of shrubs to clusters of trees. Over the brick wall a basketball made a brief appearance, and the neighbor kids began yelling as a basket was made. It was there, Barry thought, that David was going to play. But he never asked him to go along. It would be fun when he was old enough to throw a real basketball. He’d be tall and strong like Reid, and he’d make a basket every time.

“Barry. Barry.”

Barry jumped. For a moment he had almost forgotten that he was looking for them. Now he could tell the voice was coming from the house.

He ran into the kitchen, and Mrs. Ashley said, no sooner than he was into the room, without even looking around, "Shut the screen door, Barry. I've got a light on. You want the bugs coming in to my light? You want bugs in your casserole?"

Barry backtracked and shut the screen door carefully to keep the bugs out, then he ran on into the darkening interior of the house, and through the hall to his bedroom. They were standing in the darkest corner as though they didn't want to be seen, Reid tall and straight, and curled on his feet was Juno, his long cat's whiskers testing the air and trembling. Sometimes they writhed like thin, colorless worms, each whisker reaching and feeling in a different direction, and Barry didn't like looking at them. Juno's eyes, flat and black, watched Barry come into the room, and Barry saw the eyes and stopped, well away. Reid and Juno might be Barry's best friends, but Juno was Reid's friend first of all.

"Why are you calling me?" Barry asked.

"The lady won't scare you anymore. She's gone."

"Did she go home?"

"She's gone. She won't touch you again."

Barry drew a long sigh and went to look into his toy box. He put the lid back and saw the interior was too dark. He crossed the room to the overhead light switch and turned it on. The light made a golden spot on Reid's pale forehead, and glittered in the black eyes of Juno. The whiskers were reaching farther, testing the light from above. Slowly, the animal crept off his master's feet and came slinking out into the room.

Barry stood still, watching him, his trust ebbing. He looked up and saw that Reid was smiling, almost, yet not quite. When Reid looked at him that way Barry felt strange, as though his friend was changing and becoming someone he didn't know.

"I'm going to play now," Barry said. "With my toys. Do you want to play with me?"

Reid stood still. Only Juno moved, his long tail beginning to unwind, the end of it twitching like the end of his whiskers. Barry stepped closer to his toy box.

"We will make the others go away too."

"What others?"

"Shannon and Mrs. Ashley."

"Shannon is already gone. She went home. And Mrs. Ashley has to cook." He looked with puzzled eyes at his friend Reid, feeling small and confused, feeling he didn't know what Reid meant. There was a look on Reid's face that had not been there before, that Barry had not drawn there. His chin was sharper now, like Juno's, and his eyes flatter, like Juno's, as if there were no light behind them. Maybe Reid's face made changes of its own because Barry had not finished drawing his face. He had thought about it, and he meant to make his eyes blue, with lights in the back made with the point of his pencil. He hadn't planned to make them mean and flat. Tomorrow, he told himself as he sat down by his toy box, he would draw some more in his book and make Reid a pretty face.

"We'll make Shannon go away forever, so that you won't have to see her anymore."

Juno rose from his crouch, and his long body began to twitch eagerly. His whiskers curled and uncurled, his nose, black-tipped and pointed, moved, twitching like his body. In another minute he would be gone, leaping through the wall, with Reid following behind him, and Barry would see them no more for hours or days sometimes, although they weren't supposed to stay away that long. Sometimes though, when he thought they were gone, he'd find Juno curled into a furry ball in a corner, his face and tail hidden inside the curl of his body. And he would stay there, for hours and hours, sleeping, Barry guessed. Or maybe just resting, because he thought that Reid and Juno didn't need sleep, or food, or water. *She* had said they wouldn't.

"No," Barry said. "Shannon has to take care of me up at the lodge."

"We will take care of you."

Barry tried to imagine Reid driving the station wagon, and unpacking the clothes for the summer, and pouring his milk, and doing all the things that had to be done by whoever took care of him, and he laughed.

"You can't take care of me! Shannon has to drive the car."

"Shannon touches you."

"No, she doesn't!"

"She wants to."

Barry dug down into the toy box and brought out an old top. It had the remnants of a merry-go-round painted on the top, horses with children riding and laughing and having a good time. Barry laid the top aside and leaned over the side of the box to see what else was on the bottom. Sometimes he didn't see the toys in the bottom for a long time. There wasn't anything in particular that he wanted, but he felt a need to keep busy. He brought out a small car that had two wheels missing.

"I wonder where the other wheels are," he said, and leaned over the toy box again. "They're down there somewhere." The toys rattled as he moved them around. Still, he could hear the swish-swish of Juno's tail as it moved impatiently. They were getting ready to leave, he knew, and he turned and looked up at Reid. "Where are you going?"

"We'll be back."

Reid stepped backwards through the wall, and Juno crouched and sprang, a mighty leap that made only a whisper of sound as he too disappeared.

Barry sat by his toy box idly fingering the car that had two wheels missing, and strained to hear the sounds made by Reid and Juno. But they were gone, and there was no sound in his room except the soft ticking of the small clock on the desk.

SHANNON DROVE SLOWLY ON THE WAY HOME, TRYING TO REMEMBER if she had anything in the refrigerator that she could fix for supper. She'd been trying to get rid of all the food, and had been having some strange meals on the odds and ends in the freezer. She would have to unplug the appliances while she was gone for the summer. For awhile she had toyed with the thought of closing that apartment entirely—why pay rent for two or three months on something she wouldn't be living in? But she had decided that she'd have to have somewhere to live when she returned, and although it wasn't exactly next door to the university, it wasn't too far away. Getting an apartment just when you wanted it wasn't always easy either.

She drove into the carport and swung her small car around toward its slot. There were few other cars, but she did notice that Edie's car was one of them. She had to pass Edie's car on her way to the staircase, and she instinctively laid her hand on the car's hood as she went by. The hood was still warm, so Edie herself had just recently come home. She'd stop by, Shannon thought, and try to explain about the child's behavior this afternoon.

A row of lights had come on overhead, creating shadows around and beneath each car. Shannon passed by them quickly, going down the aisle in the center of the carport.

She almost stepped in the blood. It glistened darkly under the light, like spilled oil, and with a small cry in her throat she sidestepped the spreading pool. Then she saw that something lay in the edge of it, just out of sight behind a car. She moved over. Her mind grasped several things at once, yet individually, and with a sense of shock. A woman . . . face turned away . . . dark curls soaked where they lay in the . . . blood, not oil. A plaid skirt. A blue blouse. As familiar as some of the clothes in her own closet.

Edie!

She lay face down, her left arm awkwardly beneath her, the other arm flung out. Beyond the tips of her fingers was her purse, still firmly latched. Whoever had done this to her had not been after her purse this time.

Shannon bent over Edie, calling her name. Her head, turned to its side, revealed her face, mouth lax, blood laid down from the lower corner like a red ribbon. Edie's eyes stared into the darkening distance without expression.

"Oh no," Shannon murmured, making sounds of protest she did not hear. "Oh God, no."

She began to run. She started up the stairs at the end of the building, going automatically toward her own apartment, when she changed her mind and ran down again. The manager's office was on the bottom floor, and she would need him to call the police, to call an ambulance. She needed someone to assure her that Edie was not dead, that the side of her face and head were not crushed in.

She passed darkened apartments, and two others with pale lights behind drawn draperies. Otherwise, the complex seemed deserted, and she felt as though she were running through a shadowed land where there was no life, and no landmark of familiarity, nothing but the horror of a friend's death.

She reached the door of the office, and saw with relief that a light burned brightly in the uncurtained window. She tried the knob and found the door unlocked and burst into the small front room crying out, "Mr. Collins!"

The room was empty. There was a desk holding a notebook and a basket of papers. The wall behind the desk held a hodgepodge of calendars dating back for five years. In the corner was a black leather chair, and beside it a table and lamp. Stacks of newspapers and magazines suggested this was the place the manager spent a good deal of his spare time.

A door in the back of the room stood half open, and the floor there was carpeted in a more expensive carpet than the old green on the office floor. From the open door came the odors of cooking, and a sound of activity in the kitchen, of pots and pans and china.

A feminine voice said, "George. Someone's in the office."

George muttered something negative, but his footsteps made dull, slow sounds on the carpet as he came to the door. He looked through, his square, ruddy face unwilling at this time of day to show any pleasure at being interrupted. Yet on a harder look at his client, he became more alert.

"Is something the matter?" he said.

Shannon suddenly found that her legs were weak and her heart thudding dangerously. She reached for the straight-backed chair in front of the desk and leaned with her hands on its back.

"Edie . . . the girl who was mugged. She's been hurt again. She's lying out there . . . I'm afraid she's d-dead this time."

The man's ruddy face lost all its pinkness. With long steps he began running toward the outer door. He jerked his thumb over his shoulder at the desk.

"Use that telephone. Call the police. Call the ambulance. If you can't make the calls, get Marge. Marge!" he shouted as he went out the door. "MARGE!"

The woman came in from the apartment, wiping her hands on a colorful little kitchen towel. The smell of frying chicken came with her, and Shannon put her hand to her throat to hold back the feeling that she might vomit.

"What is it?" Marge cried, going nevertheless to the phone and beginning to dial. "Are you sick? Maybe you'd better sit down. My Lord, I wonder what's happening to this neighborhood. Was someone mugged again? When we moved here, seven years ago, you couldn't have found a cleaner, safer neighborhood. Lord knows we've done everything we can to keep it that way. Plenty of lights in the carport, but those bums, they don't let the light . . . hello? Send the police to the Concord Apartments, and hurry. That's on Beamont Terrace and Dixieland. We need an ambulance too, someone has been badly hurt."

Shannon ran her tongue over lips that felt as though they had been hours in desert dryness. Her stomach was still feeling as though it would revolt any moment. She needed water. A glass of ice water. But most of all she needed to go back out and be with Edie until she was taken away.

She gave Marge a nod of appreciation and murmured thanks. "I have to get outside," she said. "The night air . . . and Edie was my friend. I have to go there."

"Of course you do. Is there anything I can get you first?"

Shannon almost suggested a glass of water, then felt she had to vacate the odor of frying chicken. She shook her head and went out to the walk that edged the first floor of the apartment house. The railing felt cold as she touched it.

Marge was following behind her, and suddenly the rest of the complex was no longer deserted. As though trouble had been sensed, doors were opening, people were peering out, and a small group had gathered on the west section of the lawn and was looking toward the carport.

Shannon went only as far as the corner of the building. She leaned there, seeing Edie still in her position of death, the blood congealing now in its shallow pool and looking even more like spilled oil.

"What happened to her?" Marge asked at Shannon's shoulder, standing on her tiptoes to peer over her at the scene of death. "Did you see it happen, or was she already there?"

Shannon shook her head, reminded that these questions would

undoubtedly be asked of her by the police. Marge gathered courage and went on past Shannon to stand by her husband within arm's reach of Edie's out-flung hand. They stood looking down and talking in low tones. After a few moments Marge turned away and went to join the group on the lawn.

There were sirens in the air at last that screamed in beneath the roof of the carport and then whined away to silence.

Shannon waited only long enough to see the paramedics turn Edie onto her back, revealing the flattened side of her head. She saw them transfer her body to the carrier and cover her, and knew now without a doubt that Edie was dead.

But she hadn't died from a simple fall, even Shannon could see that. A fall wouldn't have done that to her head.

Slowly she climbed the stairs to the balcony and went along to her apartment. They knew who she was, and where she lived. When they were ready to talk to her, she would be waiting.

She found no comfort in her apartment. At first glance it seemed foreign, as though it were simply a room at the end of the unfamiliar path. She sat down in her favorite chair and looked at the photographs of her dead husband and son. But the lingering horror of this nearer death strangled the sense of comfort she usually gained from the pictures. She set the frame aside and folded her hands in her lap. She stared at the door, waiting.

The knock came several minutes later. Relieved, she got up to let in two police officers. They were neat and trim, as uniformed people usually are, and they were male. She noticed nothing more.

"I think I arrived home just minutes after Edie did," she said, after she had given them her name, age, and address. "I put my hand on the hood of her car, and it was still warm. I saw no one else in the carport, or anywhere near the apartments. I was afraid when I looked at her that she was dead this time, and I ran straight to the manager's office."

"Can you give us any information on relatives of the victim, or friends?"

"I was one of her closest friends, I guess. She was divorced, and kept pretty much to herself, and her job. But I'm sure the police files have all the information I could give now, because she was mugged a couple of months ago. But that time she lost her purse. And, of course, she wasn't struck so . . . so hard."

"The lady wasn't just struck, she was battered. Repeatedly, on the cement floor."

"But . . . but why?"

"That's what we would like to know. If you remember anything that might give us a clue to this, please contact us immediately."

"Yes, certainly."

With a thoughtful and worried frown on her face, Shannon let the policemen out the door.

"But maybe it was only a fall," she said, unwilling to admit that anyone would so brutally kill Edie. Harmless, reclusive Edie. "Maybe it could have happened that way."

One of the men gave her a sympathetic smile. "Maybe," he said. "The examiner will determine that. You'll be here if we need to talk with you again?"

"Yes, I . . . but no. I have a summer job taking care of a little boy, and I'm supposed to take him to a lodge on Big Bear Lake Monday morning to spend the summer."

"Do you have an address or phone number for the lodge?"

"No, I don't. But I can give you my employer's name and number. He has the others, and can reach me there. But what more can I tell you? I know nothing that I haven't already told. Her folks are in the east, and the police already have their name and address, and I'm sure they'll want to take her body back there for burial. I can't help Edie here. Not now. I might as well go on with my summer commitment, shouldn't I?"

"I don't see any reason why you couldn't. You'll be here tomorrow? If there is anything else, we can get in touch with you then."

After they were gone she wished they had stayed longer. With the door of her apartment closed, the silence seemed smothering. She remembered her thirst, the dryness of her mouth, and went to the refrigerator for a glass of ice water. Carrying it, she went into the bathroom and looked into the medicine cabinet for a leftover nerve pill, a sleeping pill, a tranquilizer, anything to take away some of the horror, the shock, and the familiar sting of early grief. It was unbelievable that

Edie was dead. Just this afternoon she had been so emotional, so full of love, as she reached out for Barry. She had wanted a child. How sad that her life had ended without that yearning being fulfilled. Was anything fulfilled in Edie's life? She had few friends and no enemies. No one would want to kill her. No enemy had waited for her.

"Then who?"

"A fall couldn't have done that. And yet, it had to. There was no other answer."

Shannon held three bottles in her hands. The dates on all three were almost a year old, when the doctor had felt she needed something to help her sleep, something else to keep down daily anxiety. But those two bottles were empty, and could not be refilled. She dropped them into the wastebasket. The third bottle held aspirin. She looked at it for a moment, and then placed it back on the shelf.

She walked the floor and sipped the ice water. Scarcely noticing where she walked, her eyes on the carpet near her feet, she went from the silent bathroom to the living room, to the bedroom. She walked from the door to the window where she had left the drapes pulled this morning, every morning, dressing in the privacy of a darkened bedroom, sleeping in the safety of that privacy. But something now was different. The curtains were not closed in the middle, and a streak of light came through from the yard light on the lawn beyond the balcony. It was a broad streak of light angling down across the floor, up the side of the bed, over the blue bedspread.

She had a sudden, overpowering feeling that someone was in her apartment. Her skin chilled and she turned, her back to the partly opened draperies. The light in the room was dim, provided only by the glow from the living room lamp, and the yard light beyond the curtains. To her surprise no one stood in the corners, or against the wall across the room. The closet door was shut . . . she stared at it, knowing she would have to approach it, touch it, and open it. The sounds that entered the room came from outside the apartment. Automobile sounds on the street, just as if everything were normal, as if no one had been killed this evening, as if no one but herself had entered her apartment.

She forced herself to move. She went to the door and snapped on the overhead light, then she crossed the room to the closet door, her footsteps silent in the shag carpet. For a moment she held the knob of the door, but it was only delaying the inevitable, she told herself. If you have to do something unpleasant, do it in a hurry.

She jerked the door open.

Dresses on the hangers swayed gently, and then hung still. She could see beyond them to the back of the closet, and there was no one waiting to leap out at her. She sagged with relief.

But the feeling remained of being not alone. The shadows in the room were gone, yet she felt edgy and uncomfortable and something pulled her to look over her shoulder.

She remembered having this feeling before, but where? When? The other day, in Barry's room.

Suddenly the weekend stretched long ahead of her. She wanted out of here, away from this apartment. Edie was gone, all the other tenants were strangers, nothing held her here.

A pink dress, a summer cotton with a full skirt and embroidered bodice, on a hanger within reach of her hand, suddenly moved. It slid off the hanger and crumpled to the floor, softly, whisperingly, almost as if it had been let down by an invisible hand. Shannon stared at it, knowing in the most logical part of her mind that it had happened accidentally, yet instinctively recoiling in a new burst of fear.

The phone rang. Its sound released her, and she turned toward the living room in relief.

It was Ramon Frederick. She hadn't noticed before how warm and comforting his voice was. In her heart she welcomed his call as if he were an old friend.

"I hope," he said, "that I'm not interrupting something important."

"No, not at all. I was just wandering about the apartment. There's been a terrible tragedy this evening, or this afternoon. A friend of mine, a lady who lived a couple of doors away, was killed."

"I'm sorry," he hesitated. "Maybe I shouldn't talk about the summer now, then."

"It's all right. I was planning to call you, but this other made me forget."

"First of all, is there anything I can do?"

"No, nothing. Edie and I met when I moved into this apartment last year, and we weren't terribly close, just casual friends. I have to continue my summer plans. In fact, I have decided to put my things in storage and let my rent run out and not renew it. When I come back in September I'll find another place to live."

"Then you do plan to spend the summer with Barry?"

"Yes, if you still want me to."

"I was worried that you had decided you'd rather not."

"I thought Barry and I did very well together for only one week."

"I'm glad to hear that. I know it's a heavy responsibility, and the other kids can be rascally sometimes."

"We'll be all right, Mr. Frederick, I'm sure. Actually, I can hardly wait to get started Monday morning."

"Call me Ramon, please. And you don't mind if I call you Shannon, do you?"

"Of course not." She smiled faintly, thinking they hadn't been calling each other any name at all to their faces, but they had been meeting rarely, and then usually only when she was driving away from his house and he was driving in. There, with motors humming, they'd say such things as, "How'd it go today?" and "Fine, no problems." Even when there were little problems, puzzling things she might have liked explained, still, in a hurry to get home, they no longer seemed like problems at all.

"Can I help you with your storage this weekend?" he asked.

"No thank you. I've only kept a few personal things. I had to arrange to travel lightly, as the saying goes. But thanks anyway."

"Then I'll leave instructions for getting to the lodge, and household money for a week, and I'll see you at the lodge next Friday evening."

She hung up the phone, reluctant to let it go, wishing briefly that she had said yes, I need help.

But of course she didn't really.

CHAPTER 4

Barry sat in the middle of his bed drawing in his book. He made more webby things up in the corner, and then he drew into it another eye, a three-cornered eye. It was not a new eye, but an old, old one, like the eyes *she* had shown him, the eyes that had lived back when the earth had no light, no sunshine, and no little boys nor other people for the eyes to devour with their mouths that had no bottoms. This eye, though, would not devour little boys. But it would be there to watch, to see all that went on, and to protect him. But the monster needed lots of ears too, so that he could hear. Then he could listen. While the eyes watched, the ears could listen. And his webby body could move into the dark places of the house and no one would ever notice.

The door opened and David came into the room. He sat down on the side of the bed, lifting it slightly, and tipping Barry's knee that supported his book. He made an accidental mark with his pencil, right through the new eye of the monster. Barry frowned, looking at it. Now the eye looked as though it had a dagger in it.

"What are you drawing?" David asked.

"A monster."

David leaned over with his head next to Barry's. He saw the light strokes of a body unformed, a mess of marks that weren't aimless, but intended to create an airy creature. He saw things that looked like eyes, some ears, and sharp things that could be horns scattered in and about the page. Far back in the midst of it he saw a snout with long fangs, and at the bottom of the airy body clawed feet with bumpy, scaly skin.

"Yuk," David said. "That's an ugly thing. Why did you draw him so ugly?"

"Because that's the way he is. I'm just making his picture."

"Oh. You mean he already exists, and you're just making his portrait?"

Barry nodded. "His portrait."

"What's his name?"

"Monster."

"Nothing else?"

Barry thought a moment. "I don't remember."

"He had a name that you don't remember?"

Barry nodded.

"Who told you his name?" David couldn't hide his grin any longer. He tipped his head so that he could see into Barry's face. His little brother's imagination could be fun sometimes, because Barry would carry it on and on until all kinds of characters and tales would emerge. And this monster had all the earmarks of being one of his best tales.

But instead of playing along, Barry suddenly straightened his bowed body and snapped the book shut.

"I don't know!" he shouted. "Don't ask me those questions!"

He slid off the far side of the bed, ran to the book shelves and pushed the plain blue book into its slot. He ran on out of the room.

David shrugged and got up. He stood for awhile with his hands in his pockets. The blue spine of the book stood out among all the other books. It was Barry's private book, just like he had his own book and Becky had hers. Their mother had started that tradition in their family. His own book had messy little drawings in it that were dated age one, age two, and so on, and his mother had made notations of special dates until he was old enough to do the writing himself. Even though she hadn't been here to help Barry with his personal book, his childhood diary, he and Becky had reminded their dad to get the book for Barry. But he didn't know who had helped Barry with it.

Curiosity finally overcame his reluctance to snoop, and he drew the book out from the shelf.

On the front someone had printed BARRY'S BOOK. Their dad might have done it, but David somehow didn't think so. Maybe Mrs. Ashley? Or maybe one of Barry's teachers.

He opened the book. There was a drawing of a husky boy with a blank face, and printed at the bottom of the page was the name, REID. On the opposite page was one of the most imaginative and mean looking animals David had ever seen. And its name, it seemed, was JUNO.

The next page held the monster, unnamed.

David put the book back into the bookcase.

His own book was nothing like this one. His mother had pasted flowers and pretty little pictures here and there around the edges of the pages, and she had held his hand to help him draw. The animals they had drawn had sweet faces and round eyes, like angels and cherubs. There had been times in recent years when looking at the now neglected book made him blush with embarrassment that he had ever been so . . . well, *young*. But now he thought his own book was not so bad after all. Maybe he would change his mind about throwing it away someday.

He put his hands into his pockets and walked about in his little brother's room. Other than a few toys on the floor near the toy box in the corner, the room was neat and clean, everything else in its place, the bed even made. Who made Barry's bed? Nobody came to *his* room and made up his bed, no way. It hardly ever got made on the weekends when Mrs. Ashley didn't come to work. Sometimes he got in trouble with his dad, but if he remembered to close his door he was usually safe.

He noticed a small clock, and saw that he had an hour before lunch time. If he hurried he might be able to shoot a few baskets.

He went down the hall to his bedroom, passing on the way the open door of Becky's room. He saw her removing folded articles from an open dresser drawer, and remembered he was supposed to pack things for the summer. But what the heck, he could do that tomorrow.

"Hi, Beck," he said as he went by her door. He didn't wait to see if she answered.

In his own room he had to step over clothes he had worn yesterday. His unmade bed looked messier than it had when he left the room, and he made a bored motion of pulling up the spread. But time was passing, and the bed could wait. Using a hand and a knee as leverage, he leaped over the narrow bed and scooped up his basketball from the corner. Whistling, he started toward the door again.

His dad appeared suddenly in the doorway. "Leaving your room in a kind of mess, aren't you, son?"

"Well, no, it's not so bad."

"I hope you're not planning to go outside with that ball."

"Yeah, I was," David answered tentatively.

"Have you got your packing done?"

"Tomorrow, I'll get it done."

"Tomorrow you're leaving. Today you pack and clean up your room, don't leave it like this."

"Aw, Dad, I wanted to shoot some baskets. When am I going to get another chance if I have to spend all day packing?"

"There's a basket up at the lodge, and you'll have all summer. And if you stop wasting time you might have your packing done early enough to go out this afternoon."

"Aw . . ."

"David."

"Okay."

David aimed the ball for the corner again, and thought better of it just before he released the ball. He dropped it instead, then nudged it with his foot back under his bed.

"Have you seen Barry, David?"

"Yeah, he was in his room drawing in his book."

"He isn't there now."

"Well, he ran out. I don't know where he went."

David heard his dad go on down the hall, and now that he could politely do so, he shut his door. Then he sat down on the foot of his bed and looked at the chest of drawers and the open door of the closet.

This packing business was the worst thing about going up to the lodge. It had to be done and undone, twice. He didn't know which he hated more, doing, or undoing.

He noticed suddenly, among the litter on top of the chest, his old piggy bank. It had been a Christmas present from someone years ago, and it had started out with some loose change that jingled when he shook it. Since then it had gained more odd change on his birthdays and other holidays when visitors and relatives came. He had almost forgotten it was there.

An idea struck him, and he dug into his pocket to see how much of his two dollar weekly allowance he had left. Nickels, dimes, a quarter. Why didn't he ever hold onto his money for three days? He could have saved a dollar. But maybe, just maybe, he wouldn't even have to pry into his old piggy bank if he handled it just right. He counted his change. Sixty cents. Not much money, considering inflation. But to Beck it might be the difference between getting something she wanted and not getting it.

"Hey, Beck!" He yelled before he had gotten completely out of his room. But then he remembered his dad was in the vicinity, and this was one deal he'd like to keep private. He continued his trek down the hall to his sister's room in silence. Her door was still open, so he took two uninvited steps over her threshold.

"Stop right there," she said, without looking at him directly.

She was busy at her desk, gathering stationery, pens and other little items into a neat pile. She wasn't smiling.

"Hey, you already got your things packed?"

"Almost," she said. "And you're bothering me. What do you want?"

"How can I be bothering you? I'm just trying to be friendly."

"I'm not in the mood for friendly. What do you want?"

"Why are you so grouchy?"

"I am not grouchy, I'm busy. And if you've come to ask me to help you, the answer is no."

"I'm not asking for help. Not free help anyway. I'm willing to pay."

She paused and looked at him directly. "Oh yeah? How much?"

"Sixty cents?" he held out the coins on the palm of his hand, hoping the sight of it would increase its value.

"Sixty cents!" She tipped her head back and laughed at the ceiling. Almost as abruptly then she was scowling at the top of her desk again. "You've got pennies for brains. I'd have to have at least five dollars."

That was partly what he was afraid of, although not in his wildest fears had he imagined five dollars. "What! You've got dollars for brains. Doesn't the fact that I'm your brother have anything to do with it?"

"Not a thing. I'd charge the pope five dollars."

"Well, all right, maybe I'll just make a deal with you on that. Wait a minute. Don't go away."

"Are you kidding? The way it looks I'll be here the rest of the day."

David ran back to his room and took the piggy bank down off the chest. It was made of plastic and there was no way to get into it. If he cut it open it would be destroyed, and he'd probably get into trouble. However, he might be able to widen the slot with his pocket knife just enough to shake the change out.

He began to cut, widening the slot but little. The plastic was hard, and his knife dull. He eyed the blade of the knife. It was probably dull on purpose, made that way for the protection of somebody.

He hacked a bit more and decided it would take all day to open the slot enough to get the money out.

He shook the bank, then held it up to the light of the window to see through it. There was a faint shadow of money in the bottom, and he estimated there might be a couple of dollars there, give or take a few cents.

He set the bank down on his knee and looked at the outside of the piggy bank. It was an animal of some kind, a cat maybe, or a dog. It was hard to tell. Whatever it was stood on its hind legs, the front legs molded against its fat middle. The face was cute and round. The slot was in the top of the head, between two molded ears.

He tucked it under his arm and went back to Becky's room. Remembering her earlier orders he stopped on the threshold.

She glanced at him. "What have you got? Something of mine?"

"It could be, if you want it. It's my piggy bank, and it's almost full of money."

She stopped working at the desk and gave him her full attention. "Let me see."

"Do I take that as an invitation to enter your domain, Princess?"

"Well of course you're supposed to enter, idiot. How can I see the money if you don't bring me the bank?"

She came to meet him, hands out. He edged the bank around behind his back.

"First, I've got a deal to offer you. All the money in this bank if you do my packing."

"How much money's in there?"

"A lot."

She put her hands on her hips impatiently. "David! Let me see the bank."

David handed it to her. She tilted it, shook it and tried to peer into the slot.

"Hold it up to the light," he suggested. "You can see it's got a lot. There might even be ten dollars, or twenty."

She held it up to the light, then tried again to peer into the slot. She turned it bottom side up and checked it out. With a snort she said, "There's no way to get into this bank."

"Sure there is, just cut the top off."

"Cut it off then, and let me count the money."

"No. You have to take it like it is."

"Take it like it is? How will I know if there's as much as you say?"

David shrugged, as if he didn't really care much if she took the deal or not. "That's just part of the deal. My old piggy bank, and you do my packing."

She looked at the wall and weighed the bank in her hands, thinking. "No," she decided, returning to him the bank. "Not worth it. Dad would probably not want the top cut off it or you'd have had it off by now. What would you say? You gave it to me, that's what you'd say, and you couldn't help it if I cut the top off. And there's probably nothing in there but pennies. Now go away and let me finish my work. I don't want to find myself up at the lodge this summer with nothing to wear."

"Would you—"

"No," she said firmly.

He started back down the hall to his room, feet dragging. How many pairs of undershorts would he need? And socks?

"Hey!"

David looked back. Becky was leaning out the door. "The five dollar offer still stands, for the rest of today. Tomorrow, the price is doubled."

David put the bank back on the top of the chest, and another idea struck him. Since he would be leaving sometime tomorrow, Dad might be more lenient today. He hurried out in search of his dad.

He looked into Barry's room, and found it quiet and empty and almost unnaturally neat. He looked into the den. It was shadowed and cool, the draperies drawn. Dad's leather chair was twisted away from the desk, as if he had recently been resting there, but the room was empty except for the books and the furniture. He closed the door and went out through the kitchen to the patio.

They were coming across the lawn, Barry's hand in Ramon's.

"I don't want to go," Barry said, his face crumpling, on the verge of tears.

Ramon picked him up and held him in his arms. Barry's arms encircled Ramon's neck closely.

"But you'll have so many interesting things to do," Ramon said. "You can walk in the woods and play in the lake. And Becky will be there, and Mrs. Ashley and Shannon, and David. David is looking forward to going to the lodge, aren't you, David?"

David watched his dad come onto the patio with little Barry in his arms. "Yeah, sure," he said, although his feelings were closer to Barry's than he had admitted even to himself. It wasn't so bad around here in the summertime. There were plenty of things to do, kids to play with.

Ramon put one arm across David's shoulders and drew him along with them toward the house.

"And David will come along to your bedroom and help choose the things you want to take along this summer, won't you, David?"

David saw this last plan too going down the drain. Asking for an advance on his allowance hadn't been too great an idea anyway. "Sure," he said. "You can take your teddy bear and your own personal book so that you can finish your drawing. Wouldn't you like that?"

Barry relented slowly. His arms came away from his daddy's neck. "Okay," he said. He struggled to get down. When he was standing on his own feet, he put his hands up into theirs. He entered his bedroom walking between them.

But once he had crossed the threshold he broke free and ran into the quiet room. He looked for Reid and Juno, but the room was empty, and almost scary in its emptiness. Reid and Juno were gone. Gone to the places they went whenever they left him, and he didn't know where that was. Would they know he had gone to the lodge? Would they ever find him? Would they come when he called? Or would he be left alone again, the way he used to be when he went to school.

SHANNON SURVEYED THE APARTMENT. NOW IT LOOKED MUCH THE way it had when she first saw it, with no personal ornamentation, no sign of recent occupation. She had even given her flowers away to the landlady. The two cushions she had made for the couch were packed away in a box and stored in a nearby rental storage. All she had left in the apartment was one packed and closed suitcase standing by the front door, and one open suitcase in the bedroom. Only her nightgown and robe remained hanging out.

She looked through the kitchen once again to make sure she had gotten everything that was hers. A few dishes had been in the cupboards when she rented the apartment, as well as one fry pan and one stewer. The apartment had been advertised as fully furnished because of those items. A housekeeping apartment.

She pulled the blind on the kitchen window and adjusted the curtains. It seemed uncomfortably quiet within these walls, and she regretted suddenly that she had returned the television to the rental agency. She should have kept it for Sunday night viewing and taken the time to return it tomorrow morning.

She turned out the suspended light over the small round dinette table and left the kitchen. In the living room she pulled the draperies and turned out the table lamp after a moment of wondering how she would spend this evening. She would take her bath, she decided, and get into bed. She had purchased a paperback novel at the supermarket this afternoon, and although she didn't feel in a mood to read, it would fill the evening hours.

A hot tub bath would be nice, she reflected. There was plenty of time. There would be no bubbles, all of that had been packed into the other suitcase, in the bottom as she recalled, and she didn't want to disturb the carefully folded blouses, dresses and other things just to get the small jar of bubble bath. She had remembered to keep out a towel and washcloth, at least.

She undressed as the tub filled, and folded her clothes into a plastic bag. She carried it into the bedroom to the open suitcase, and stuffed it down into one corner. She would launder them at the lodge.

Suddenly she felt overly aware of her nakedness, as if someone had come out of the living room to the bedroom door and stood there watching her. She straightened abruptly and whirled. No one stood there, and no foreign sound had entered her apartment. If someone had unlocked her apartment door and crossed the living room, they had made no sound. Yet as she stared at the empty shadowed rectangle of the living room doorway chills were raised on her body, and she hardly dared breathe. Her robe was in the bathroom, and to reach it she would have to pass the living room door.

Her heart pounded, and her throat grew dry. She thought of calling out, *is someone there*? Yet knew she could not speak.

She began to move, stealthily, her eyes searching the parts of the living room that were visible beyond the bedroom door. Eventually she reached the bathroom, and pulled her robe around her. But there was no way she could get into the tub of water until she knew for sure if someone had entered the apartment. With all her senses alert, she began to reason that it was all her imagination, yet the feeling that she was being observed lingered, too strong to ignore.

With her courage raised by simple logic, by explaining to herself that no one was likely to have unlocked her door without making a sound, she went out of the bathroom, across the bedroom, and into the living room. She stopped just inside the room and searched it hastily with her eyes. There was enough light from the bedroom to see from wall to wall in the living room. The couch was against the wall across from her. A chair sat to the left. To her right was the empty corner where the television had stood, and just beyond that was the bar that separated living room from kitchen and dinette. There were no hiding places. No one was there. The front door was still locked, the chain in place.

She turned on the table lamp, expelling all shadows in the adjoining rooms.

She returned to the bathroom wondering at herself. She still felt edgy, still felt that someone was watching her.

She looked at the tub of water, and knew she could not remove her robe long enough to take a bath. She released the plug, and listened to the water draining away. When it was gone the awful silence returned.

With the bathroom door firmly shut and locked, she quickly put on her nightgown, then she wrapped her robe securely over that. She was being neurotic, she told herself, and then rationalized her feelings the best she could. It was Edie's death. She had not felt safe in this apartment since then.

Perhaps a summer at the lodge had come just in time to save her sanity.

CHAPTER 5

SHANNON DROVE the Frederick family station wagon up the highway into the mountains, driving out of the smog and heat into sharp clear air, refreshing coolness, and the pungent aroma of tall pines. She rolled down the window and smelled the mountain air. Now that she was here, breathing deeply of the different air, with the kids in the back seat and the housekeeper, Mrs. Ashley, sniffing the air on her side, she felt that at any moment she would begin to relax. It had been hectic for awhile, getting everything and everybody into the car. Behind the kids were stacks of luggage, with more in the luggage racks on top the car. As the highway steepened, and the canyon dropped farther away on the right side of the road, Shannon felt herself leaning forward, as though to help the car upward and onward.

"Lord," Edna said out the window, "it's a long way down there."

"Don't tell me!" Shannon said.

The steering wheel, that had felt cool in her hands from the air conditioner; now began to feel hot, slippery and sweaty, even though the outside air here was cooler than the air conditioner had been.

"Isn't it great, Barry?" said David from the seat behind Mrs. Ashley. "Aren't you glad now that we came? See how tall the trees are! And how blue the sky."

"How much farther is it?" Becky asked. She pulled herself forward behind Shannon, jouncing the seat, creating more unsteadiness in Shannon.

"Not too far," Shannon answered, trying to concentrate on the uncurling strip of road ahead. "I hope."

Driving into the mountains, she thought privately, was another new experience for her. Before this, on their annual trips "upstairs" as Kelly had called it, James had done the driving. It was on one of their trips back down, just as they were coming into the smog and heat of the valley, and the madness of heavy traffic, that the fatal crash had come.

Maybe, she thought now, a season back to a place similar to the one where she had spent the last two weeks with James and Kelly might be as therapeutic for her as for Barry. Of course, she had no intention of taking her problems along. The memories were at last being glazed over, so that it seemed a plate of glass was between her heart and their faces, allowing her a clear vision, but without so much pain.

It was little Barry who mattered now.

He sat in the middle of the back seat, securely buckled in, saying nothing. She had glanced back at him occasionally during the trip, almost unbearably aware of her responsibility. He was so small, so . . . *motherless.* Still so much a baby, in his speech, the shape of his face. He had an exceptionally beautiful little face, on its way to becoming one of the heart-breakingly handsome boys that nature produces now and then. His eyes were almond shaped and rimmed by thick, golden brown lashes. But the blue irises, the silent depths, when he looked at her seemed distant and unfriendly most of the time. The distrust was still there, belying her sense of accomplishment Friday when he had wanted her to join him for an ice cream cone. For a brief time then he had seemed to be relenting toward her, separating her in his mind from the woman, or women, who had abused him. But now it was obvious again that she would have to let more time lapse. Their separation over the weekend, perhaps, had worked against her. She could see and compare his gaze at her now with the much softer look in his eyes when his attention was on his brother or sister, for example. But there were many times when she saw an expression in his eyes that made her heart ache, a fear, a vulnerability that made her want to pick him up and hold him close and assure him that all was well with the world after all.

He hadn't wanted to come on this trip. When David helped him into the car, little Barry had looked back toward the house with desperation in his eyes. At first it seemed that he was looking for someone. But she had misinterpreted, she decided, for everyone who was going along was there. It was all Shannon could do to keep from taking him into her arms and trying to comfort him.

During the trip up from the valley he had ridden in silence.

"Are you getting hungry, Barry?" she asked.

"No," he answered faintly, trailing the O off into silence in a way that reminded Shannon of her own little Kelly. "No" had been one of his first words, and he had used it for both affirmative and negative answers.

"I am," Becky said.

They reached what appeared to be the summit of the mountain range and the road leveled off. Following directions written down by Ramon, as well as somewhat shambled instructions from David and Becky, Shannon drove into the pine shaded little village on the western shore of the lake.

"There," said Becky, pointing at a surprisingly large and modern supermarket. "That's where we shop."

Shannon drove in. Edna was digging into her purse for the long grocery list she had prepared.

"It's going to take awhile to get this stuff," she said, getting out of the car, stretching her legs and back. "Now if any of you kids want anything special that I don't have down on my list, this is the time to speak up."

"I'm going in with you," Becky said, opening the car door and leaving it open behind her.

Shannon looked back at Barry. "Would you like to go into the store, Barry?"

He twisted in his seat belt and looked into the rear of the station wagon. Shannon saw him smile. He began to work at unfastening his belt. David reached to help him, but Barry edged a shoulder against him.

"I can do it myself," he said.

David rolled down his window, but did not open the door. Barry crawled out on Becky's side. His sister had gone on and was now standing outside the window looking at something on display. Mrs. Ashley was headed for the door, examining her list, talking.

"I don't suppose there's any need to over-supply. We probably won't be that far from the store. There ain't no chance I'll be getting everything I need, for soon as I think I've got it all, one of the kids wants something I ain't got—"

She went out of hearing. The double doors at the front of the store slid open ahead of her.

Shannon leaned into the car. "Are you staying out here, David?"

"Yeah."

Shannon put her hand down to Barry, but he threw both arms behind his back and ran to catch up with Becky and Mrs. Ashley as they disappeared into the store. Shannon followed him in silence. Down in the valley she would not have dared let him slip from her sight into a large store, but here the customers at the time were scarce, the store not quite so large. Keeping up with a three-year old would not be so difficult.

They each took baskets, and followed Edna along the aisles. Barry trailed behind, sometimes stopping to look at the toys that seemed to be displayed at regular points along each aisle, then running to catch up, his footsteps quick and light. At the delicatessen they chose food for lunch, fish, meat, prepared salads. Barry put his face against the glass of the display counter and pointed at a dessert. The clerk added it to the collection.

With three grocery carts loaded with food supplies, they went through the checkout counter. Shannon watched Barry run out the doors that opened for shoppers going in or out. At the car he ran on out of sight behind it, and in sudden alarm Shannon followed him. But by the time she had reached the car she saw David's door open. Barry crawled in over him and sat obediently in the middle, refusing David's help in fastening his seat belt. He smiled in satisfaction as he clicked it shut, and Shannon saw that to Barry self-sufficiency was as important as to an adult.

"I wanted to do it myself," he said. "And I did!"

"Yes, you certainly did," Shannon said, relieved that he was safely back in the car. After this when shopping was needed, Edna could take the car and go by herself.

The grocery boy stacked the sacks of supplies in whatever crevice he could find, and at last they were on their way out of the village. Becky and David directed Shannon to the private road back to the lodge, around the northwestern curve of the lake. Tall conifers grew close against the narrow road, shutting out all sunshine. Occasionally they passed a private lane to a summer home, as the road curled on into the depths of the forest. The lodge was, according to Becky, three blocks from the lake. It seemed to Shannon that, so far as she could judge by the odometer and in consideration that the road turned a short distance from the blue and sparkling shore of the lake, that it was about one-quarter of a mile.

"It's so far," Becky groaned.

"Just a nice walk," Edna said.

"You get all hot again after a swim," Becky said, "just walking back and forth."

"Bosh," said Edna. "In this here air? It's downright chilly."

"Well you just try walking back after a swim in August," Becky said, "and I'll bet you won't think it's so chilly. That's when we usually come up here. August."

Shannon pulled the loaded station wagon to the circular end of the lane, which edged as closely to the front door as the steps up to the porch allowed. The kids piled out of the car and began taking from among the articles in the back things that were crucial to them at that moment. Barry too reached back and gathered up an armload of his toys before he crawled backwards out of the car. Edna went ahead of them up the steps, separating the key to the front of the house from the others on her key ring.

"Don't make yourselves absent now, kids. There are a lot of groceries that have to be carried in."

Shannon climbed the steps to the long cedar-posted porch of the log lodge and breathed in deeply of the fragrant air. Glimpses of the lake were visible from the porch, she saw, although most of the view was blocked by the tall trees whose dark trunks stood like Easter Island statues, solid and permanent. How marvelous, she thought to herself, with the lake like bits of blue-white diamonds sparkling in the sun, and a breeze that arrived from it in drifts cool and tangy, like a frosted drink.

Yet there was no sun here. The house would be perpetually shaded by the tall trees that became a trackless forest that closed in at the sides and back and deepened from light shadow to dark.

A sudden depression struck her as it seemed a shadow from the depths of the forest fell upon her and darkened further her strange surroundings. The sense of freedom she had hoped to gain seemed to be eluding her after all.

She bent to reach a hand down to Barry, who was trying to climb the five wide steps with his arms full of a teddy bear, a red dump truck, and a plastic bucket with spade. She touched his elbow and felt him recoil. She felt too, an instant later, the push of something against her leg, a sudden, hard push that almost toppled her down the steps. She grasped the banister and regained her balance. Barry had stopped and was staring at a point behind her. She turned, expecting to see someone there. But the porch was empty except for Edna Ashley at the door, inserting her key, pushing it open.

Barry directed a brief steady gaze at Shannon, then readjusted his toys in his arms and finished climbing to the porch. Behind him came Becky and David, absorbed by their own loads, their own approach to the house.

"Whew-oo," said Edna, wrinkling her face. "I can see right now we're going to have to air this place out. Leave the door open. And you kids, put down your things then go around and open all the windows. I'll have to find the kitchen before I'll know where to bring the groceries."

"It's straight back down the central hall," Becky said. "And all the bedrooms are on the second floor, except for Daddy's room and Aunt Lynn's."

Shannon stood trembling, her hand grasping the upper end of the banister. Someone had pushed her, yet no one was there. Still, she felt the presence of something hostile as forcibly as the invisible breeze that pushed against her suddenly from the lake, bringing with it a chill that suggested a lingering of winter ice.

Barry had gone past her into the house. She followed him.

They entered a large room with a fireplace of native stone on the right wall, and a staircase on the left banistered in knotty pine. The walls too were of knotty pine paneling, darkened by years, and dulled by smoke from the fireplace. The furniture was mostly of dark leather, and the rug on the floor was a woven cotton twelve by twelve square that pulled together its arrangement in front of the large fireplace. The rest of the floor was uncovered, although each chair that had been placed around the perimeter of the wall had its own throw rug made of yarn. At each chair was a table and a table lamp. Bookcases built into the wall had a scattering of hardbound and soft-bound books.

Edna was on her way back to the opening that evidently was the central hall that Becky had mentioned. "These houses that are left shut up all winter," she was saying, "always get a smell of their own, like a cave. Put them things down, David, and see if you can open some windows."

"Just a minute," he said. "I'll have to take them up to my room."

Shannon took a look into the kitchen, which seemed almost as large as the living room, with an unnecessary number of cabinets built along the walls. At one end of the long room was a plank, trestle table built of the same kind of pine that was used for everything else in the house from floors to ceiling, to cupboards to window frames. Shannon had a feeling that she would find her bedroom paneled in pine also. She could see why some houses were intended only for vacation use.

Edna unlocked and opened a back door. Beyond it Shannon could see a deck with cedar banister, and not far beyond it a shed with a basketball hoop nailed over the door, and the thick, dark forest of tree trunks.

"Maybe we should help the kids upstairs with the loads they're carrying before we go out to bring in the groceries and the luggage," Shannon said.

"You're probably right. That way we'll find our own rooms."

The second story, Shannon found, was as dark as the first floor. A long hall separated the bedrooms into east and west. There were at least eight small bedrooms, all of them very much alike. At opposite points on each side of the hall were two bathrooms.

"This is the girls' and this is the boys'," Becky said, "and the only one who is allowed to make a mistake is Barry. He hasn't been up here since he was two years old, and he used both bathrooms then, depending on who helped him. David and Barry have to take the bedroom with twin beds, cause when Aunt Lynn and Ted and Jason come they sometimes bring a friend, and those bedrooms at the end of the hall are always reserved for them. You, Shannon, take the front bedroom. Either one. Mrs. Ashley can have the other. They're the nicest rooms because they have two windows."

Becky stood in the center of the narrow hall giving her instructions with all the poise and assurance of an experienced hostess. Watching her, Shannon realized she wasn't a little girl at this moment. She was a beautiful young lady. But a moment later, when Becky saw David looking into the room next to the west bath, the illusion was destroyed. Her temper flared and exploded, beyond justification, as it usually did when David was involved.

"Hey! That's my room! Out!"

"Since when!" he returned, equally put out. "This is where I stayed last year."

"It is not! You stayed across the hall."

"No I didn't!"

"Yes, you did!"

What, Shannon wondered, was she supposed to do when those two squared off at each other? She hadn't discussed this with their father. Was it her responsibility to see to it they didn't kill each other, or was Mrs. Ashley the referee?

Edna Ashley had gone into the east front bedroom and was looking it over. A moment later she came out and went down the long stairs with a glance at Shannon, a brief smile, and a shake of the head. Shannon looked from Becky to David.

"You have to share a room with Barry," Becky was shouting, her face pink. "I told you, you have to share with him, and—"

"Who's making the rules?" David responded. "Who gave you authority?"

"I did!"

Suddenly David turned to Shannon. "Am I supposed to share a room with Barry?"

To Shannon's amazement Becky hushed and looked at her also.

"It would probably be better for Barry if you did," Shannon said. "But why don't we ask him what he wants? There will be enough bedrooms for your cousins even if Barry has his own room."

"He had his own room last year," David said.

"But there were fewer of us," Becky said. "And besides, Dad said to be considerate of Barry. He wouldn't want to sleep alone in a strange place, would he, Shannon?"

"Where he is?" Shannon asked, calling, "Barry?" Becky and David, suddenly working together, added their voices to Shannon's. They went along the hall looking into rooms. Shannon joined them.

They found him in a rear room, where the slope of the roof created an attic closeness over the single bed. The one window let in little light, the dark green boughs of a fir tree pressing closely against the pane. Barry sat in the corner, his small hands on his bent knees.

"What are you doing here?" David asked.

"Reid likes this room," he said.

There was a silence, then Becky asked, "Who's Reid?"

"He's my friend."

"Well, you tell Reid," Becky said, "that these rooms are always reserved for our cousins."

"No."

Shannon looked more thoroughly into the room. It was hardly larger than a closet. The one bed took up a good deal of the center space. But it had a cozy look that would be attractive to a child.

"Perhaps the cousins would as soon have a room farther along the hall. I don't see that it matters that much. But Barry, wouldn't you rather share a room with your brother?"

"No."

Shannon looked at David and Becky, and each in turn shrugged. Becky conceded, "Well, I guess if they bring company that's their problem. I'm going to move my things into my room." She gave David a sharp, significant glare. "The west one right next to the girls' bath."

He shrugged. "Okay, so go ahead, I don't care." They went down the hall, and David suddenly switched course into the alcove that held the landing of the stairway and began running down, his feet pounding on the uncarpeted steps.

Behind her, as she followed Becky, Shannon heard Barry talking softly to himself, or perhaps, she thought smiling, his imaginary Reid.

"DON'T LET THEM TELL YOU WHAT TO DO."

"They didn't."

"Stay away from them, they want to touch you."

Barry sat still, his hands gripping his knees. Reid stood in the corner between the bed and the wall by the door, in the dark spaces where his head came all the way to the sloping ceiling. His face looked sharper than it had before they had come to this strange place. Beside him Juno stood alert, his tail coiled, the end switching back and forth slowly, his sharp nose testing the air. He looked the way he always did just before they left to go to the mysterious places Barry knew nothing about. They wouldn't tell him where they went, or what they had done. They wouldn't tell him where they lived when they weren't with him.

"They're not your friends. You can't trust them. Shut the door so they can't come into your room anymore."

"David can come in."

"No, not even David. He's not your friend."

"My daddy can come in."

"Your daddy sent you up here with that woman, Shannon. He's not your friend. We're your friends. We'll make all the others go away, forever."

Barry sat huddled into the corner thinking of how it would be if Reid and Juno and he were all alone, the others gone. He felt confused, and suddenly terrified. There was something too frightening about the thought. There were so many things he couldn't do. There were even some doors he couldn't open. The knobs were too high, and too hard to turn. And he couldn't go through the walls the way Reid and Juno could. He began to cry, his head nodding over his knees.

He heard footsteps approach his room and enter, and come near him. He knew without looking that it was not Reid, for Reid never made a sound when he moved, unless he wanted to. Besides, Reid was already in the room just a minute ago.

"Barry, sweetheart, what's wrong?"

Barry looked up through blurry eyes, and saw Shannon bending over him. But she was not touching him, not yet. He pushed harder into the corner. Beyond her he could see Reid and Juno. Juno had moved on his silent feet to the foot of the bed, and there he crouched as though getting ready to spring, his black eyes fastened on the back of Shannon's head. A new twinge of fear made Barry tense. His tears froze.

Shannon looked behind her, as though she could see Juno. But then she turned again toward Barry and held out one hand, palm up.

"Why don't we go downstairs now and get something good to eat? Maybe that will make us feel better, and it won't seem so strange and scary here in this place. All right?"

The thought of food made Barry aware that he was hungry. But that was something Reid and Juno would never understand, because they didn't have to eat. But more than he wanted food, Barry wanted to get Shannon out of his room, away from Reid and Juno. He didn't want Juno to leap at her, the way he was going to if she didn't leave the room.

Without touching her hand he slipped past her and ran to the open door. He paused there just long enough to see that she was following him.

At the head of the stairs he looked back again. Shannon was coming along the hall, and slinking behind her was Juno, but as he watched, his breath held, Reid appeared in the hall. He called, and Juno turned back. Together then they disappeared.

Barry went on down the stairs to the lower floor.

CHAPTER 6

THE NEXT TWO days were too busy for Shannon to decide just how much she might like a summer at this particular lodge. She unpacked and put away all of Barry's clothes as well as her own. She made the requisite phone calls to Barry's father to let him know all had gone well, and that they had safely arrived. She didn't tell him about the controversy over the rooms, and Barry's choice of one of the rooms most distant from the rest of the family, nor of finding him crying there alone. He would settle in with time, she felt sure, and she had attuned herself to listening for his every move without letting him be aware of how closely he was watched.

At one point, though, he was the one who surprised her.

She was in her room adding the last, personal touches. A special pillow case for her bed. And the photographs of her husband and son on the bedside table. She was engrossed by their faces when she became aware that she was not alone.

Barry stood in the center of her room staring at the picture of Kelly.

"Why, hello, Barry," she said. "Did you come to visit me?"

"Who's that?" he asked.

She picked up the photograph and offered it to him. After a hesitant moment, he took it.

"That's my little boy," she said. "His name was Kelly."

"Your little boy?"

"Yes."

"Where is he?"

She hesitated. How do you tell one small child that another one has died, she wondered. Had death ever been explained to Barry? "He . . . lives with God," she finally said.

"Oh," Barry said with an odd finality. He went to the table and carefully set the photograph where it had been. "Did somebody kill him?"

Shannon was too stunned for a moment to reply.

"No," she finally said. "Kelly died with his father in a car crash."

"Oh."

He turned away and left the room, and Shannon remained looking after him in bewilderment, still not knowing his concept of death, or living with God. She had a feeling she had failed in her communication. That he was far ahead of her. But Barry seemed satisfied with the answer. She felt chilled that Barry had assumed her child was killed by a person.

She returned to her task, putting out onto the dresser the small figurines she had tucked into the corners of her suitcase: the little ceramic blue bird on the green, leafy perch; the cherubic child looking into the robin's nest where three tiny eggs nestled. Both had been Mother's Day gifts from Kelly, chosen by him when James had taken him shopping.

The ceramic figurines looked peaceful and lovely, their images reflected in the dresser mirror, and to a lesser extent in the polished surface of the dresser top. But the sight failed to lighten Shannon's heart. She was hearing again Barry's question:

"Did somebody kill him?"

He had spoken so matter-of-factly, as if the act of killing were nothing new to him.

Shannon let down her sense of responsibility for Barry only when she took her nightly half hour in the bathroom. She informed Edna, as well as David and Becky, that she would be unavailable for awhile, and then took her towel, washcloth, and the small tray of lotions and creams and locked herself into the girls' bath.

She hadn't realized she was so tired.

In comparison to the bedrooms the bathroom was large, as though it had become a bathroom only as an afterthought, having first served its time as another bedroom. For such a roomy bath, it was poorly lighted. There was one small ceiling light that should have held two bulbs, but a shadowed area on the left side revealed that one of them had burned out. The cleaning crew that had supposedly gone through the house from top to outside porches had missed the bathroom light fixture. The other lights above the medicine cabinet weren't much better. As a result, shadows lurked heavily in the corner behind the stool and in the recessed alcove of the bathtub. The tub didn't quite fill the space allotted to it, so that an area of about three by three at the end of the tub held a wicker clothes hamper, and one standing towel rack. Shannon threw her bath towel over the rack and stepped into the tub. There was, she found, plenty of hot water tonight.

The lights over the medicine cabinet began to flicker threateningly. Shannon watched them. The one light in the ceiling was steady, so, Shannon deduced, there was trouble with the wiring behind the medicine cabinet, or, perhaps, the bulbs both happened to be loose.

She got out of the tub, dried her feet on the towel, and turned off the water. The lights over the medicine cabinet steadied, and Shannon paused to watch. After a moment it seemed they might continue to burn, but to be on the safe side she reached up to tighten each bulb. The heat was too much for her fingers, so she looked around for a dry washcloth. Her own washcloth was floating in the tub of water. There was no other, so she used her towel. Both bulbs seemed to be firmly attached. She returned to the tub, and sat down in the hot water with a long sigh. She leaned her head back and slid down so that she had a bed of water. She closed her eyes.

It had been a long day. Becky and David had dug out and dusted off a couple of bicycles from the shed in the trees at the back of the house, and spent most of their time riding back and forth to the lake. In the afternoon they had gone in their bathing suits, and because

Shannon wasn't comfortable about letting them swim unattended, she and Barry followed them. She had found a shore line with a small beach where the water was fairly shallow, but nearby, in both directions, there were boulders and deeper water. She had persuaded both Becky and David to promise never to go in alone, but she couldn't get them to agree to wait until there was an adult around.

"We've been swimming here since we were babies," Becky said with some disgust finally edging into her voice. "Really, Shannon, we know how to take care of ourselves." David was nodding in agreement. Becky looked pointedly at Barry, then at Shannon, and although she didn't say it, Shannon literally read her mind. *You're being paid to take care of Barry.*

Shannon let her body relax in the soothing water of the tub, feeling the strain of the day melt away. She'd have to have a talk with Ramon, she decided. It was true that Barry was her biggest worry, but that didn't mean she didn't also feel responsible for David and Becky, even though both of them were almost as tall as she, and certainly seemed to know their way around that rocky shore and feel at ease with it. But how deep was that water just beyond the boulders? And how quickly did the land slope away at the sandy, pebbly little beach? The waves washed over from the far shore with whitecaps almost ocean-like, and Shannon had to admit she was a little bit afraid of strange waters.

Barry, thank heaven, had been no problem. He had stood well back from the edge of the water and seemed to have no interest even in wading. When Shannon had turned away at last, with a caution to be careful to Becky and David, Barry had run ahead of her up to the quiet little road that led back into the forest where the Frederick lodge was located.

As it turned out, Becky and David had decided it was much too cold to swim and had changed back into jeans and sweaters. But that was today. Another day, on toward summer, the weather and the lake would be warm enough for swimming.

Barry spent most of his time playing in and around the house. He seemed quite happy alone, although he did talk to himself a lot. But perhaps because he could talk to himself, to his toys, was the reason why he played so contentedly alone. He seemed uninterested in following either Becky or David, or demanding attention from anyone. Although that made him very easy to care for, Shannon felt it wasn't normal. She wished he would at least come to her with a storybook to be read.

Suddenly all the bathroom lights went out. There had been no warning flicker, no dimming beforehand. Shannon sat up in the tub of water looking ahead at a wall of blackness. An icy chill sped up her back like long fingers trailing upward, spreading drops of water that turned cold in the darkness. She was not protected, not a part of all things that had gone invisible in the total lack of light. Instead she stood out, she felt, seen by the eyes that watched her reaction. Fear coiled in her stomach and crawled over her skin.

She always carried a candle along for emergencies. It was a habit learned from her grandmother, who had lived through the era when electric lighting was not always dependable. Now, for the first time in her life, she needed that candle, but it was tucked into the corner of her dresser drawer in the bedroom.

At the bathroom door a thread of light became visible. The lights were still on in the hallway. Unwilling to leave the relative safety of the water, the feeling that at least part of herself was not exposed to whatever dangers lurked in the darkness surrounding her, she forced herself to move. She reached over the end of the tub and fumbled for the wood rack that she had thrown her towel across, but although her fingers finally grasped the wood bar at the top, there was no towel. Had she moved it? She thought she might have. The bathroom door was the most sensible thing to reach for.

She climbed out of the tub and took hurried steps toward that sliver of light that lay like a jewel on the floor beneath the door. Something brushed against her ankle and she cried out softly, a gasp more than a cry. She paused in her surprise, visualizing in her blindness the room, the fixtures, even the rugs. There should have been nothing there where something had touched her.

Her fear was unreasonable, one part of her mind was sure of that. She had locked herself into the bathroom and the door had not been unlocked since.

She reached the door and found her hands awkward and fumbling.

The lock resisted her efforts to open it. The knob turned, yet the lock held. She heard a movement behind, a soft, drawn out slither across the floor, as of something being pulled, or something crawling.

In desperation she used both hands on the knob and at last felt the button lock yield. The door lurched open, almost causing her to lose her balance and fall backwards. Beautiful light spilled into the darkness. Shannon looked behind her in the bathroom and saw only that a throw rug had been disarranged and now lay in a heap. Was it that which had brushed her ankle?

She felt weak and tired, all her strength left behind with her fear. That silly, irrational fear. Just because the lights had gone out. She had thought her anxieties had been left behind at the apartment.

She pushed the door wide open and looked into the shadowed room for her robe. It still hung on the hook where she had left it. She put it on and went downstairs to look for new light bulbs. Yet it wasn't probable that the bulbs were at fault. It had to be the wiring. Tomorrow she'd call in an electrician.

Mrs. Ashley and the children were in the living room watching television, so absorbed that none of them heard Shannon come down the stairs and go into the hall that led to the kitchen and pantry at the rear.

Shannon found the bulbs in the pantry, and took them back upstairs without speaking to the group in front of the television. They looked so comfortable. Mrs. Ashley and Becky sat on opposite ends of the long sofa, only the tops of their heads visible! To the right end of the sofa David and Barry sat in a large chair that had a matching ottoman. Although the sides of their faces were visible to Shannon, neither of them noticed her. Shannon glanced at the television and saw a car race in progress. It was no doubt one of those shows so common to television where the battles are more between automobiles than between people.

Shannon reached the upper hall and walked a third of its length, then halted in surprise. The bathroom was no longer a room of shadows beyond the open door. The lights had come back on.

With a grimace of annoyance she went on into the bathroom, going in gingerly and looking into every shadowy corner, as though lurking there was a presence that did not belong. Satisfied that she was alone, she put the bulbs away in the shelves beneath the wash basin.

She bathed without dawdling, hurried by a touch of anxiety that the lights would go out again. If the trouble were in the wiring, the extra bulbs would not help her.

She released the drain. The water gurgled away noisily, as though dropping straight downhill. She stepped out of the tub and looked again for her towel. It was not on the rack, nor even on the floor. Puzzled, she searched the room for it. She straightened the throw rug that had brushed her ankle. She noticed the toilet seat was up, as though it had been used while she was out of the room looking for light bulbs, and hanging over the edge of the white porcelain bowl was a corner of something dark. With a frown of perplexity, she looked into the bowl, and saw it crammed with her dark blue bath towel. With her fingers gingerly gripping the dry edge that hung over the side of the bowl, Shannon slowly pulled the towel out of the water.

Water dripped from the laden towel into the bowl as she held it up. How had it gotten into the bowl? She thought briefly of David, or Becky, of tricks being played with secret amusement, and immediately rejected the idea. For one thing she had seen them absorbed in front of the television with Mrs. Ashley. And for another, they weren't the kind of kids to play practical jokes.

Another explanation was that someone had come into the house. But she rejected that idea also.

The third possibility was that in her anxiety over the lights going out she had tossed the towel over the stool herself. It was the only explanation.

Yet she felt uneasily that it didn't fully explain what had happened. It didn't explain the fear that had been plaguing her since Edie's death, both back at her apartment and here, tonight, nor the little annoying happenings that didn't seem to have any human reason behind them.

Shannon wrung the water out of the towel over the bathtub, and then hung it over the edge to dry. She gathered the things she had brought with her, wrapped herself in her robe and went back to her bedroom. The feeling of anxiety dropped away gradually as she dressed in pajamas and short, matching cotton robe.

By the time she went down the stairs to join the others the incident of the lights and the towel had been filed in the back of her mind, along with the other disturbing but unexplainable happenings that had been occurring lately with increasing regularity.

She watched the last ten minutes of the show. There was another car chase, and at last a shootout between the good guys and the bad. Barry sat close against David, the changing lights from the television flickering over the features of his face. Like David, his legs were stretched out in front of him onto the ottoman. David's legs looked long compared to Barry's. Together they made a touching picture. Shannon wasn't sure that Barry should be watching the television at all. What effect would the violence have on him? Some of the experts made dire sounds against the violence on television and its influence on young and impressionable minds. But she remembered the fairy-tales and stories and television shows of her own youth, and felt that none of it left negative results.

At nine o'clock she stood up. "Bedtime, Barry."

He slid obediently off the chair.

"Are you going to give goodnight kisses to David and Becky and Mrs. Ashley?"

"No," he said.

"All right. Tell them goodnight."

Goodnights were exchanged, and one television commercial faded into another. Mrs. Ashley changed positions on her end of the sofa, and David kicked off his shoes and pulled both feet up onto the ottoman. He sprawled out over the chair, an elbow on each chair arm.

Barry went ahead of Shannon up the stairs. In the upper hall she switched on the lights from the master switch. Three ceiling bulbs spaced evenly along the length of the hall ceiling put forth a muted light. Barry ran down the hall, his footsteps clattering on the pine floor.

Shannon turned on the bedside lamp in Barry's room, and from the top drawer of the chest took a pair of clean pajamas.

"Bath time, Barry. Do you have some water toys that you'd like to take along to the bathtub?"

There was no answer. Shannon turned to see that Barry had pushed himself protectively into a corner.

He stared at her.

Shannon sat down on the side of his bed, and smoothed the pajamas out across her knees. They were approaching another difficult time, she could see.

"Won't you let me help you with your clothes, Barry?"

He shook his head.

"Bath time can be fun time, but if you feel that you'd rather not bathe tonight, you can bathe tomorrow morning instead. It is rather late, isn't it? Maybe you'd just rather go to bed?"

"Yes."

"And tomorrow morning you'll let me help you with your bath?"

Again there was no answer. He seemed even more melded into the corner, the palms of his hands flat against the wall on each side; his eyes bright with fear and tears coming close to the surface. Shannon's heart went out to him.

"Oh, Barry, baby, it's all right. However you feel most comfortable, that's how we'll do it."

He drew a deep breath, and she saw his small chest jerk with it. She held out her arms.

Her sudden movement, the reaching toward him, was like a trigger to his emotions. Suddenly he was whimpering and crying. He sat down abruptly on his heels, and covered his face with his hands. She knelt beside him and drew him into her arms. His small body was unyielding and stiff.

She held him only briefly. She drew away and picked up one of his stuffed animals. It looked like a cross between a lion and a lamb, with a red yarn mane down its back and a sweet, blunted face.

"Oh look, Barry," she said, forcing eagerness into her voice. "Brewster wants you to get into your pajamas and take him to bed with you, so that he won't get cold tonight."

Barry grew still. After a moment he looked out over his hands at the stuffed animal Shannon held.

"That's not Booster," he said, his voice jerking with a last sob.

"Oh, I'm sorry, did I get his name wrong?"

"Yes."

"What is his name?"

"I don't know."

"You haven't named him yet?"

"No."

"Is he a new toy?"

"Daddy brought him to me yesterday."

"You mean the day before we came up to the lodge?"

"Yes."

Shannon went back to the bed, removed the spread and turned down the blanket and sheet. She laid the stuffed animal on the far end of the pillow.

"I think he wants you to name him. Shall I help you?" She glanced back. Barry had risen, had come a few paces away from the corner. Shannon sat down on the end of the bed, and held out Barry's pajamas toward him. "While you change into your pajamas we'll think of a name."

Barry clasped his pajamas against his chest, his arms crossed over his body. He took a step backwards.

"No, I can do it," he said. "I can put on my own pajamas."

"Wouldn't you like me to help you with the buttons?"

"No. Reid will help me."

"Oh, I see." What difference did it make, she thought to herself, if he slept in pajamas that were buttoned crookedly? His sense of safety and comfort were the important issues. "Well, while Reid is helping you change your clothes we'll think up names for your animal. All right?"

His eyes were suddenly directed past her, and upwards, as if he were looking at someone standing behind her. An instinctual quiver edged coldly over her back. She fought a desire to turn and look for whoever stood there.

"Reid wants you to go away now," Barry said, without bringing his gaze back to her. "Reid will help me think up names."

Shannon rose from the bed. "All right. Good night, Barry."

His face changed expression, softened, lost the tight look of anxiety. He moved closer to the bed.

At the door Shannon said, "You'll call me if you need me, won't you, Barry?"

Barry didn't answer. He leaned now against the bed, one foot up, knee bent. He looked so small and defenseless, the pajamas still clasped against his chest. What terrible things must have been done to this child to make him so distrustful of women, Shannon thought, and felt a burning anger against that unknown person. She said good night once more just before she closed the door behind her, and she heard a murmuring reply.

She stood for a minute in the hall, listening to the sound of his voice as he talked to his imaginary Reid. He spoke short sentences and then waited in silence for long moments as though listening. But the words he spoke were mere murmurs beyond the door, too softly spoken for her to understand. With an ache in her heart that he must resort to non-existent friends for comfort, she went slowly to her room at the far end of the hall. At least, she thought as she got into bed, those friends were harmless.

CHAPTER 7

Becky had never been so bored in her life. Riding the bicycle back and forth to the lake during the mornings when it was too cold to swim wasn't nearly the fun it had been last year. She was afraid someone would see her riding with her brother, yet wondered why she worried, for the other houses were still closed. Usually they came up to the lodge in August. This year it was mid-June, and there were no other kids around yet.

She rode slowly along the narrow lane, the bicycle hardly balancing, one hand on the handlebars to keep it from straying into the trees at the side of the road. David rode on ahead of her, standing up on his pedals and pumping hard, his narrow rump pointed at her. Then, as though showing off, he sat down abruptly and spun the wheel sideways. Pine needles sprayed into the air, dust fogged. The bicycle made the abrupt turn without toppling. David grinned at her.

"Grow up, David," Becky said.

David stood up on his bike again, pumping hard, and came back to meet her and went on up the lane toward the lodge.

Becky drew a sigh of relief. There were times when she enjoyed being alone. Times when she felt a strange yearning to just go away and sit where she had a beautiful view and just . . . feel.

She was suddenly and ambivalently glad that the other houses along the lake were still closed, that she could lean her bike against a boulder on the shore of the lake, and sit on the sun-warmed rock and stare out across the water.

She shivered from the cold wind that swept across the water and hugged her knees close to her chest. With her chin resting on her knees she looked at the shoreline in the distance. Among the trees were bits and pieces of buildings visible in the overpowering forest. At the edge of the tree line, a hundred yards or so beyond the water, was a paved road similar to the one that continued on around the end of the lake and passed behind the boulder on which Becky sat. She supposed the road went on around the lake, a black strip of pavement without a center line, just a little country road from which led all the lanes to the houses and summer lodges hidden back among the trees. No car passed on the road behind Becky, but across the lake she saw the occasional silent movement of an automobile along the lake road, and farther in among the trees glimpses of blue, red, green movements that she knew must be cars going to the market, or to the bars that clustered along the one main street of the village. Occasionally there was a person or two walking down to stand for a moment at the edge of the lake.

She saw a bike rider, and sat up in surprise. Could it be David? Had he ridden all around the end of the lake to the village? He wouldn't dare. Their dad hadn't given permission to go so far. The rider was much too far away to be recognizable. He was only a tiny figure against the tall green conifers that stretched their spiked tops to the brilliant blue sky.

It was, however, an idea. A ride around the lake, or at least around the end and over to the village, would be fun. She might even meet some new boys in the village. She wondered how far it was to the village. Two miles, three? Even if it were four, it wouldn't take long to ride there and back.

She climbed down off the boulder, no longer wanting to be alone. She mounted her bike and pumped hard toward the lane, yelling, "David! David? Come here, David."

She left the warm sunlight, the smooth pavement of the lake road, and rode into the shaded lane that was carpeted in pine needles. The lane curved, so that only glimpses of the lodge were visible, and less than half of the lane.

The curve was straightening out in front of her when a noise other than the sound of her tires on the pine needles came to her attention. Behind her came the sound of larger tires munching their way along, and the sound of a motor. With a spurt of energy, a burst of heartbeats, Becky jerked her bicycle out of the road. She stopped and looked back.

She didn't recognize the car. It was a sedan, a two-tone lavender and gray Cadillac. Nor did she recognize the good looking boy who was smiling at her out the passenger's window. But then she looked at the driver. Aunt Lynn! With the same puffy, cream-colored hair, the same sunglasses, almost, although these sunglasses seemed larger and with a more elaborate shape than the old. It was Aunt Lynn with a new car, and new sunglasses—didn't she always have a new car and new sunglasses? Sometimes she even had a new hair color, but otherwise the style stayed the same. But who was the good looking boy in the front seat?

The car stopped, the engine idled. The door opened, and the boy got out. He was taller than Becky, and had wide, straight shoulders. His black hair waved interestingly, and there was a fuzzy new growth along his upper lip.

Recognition hit Becky with an electric jolt. "Jason!" she screamed. "Is it *you?*"

He stood smiling at her. Behind him Aunt Lynn leaned across the seat, one elbow sinking into the soft leather.

"Becky," she cried. "How good to see you, dear. Weren't you expecting us?"

"Gosh no! I mean, I don't know." Having Jason stand there smiling down at her like that made her stammer. "I mean, Auntie, we hoped you were coming, but you usually don't come until August, do you?"

"No, but then neither do you. Ramon called me and asked if we could come earlier. He told me you were here. He's expected this weekend, isn't he?"

"Yes."

Becky pulled her eyes away from Jason. In the back seat, in a small space that wasn't taken up by luggage, sat Freddy. He was only ten, and didn't look that old, he was so scrawny. Becky had hardly ever noticed him. He was just one of the younger cousins that she had to put up with being civil to once a year or so. Sometimes they spent the Christmas vacation together, too, but hadn't this last year.

"Hi, Freddy," she said, then looked her older cousin up and down. Last year he had been shorter than she, and almost as scrawny as his little brother. But now, wow. "Golly, Jason, have you ever grown."

He kept grinning in silence, but his mother said, "Hasn't he though? Four inches."

"Five," he said, in a voice that Becky would not have recognized at all. It sounded almost comically deep and masculine.

"I can't believe it," she said. "You're so *tall!*"

Aunt Lynn said, "Do you want to ride up to the lodge with us, Becky? You can come back for your bike later."

Jason reached behind him and shut the door. "You drive on, Mom, I'll walk with Becky."

"All right. But do come on right away and help unload. We've got a lot of unpacking to do."

The long, sleek automobile moved on, its wide tires crunching the pine needles, its motor humming softly.

Becky looked at Jason with new admiration. The way he had made the decision about walking was downright masterful. Becky felt her boredom suddenly replaced by a strange, new excitement.

BARRY PLAYED ON THE GROUND WHERE THE STEPS OF THE FRONT porch joined the boards of the porch, creating a corner where pine needles collected in a heap, driven and pushed by the winter winds that swept over the lake. He had scooped away the needles to make little curling roads in the soft, black soil, and he had carried down from his room all his wheeled toys. Even the little plastic pony that had wheels on its hooves. Shannon had helped him, and now she sat on the top step of the porch. Sometimes she watched him play, and sometimes she just looked out through the trees toward the lake. Barry was almost forgetting that she was there.

He built a city, and returned to his room for some people to put in it. He had just settled down to serious play when he heard the sound of the car in the driveway behind him. He twisted around to look.

He saw the shining grill, and the license plate on the front bumper. Then through the slanted windshield he saw the woman with the pale yellow hair puffed up above her low forehead.

Her.

She had found him again. She was coming for him. She would take him back to her house, and Reid and Juno wouldn't know where he was, and his daddy wouldn't know. Not even Shannon could help him then.

He was paralyzed. He couldn't move. He could only stare at her getting out of the car, could only see that she was coming toward him. He felt a whimper of terror in his throat, but it was soft and low, for crying wouldn't help him. Crying had made her hurt him more. He dared not cry.

He saw her smiling at him, and he saw that she was smaller, thinner, but mostly he just saw the hair.

Shannon was coming down the steps, saying, "Barry. Barry, baby, what's wrong?"

Suddenly he was able to move. He was able to lift himself off the ground and run as hard as he could for the front steps. With his hands reaching for the step above, he managed to climb them all, and at last reach the door to the house. Then he was in the cool interior and running for the stairs. He heard his footsteps, and others, it seemed, behind him, and he knew she could catch him. She always had. She always had.

He reached his room and slammed shut his door. Then he went to the farthest corner and hunkered down there, his back to the room, his face buried in his hands.

"Reid, Juno, Reid, Juno — " But his voice was only a whimper, his mouth trembling too much with his fear to speak their names.

The footsteps came behind him, hundreds of them, pounding the floor of the hall, echoing in far away places. More than Shannon's voice was calling his name. But *she* was silent. She was among them, but she was silent.

"Reid, Juno—"

But could they help? Maybe they would be just shadowy things that had risen off the paper she had helped him to draw, the way they were when they first appeared. That was the day she had taken him into the black room where the black candles burned, and where she had killed the baby rabbits. The sacrifice, she had called it, for the devil. And that was the day she had written the names on the paper for him, and then like smoke they had appeared to stand there in the black room, Reid, wavery, and without features on his face, then. No nose, no eyes, no mouth. They came later, when Reid had chosen Barry for his boy. Juno came too, like one of the dead animals *she* had sacrificed.

They hadn't helped him that day. Maybe they wouldn't help him now.

"Reid. Juno . . . Juno . . ."

Her hands were on his shoulders now, pulling him out of the safety of his corner. Her arms were around him, and he was afraid to try to push away from her. He was afraid she would hurt him worse than ever, and maybe she would kill him too, the way she killed the little helpless animals and birds.

But the voice that cried his name was not hers. It was Shannon's.

He opened his eyes. It was Shannon's face above his, and there were tears in her eyes. It was her arms that held him.

In terrible desperation he clutched her shoulders and looked past her. *She* was coming, and Shannon didn't know that she would hurt him, for *she* was his teacher, and he had to go with her. He couldn't tell his daddy, and he couldn't tell Shannon, for if he did she would kill him.

Over Shannon's shoulder he saw the woman with the pale yellow hair. She was bending down, coming closer and closer. In a minute she would reach for his hand and lead him away. His voice came true suddenly, and he screamed. Shannon's arms tightened on him. She stood up, lifting him, and turned so that he could no longer see her.

"Barry, it's your Aunt Lynn. Barry, *Barry.*"

"Barry, don't you remember me? I'm your Auntie Lynn, sweetheart, your Auntie Lynn. See, Freddie is here. And Jason. Your cousins. Don't you remember them?"

Barry looked over his shoulder. Now he saw the difference in the face. The woman with the yellow hair had a different face, a different face. Mrs. Ashley stood in the room behind the woman, and there was a tall, dark-haired boy and Becky. And David, and a smaller boy, all crowded into his small room and in the hallway just outside the door, all looking at him with faces that seemed a little scared. She was not really here, after all.

The woman stepped closer and started to touch his shoulder. He jerked away, staring at her. He realized that Shannon was still holding him, and he twisted in resistance. Her arms loosened, and she let him slide down so that he was standing on his own feet. He kept staring up at the strange woman.

"I'm your Auntie Lynn, dear boy, don't you remember me? I was here last year, when you were." Mrs. Ashley said, "A year is a long time when you're just three years old."

Shannon bent closer, and her hand brushed lightly at his hair, pushing it off his forehead. "Nobody's going to hurt you, Barry. You're safe. Your Aunt Lynn and your cousins are going to be staying at the lodge too. Don't you remember?"

He remembered. But he didn't know what his Aunt Lynn looked like. Nor his cousins. He didn't remember ever seeing them before.

Shannon offered him her hand. "Why don't we go downstairs now and see if Mrs. Ashley has a nice afternoon treat. Some ice cream maybe."

Barry looked around for Reid and Juno, but there were too many real people in the room. They didn't like a lot of people, he guessed, for mostly they came to him when he was alone. Then he saw the tip of Juno's tail ease out from under the bed. It silently swept the floor, back and forth, back and forth, as though he were crouched to spring. Then too he saw that Reid was standing in the corner, just a part of his strong body showing, as if he stood within the wall itself. But it was all right now, he didn't need them to help him. And they knew he didn't need them, not now that he was going after ice cream.

He reached up and put his hand in Shannon's.

. . .

LATER IN THE AFTERNOON, WITH BARRY FINALLY BACK IN PLAY IN his corner by the front porch, Shannon offered to help Lynn with the unpacking. Her offer was immediately accepted. She helped carry the last of the luggage to the downstairs bedroom where some of Lynn's personal things remained from previous visits. Then, as Lynn removed clothing from the suitcase, Shannon arranged them on hangers in the large, walk-in closet.

"Is that child afraid of everyone?" Lynn asked.

They were alone in the room. Mrs. Ashley had raised the blinds and made the bed, and now had gone to begin dinner. Jason, Freddie, David and Becky, having carried in most of the luggage and distributed it to the three bedrooms where Lynn and her boys would be staying, had now gone out, and the house was quiet.

"I have never felt so —so abashed in my life," Lynn said. "Imagine your little nephew acting as though you were some kind of monster out of the worst horror show! Can you imagine how I felt?"

"Yes, it was probably pretty terrible for you. And the strange thing is that he isn't afraid of everyone. In fact, I've seen him act that way only once before, and that was when a friend of mine tried to put her arms around him."

"But I didn't even do that. All I did was get out of my car."

"You must have reminded him of . . ."

"Heavens! If that's the case, I won't be able to get close to him during my entire stay here." She shook out a blue silk blouse and handed it to Shannon. "What a change since last year! He was adorable, friendly, and talked a lot for his age. Pronounced his words really well. Made complete, complex sentences. A bright little guy. He'd come and climb onto my lap and chatter a mile a minute. I adored him."

Shannon hung the blue blouse on a hanger that was padded in blue silk and trimmed in cream lace. "We're hoping this summer will see a definite, positive change in him."

"Don't count on it. I wouldn't have believed the change in him now if I hadn't seen it for myself. Ramon said the amount of the damage was not understood at this point. I'd say it was quite extensive."

"I think we're making progress," Shannon said. "Today was the first time he allowed me to hold his hand."

Lynn stationed herself in front of the dresser mirror. She touched her face, her cheek, her chin, and at last her hair. "What is there about me that frightens him, do you suppose?"

"I wouldn't worry about it," Shannon said. "Now that he knows who you are, he'll not be so frightened. He went back to play quite willingly." She looked around, saw the suitcases were empty. "If you'll excuse me now, I think I'd better check on him. If he's allowed to, he'll go back to his room and close himself in. We try to keep him interested in doing things where others are."

Shannon left the room, seeing that Lynn was still looking at herself in the mirror. She closed the door behind her.

Down the hall from the kitchen came the sounds of Mrs. Ashley, a tune being hummed, occasional footsteps as she crossed from one counter to another, the oven door closing, the clatter of spoon against bowl. Shannon smiled. Edna Ashley was a comforting soul to have around.

Shannon went out onto the porch and looked over the railing. Barry was on his knees pushing a blue and white truck along one of the roads she had urged him to build. He was making the sound for the motor, grinding it up what must be in his mind a very long, steep hill.

Down the lane David and Freddie were yelling back and forth to each other as they rode bikes. Shannon looked around for Becky and Jason, but did not see them.

At least, she thought as she sat down on the top step where she could see the top of Barry's head, the confusion had not lasted long, nor spoiled anyone's day. The kids were going on as though nothing at all had happened.

Shannon looked through the trees into the distance, seeing slivers of bright water, small whitecaps reflecting the sun. On the road near the water a car moved slowly. Sightseers. The few people who lived year-round locally drove the road much faster. The car disappeared beyond the thicker forest of trees in the east. And for a brief moment then two cyclers passed into view. Shannon recognized Becky's richly glistening dark hair. It swung across her shoulders as she rode toward the lake. Then, coming into view behind her was the cousin, Jason.

Shannon clasped her hands together. They were trembling slightly. Every time Barry reacted unexpectedly, especially when he showed fear, she felt helpless to comfort him. His needs, perhaps, were greater than her ability to understand. She yearned to help him, to draw a hand over his eyes and erase all his bad memories.

"Vooomm, voom," his voice ground out, as he pushed his truck along. Then he gave a long, deep sigh, and was silent.

Shannon looked down at him. He was slumped, his back rounded, as he sat staring at the ground as if a great tiredness had overcome him.

CHAPTER 8

THEY LEANED their bikes on the ground and walked together down to the edge of the water. Jason looked down at Becky. She gave him a glance out of the corner of her eyes, and a quick smile. He doubled his right fist and socked her lightly on the shoulder. It jolted her a bit sideways.

"Hey, you turned out to be pretty good looking," he said.

She made a fist and socked him back, and he pretended to be thrown off balance with the surprise of her strength. He stumbled to a boulder and leaned against it in mock pain.

"You're not so bad yourself," she said. "When you're not beating up on girls."

"Mean woman," he groaned, holding a cupped hand over his wounded arm.

She grasped his hand in both of hers and pulled. He yielded unexpectedly, allowing her to pull him forward. She lost her balance and fell, and he fell on top of her. For a moment his body pinned hers to the ground, but laughing she twisted away, rolling out from under him.

A car drove by, and self-consciously they got up from the ground, dusted their clothes, picked up their bikes and began to ride back toward the lodge. The elderly couple in the car only glanced at them. They idled along, pedaling only as needed to keep the bikes upright.

"I'll bet you've got a boyfriend," Jason said.

"Sure, several."

"Do you go out on dates?"

"No, my dad won't let me. Sometimes I go over to my girlfriend's house and a couple of guys come along. Her folks don't care. My dad's old-fashioned. He thinks I'm too young to date. Do you?"

"You don't look too young."

"I mean, do you date?"

"Sure, sometimes. I'm taking driver's ed. I'll be getting my driver's license the day I turn sixteen."

"When's that?"

"Don't you remember? You've sent me a birthday card every year since I was ten."

"Oh yeah. Sometime in December."

"You don't have a very good memory."

"As good as yours probably. When's mine?"

"April."

"But you don't know the date."

"Well, you don't know the date of mine, either, so we're even."

"I've got it written down on my calendar."

David and Freddie came around the bend in the lane and maneuvered their bikes past without slowing.

Freddie yelled, "Bet we can beat you to the lake and back!"

"Yeah!" David cried, standing up on his pedals and leaning over the bike handles. He slipped slightly to the lead. "Come on, you two."

Becky and Jason ignored them and rode slowly on toward the house. Goosebumps were beginning to rise on Becky's bare arms. The sun had gone down beyond the mountain, and the air had taken on an evening chill. The light of the day seemed to end at the sides of the lane where the tall conifers grew. Shadows lay heavily among the trees just a few feet in.

"Let's go to the house," Becky said.

"Okay."

The lane came to an end in a circular turn-around area in front of the house. The path to the rear of the house was so narrow and so covered with pine needles that it was difficult to ride a bike along it. They dismounted, and pushed the bicycles along the path.

"We oughta hike back into the forest," Jason said.

"It's getting cold and dark."

"I don't mean now. Just sometime while we're here."

"Okay."

They leaned their bikes against the back porch and started to climb the steps. Becky heard a sound, an unidentifiable whish of air. She turned her head and looked back at Jason just in time to see him duck. Something whizzed through the air within fractions of his head and struck the back of the house with a cracking sound. Becky stared at it, one hand gripping the banister.

"What the hell—" Jason muttered.

"A rock," Becky said, and turned to look into the space from which it had come. She saw the shed, the trees of the forest, the growing darkness. "Someone threw a rock. Who would do that?"

Jason went back down the steps and ran to look behind the shed. He disappeared from view for a long moment while Becky searched the back yard with her eyes. There was no movement, no hint of where the rock had come from. Jason came on around the shed looking perplexed.

"There's no one there," he said.

Becky finished climbing the steps to the back porch. She nudged the rock with her foot. It was the size of a softball, and one side of it had traces of soil that showed it had been partially embedded just recently, just minutes ago.

"It couldn't have been David or Freddie," she said.

"No."

"Nor Barry. He's not that strong or well coordinated." She looked at Jason as he came up to stand beside her. He shrugged.

"If it had hit you it would have killed you," she said.

She thought his face looked pale. The daylight was fading rapidly, and the growing darkness among the trees began to look ominous. Becky moved toward the door. The chill that rippled over her body was more intense than the temperature warranted.

"Let's go in," she said, and at that moment the back door opened and Edna Ashley looked out.

"What're you kids doing out here?" she said. "Did you hear something hit the house?"

"That rock," Becky said, pointing.

Edna stood in the doorway with the kitchen light outlining her body. "You shouldn't be throwing rocks," she said, "you might accidentally hit someone."

"We didn't throw it. Someone threw it at Jason."

Edna came out onto the porch. "Well, who threw it?"

Jason said, "I don't know. There's no one out there."

Edna looked from one to the other, then stepped back into the light of the kitchen. "Now don't tell me that. You'd better get your brothers in here. Supper is almost ready."

"They're coming," Becky said, and followed the spill of light into the comfortably warm kitchen. She left the darkness with a shiver of relief. No one had thrown the rock. It had come with what seemed to be excessive speed, too much for one of the younger boys. She had a feeling that something she didn't want to see was out there in the darkening forest.

It was easier to pretend it had never happened. She had learned in her thirteen years that a lot of things were easier to handle if one just pretended they had never happened to start.

She woke in the night to the sound of voices and footsteps in the hall. She recognized her father's voice, and Shannon's. She listened to their footsteps go to the rear of the hall, to Barry's room, and return almost immediately. The footsteps went down the stairs then, both pairs. Becky leaned on her elbow and looked at her digital clock. It was just past one. Her dad probably had just arrived from the valley.

She lay back. It was good knowing her dad would be with them at the lodge for the next day and a half. He'd probably leave before noon on Sunday so that he could get home before dark. A few days ago she had plans made to cajole him into letting her go back with him, but now that Jason had come, and was so much fun, she didn't care if she went home all summer.

She turned over and closed her eyes. As she drifted back into sleep, she thought of the strange, flying rock. But it had lost its importance. There was no reason to tell her dad about it.

THERE WAS LITTLE TO REPORT. SHANNON SAID GOODNIGHT TO Ramon and went back up the stairs to her room. She had been awake, reading in bed, when the car lights flashed upon her bedroom window. She had known that Ramon would arrive either tonight or tomorrow morning. Since she was awake anyway, she put on her robe and went downstairs to meet him. She had made him a cup of coffee to relieve some of his fatigue, and while they sat at the kitchen table, had filled him in on all the happenings she recalled during their first week at the lodge. In her bed again she found herself too wide awake for the hour. She was looking forward to the weekend, she realized, more than she had looked forward to anything for quite a long time.

THE NEXT TWO DAYS PASSED RAPIDLY. RAMON'S ARRIVAL CREATED A family atmosphere that was warm and pleasant. Barry stayed close to Ramon, relieving Shannon of all responsibility, bringing his toys to play on the floor near Ramon's chair, or climbing up to relax on Ramon's lap, securely encircled by Ramon's arms. When Ramon told Shannon she could have the weekend off if she desired, she thanked him, but refused. She had no desire to drive back down to Los Angeles. There was nowhere there she wanted to go. Her apartment was closed now, no longer hers. She did, however, take the station wagon and drive over to the village where she wandered in and out of the shops for a couple of hours. But she found that she was watching the time too carefully, and that she was eager to get back to the lodge.

Saturday night there were games in which all the kids, even Barry, participated. A game of Monopoly lasted about two hours, and was replaced by a game of junior Trivial Pursuit. Barry, sitting on Ramon's lap, was Ramon's partner.

Shannon went to bed at midnight feeling tired and quite happy. Half asleep, she listened to the sounds made by the others as they settled down for the rest of the night. The house grew quiet, and

Shannon slept. She dreamed marvelous adventures in which Ramon and Barry played a part.

SHANNON WAS AFRAID BARRY WOULD CRY WHEN RAMON LEFT THE next day shortly after noon, but he didn't. However, he stood on the porch, refusing to wave goodbye. When Ramon's car disappeared beyond the curve in the lane, Barry turned and ran upstairs, and closed himself into his room. The door slammed, echoing the length of the hallway.

Shannon stood undecided at the bottom of the stairs.

Edna, passing by on her way to the kitchen, said, "I'd let him alone for awhile if I were you, Shannon. You know where he is, and you know he's all right. It's natural that he's not wanting his daddy to leave. But he'll be all right."

Shannon went up to her room, and left the door open so that she would know if Barry called her, or needed her. Of course he wouldn't call, he never had. Would he ever? Shannon arranged her pillows so that she could sit leaning back against them on her bed. She started to read, but found the house lulling in its silence. She slipped down into a more comfortable position and closed her eyes. Within moments she was asleep.

"HEY," JASON SAID, GRIPPING BECKY'S ARM IN STRONG, HURTING young fingers. "What do you want to do next?"

Giggling, she twisted her arm out of his grasp. They had walked around the house to the back where two bicycles leaned against the porch. Freddie and David had already taken theirs from this convenient parking place and were riding down to the lake.

"I don't know. Go to the lake?"

"How about the walk in the woods?"

"What is there to see in the woods but trees?"

"What is there to see at the lake but water?"

"People." Becky shrugged. "I don't know."

Jason reached for her arm again, and she dodged away from him and ran. He followed, reaching for her. She laughed and ran, back toward the shed, behind it and beyond. The land sloped down, creating a long, curved hollow that was scattered with boulders. Becky followed the curve of the land, running as hard as she could, with Jason behind her. He gave a sudden leap, with a pretend animal growl in his throat, caught her and threw her to the ground. Her fall was cushioned by the pine needles, and she lay limp and laughing as he pinned her to the ground. "Let me up!"

"Uncle! Cry uncle!"

His hands held hers on the ground above her head, the upper part of his body leaned lizard-like above her. The lower part pinning her helplessly.

"Aunt! Aunt!"

"No, say uncle."

"Sexist! You're a sexist pig."

"I'm not letting you go until you say uncle."

She laughed, giggled and squirmed beneath him, but she liked the feel of his body on hers, and even though she knew she would cry uncle eventually, she also knew she was going to put it off as long as she dared.

Beyond Jason's square young shoulder she could see a portion of the roof of the lodge, and a smaller portion of the back porch railing. They weren't as far away from the house as she had thought. She half guiltily looked for someone, Mrs. Ashley, Aunt Lynn, to come out onto the back porch and see them, but then she realized that they were too well hidden to see.

She gave a sudden lurch, to overthrow him, but he clasped her more tightly, and then bent his lips to her neck.

"I'm going to give you a hickey," he threatened.

"Oh no, no! Don't you dare!"

"I am."

"You're not either!"

"You'll have to cover your neck with a scarf the rest of the summer. I'll bring a wool scarf down from the attic just to cover all the hickeys you're going to get."

"No, hey . . . she cried, only half in mock fear.

"Hey no, Jason . . . Jason . . . *Jason!*"

"Barry. Barry."

Barry raised his head and looked about his room. It was Reid calling, but Reid was not here. The call seemed to come from far, far away.

"Barry. Come here, Barry."

Barry got up from the corner where he had been huddled since his dad drove away, and went into the hall. Reid was not in the hall, and neither was Juno. The hall was empty and quiet.

Barry went toward the stairway. He saw that Shannon's door was open, and she was taking a nap on her bed. She lay on two pillows, her neck twisted as though it were broken, like the neck of the dove that was sacrificed one time in the black room where *she* had done the bad things. He paused, and thought about going in to see if Shannon would wake up, but Reid was calling him again, from somewhere beyond the house.

Barry went down the stairs, quietly, holding the posts of the banister, one after the other until he reached the bottom of the stairs. There was no one in the living room. But he could hear Mrs. Ashley in the kitchen humming a song.

Barry went out the front door and stood on the porch looking toward the lake. He was alone except for the trees. He caught glimpses of David and Freddie as they biked along the road that circled the lake. Barry looked for Reid and Juno, but didn't see them. Were they hiding from him?

"Barry. Barry. This way, Barry."

The soft, far-away voice came from the other side of the house, the side where the trees grew so tall and so dark. Barry had never been on that side of the house, and he went there hesitantly and stood near the log wall and looked into the dark forest. Still he didn't see Reid or Juno.

"Come, Barry."

The voice sounded as though it came from deep in the forest, and even though Barry didn't want to, he followed the sound of the voice.

He walked on pine needles, and went from tree to tree in a straight line away from the house. He paused and looked into the tree tops for Reid, and for Juno. Sometimes Juno played hiding games in which he hung from his tail on a tree limb, his teeth showing in a silent laugh because Barry had a hard time finding him. And sometimes Reid himself climbed a tall tree to sit on a limb near the top. Even though he urged Barry to climb also, Barry had never climbed a tree taller than the fig tree in the yard at home. But today Reid and Juno were not in a tree. Not these trees. Reid was calling from somewhere beyond. Barry followed, deeper into the woods.

He caught a glimpse of bright clothing, a flash of green against the brown needles of the forest floor. Becky had been wearing a green blouse. Now her voice came to him.

"They'll kill us, Jason. Let me go."

And Jason's voice answered deep, muffled so that Barry couldn't understand what he said.

Barry ran forward, then stopped. Jason was on top of his sister, holding her down, and his face was hiding hers. Now they were silent. Then Becky began to squirm, trying to get out from under Jason. But Jason wouldn't let her go.

"No! No!" he screamed, running toward them, seeing them both sit up suddenly, their eyes big, their mouths opened and silent. Barry stopped, staring at them as they stared at him.

"Don't hurt my sister!"

Jason scrambled up, spreading his hands palm up in a gesture of good will. "Hey, man, I'm not hurting your sister."

Barry saw it was like the television shows where sometimes people didn't hurt each other. But he didn't like seeing his sister with forest things in her hair, and her clothes twisted.

Barry turned and ran back toward the house.

Becky scrambled to her feet and ran a few long steps after Barry.

"Barry!" she called, but he went on, going at last out of sight over the rise of the ground. She stood in silence watching for him to appear again on the back porch, waiting for him to cry out again. But the woods grew quiet, with not even a jay breaking the silence.

Becky turned slowly to look at Jason. He stood where he had risen, looking past her toward the house. Then abruptly he whirled and stared into the depths of the forest, as though he had heard a frightening sound. His head swiveled slowly as he looked into the trees. Suddenly his head jerked up and back as though he stared overhead into the upper branches of the tree. His mouth fell open, but no sound escaped. Alarmed, Becky's gaze followed his. She saw one bough below another dip and rise as if something quite heavy were dropping from limb to limb, yet there was nothing there. No animal was coming down out of the tree. Only movement and sound in the tree itself. The bottom limb dipped and as though he had suddenly gone mad, Jason began to flail his arms at something invisible to Becky. He stumbled backwards, fell, struggled to his feet again and tried to run. Something seemed to grasp him and hold him back. From his throat came hoarse, low cries, groans, sobs.

"Jason, what's wrong?" Becky hurried toward him, hesitated, ran again.

Jason seemed not to know she was there, and in growing horror Becky watched his shirt rip as though long claws raked down over his back. Flecks of blood stood out on his bared back. He whirled, fighting the invisible. Then with a hoarse cry of pain and fear, he began to run toward the lake.

Becky tried to call his name and couldn't. Her breath grew raspy and short as she ran following Jason.

Jason came upon the lake road suddenly, and crossed it in front of a car. The car stopped, and as Becky reached the edge of the road, started on again. She could see the angry, red face of the driver and read his lips as he muttered, "Crazy, doped-up kid."

Jason's shirt was hanging in shreds when he reached the lake. He climbed over a low boulder and dived from there into the water. Becky followed in his path, scrambling up on top of the boulder. She looked for Jason, but he was gone.

"Oh my God," she muttered under her breath. "Oh my God." Frantically she clawed her clasped sandals off her feet. She was wearing denim jeans, and they would become waterlogged in a hurry and hamper her as she tried to find Jason. She had to take them off, even though there might be people coming along the road who would see her.

She saw that Jason's opponent was human. But in her vision his size wavered, and as they spun in the water he at times looked large and overpowering, then again he seemed no larger than Jason, and sometimes smaller. He was wearing clothing, shirt, trousers, of a neutral color, and his hair waving like water fronds from his head was as golden as sunshine. They rolled in the water, and it seemed the stranger was pulling Jason down, down, as though trying to take him into the dark recesses beneath the boulders. Jason, struggling against him, was losing the battle.

Becky kicked out with one leg, and her foot touched the boy with the pale hair, and his head swiveled backwards on his body and he looked directly at her, his face a white oval in the water. Shock spiraled through Becky, for the face she saw was the face of Barry. Thinner, more mature, with a cold, flat lack of living soul in his eyes. The same nose, the same mouth. *Barry.* And yet, not Barry at all, but something that had tried to take the form of Barry.

She jerked back instinctively and swam for the surface. Her head broke through the water and she tried to scream, but her mouth filled with water and she found herself choking.

She caught a glimpse of movement on the road, a brown pickup with a state emblem. *A ranger truck.* With a sob of relief she raised an arm and waved, but the pickup moved slowly along the road, going on. Becky swam hard for the shore and scrambled out on a sandy spot. The pickup was about to go on by when her voice found substance and she screamed. The pickup stopped.

A young man dressed in a ranger's uniform got out of the truck, leaving it parked in the road with its driver's door open, and came running to Becky. She pointed toward the water with a fully extended arm.

"My cousin," she gasped. "He needs help. *Please.*"

"Drowning?"

"Y-yes."

As he spoke, the ranger unbuttoned his shirt and threw it off, then he bent to his shoes. Dressed in trousers, he followed the direction of Becky's motions and slipped into the water between the boulders.

The water seemed exceptionally murky, as though the mud on the bottom of the lake had been disturbed. He should have radioed for help, Ken Masters thought as he swam looking for a body that seemed not to be here. But in a drowning, or near-drowning, that extra minute of delay could be deadly.

He swam near the bottom of the lake and around the base of the boulder. He saw the shadow first, a silent, floating shadow thrown from a body above him. He reversed his strokes and looked upward. The body of a boy about sixteen years old was floating slowly outward toward the deeper distance of the lake. He was unconscious, obviously, for his arms and legs were being pushed about by the water.

Ken began to swim with all his strength. He reached the body and encircled the slender waist with one arm. The body came to life and began to fight. One fist caught Ken on the forehead, but the blow was softened by the water. The boy's body squirmed in Ken's arms, but he hung on and fought for the surface. The instant he brought the boy's head above water, the boy cried out with a voice that sounded tortured with pain and fear. His opened eyes stared at Ken as if he were seeing the sentry of hell itself, then he blinked and a great relief blocked out the fear. His hands clutched Ken Master's wide shoulders, holding him for support as he was half-dragged out onto the grassy strip between the road and the lake. Ken let him down, and the boy slumped, and began to cry.

"You're all right, kid," Ken said, touching his shoulder briefly. He saw that the boy's shirt hung from his shoulders in shreds, and there were several long, shallow scratches down his back.

"What happened here?"

The man looked at Becky from friendly, hazel eyes, but with suspicion. Somebody had done a good job on the kid's back. Like someone with long, sharp fingernails. Then he saw that the girl's nails were short. He picked up his dry shirt and put it on, wondering.

Becky stared from the ranger to Jason, feeling her body shaking violently, as was Jason's, from both the fear of what she had seen, and the sharp, chilly wind that blew over the lake.

Becky pointed toward the water. "He—he—something was fighting him. An animal. A—a boy."

Jason raised his head. His face twisted with fear and strangely, with anger. “No, that’s crazy, Becky. There was nobody there. *Nothing. Nobody.”*

She looked into his eyes and saw a fear as terrible as her own. *I saw them,* she wanted to say, yet his eyes stopped her. Later. Later. Not now in front of the stranger. Jason was shaking his head. Tears rolled down his cheeks. He lifted both fists and rubbed the tears away. When he looked up again the tears had stopped coming.

“You kids are freezing,” the ranger said. “Come on, get into the truck and I’ll take you home. Where do you live?”

“There, down that lane. The Frederick lodge.” Becky said.

The ranger opened the truck door and helped them in, Becky into the center. The boy seemed as boneless and limp as the girl.

Becky looked out over the lake. She looked at the rippling surface near the boulders where Jason had almost drowned. She searched the surface for the head of the boy who had been there, for the long, swimming body of the strange animal. But the water was undisturbed except for the wind and the constant movement from one shore back to the other. She felt the ranger’s body touch her as he slipped in under the wheel. The engine started, and the truck turned, angling around and back into the road and then to the right up the narrow lane.

About halfway to the house, they met David and Freddie on their bicycles. The two boys pulled out onto the side of the road and watched soberly as the truck went by. Then they mounted their bikes and kept pace behind, following.

The ranger pulled the truck into the circle at the front of the lodge and parked behind the station wagon. Jason opened his door and almost fell out. Becky followed.

“Hey!” said David and Freddie simultaneously, looking at Jason, and then glancing from him to Becky and the ranger as he got out of the truck. “What happened to you?”

“Yeah, what happened?”

Jason didn’t answer. With his shoulders hunched against the wind, and the fiery scratches on his back, he went glumly toward the steps. Freddie ran ahead of him yelling for their mother.

“Mom! Jason’s hurt himself. Mom!”

Lynn came out of her bedroom, a novel in her hand. She had been caught speechless, it seemed, as she looked at the people coming into the living room. Her eyes swept from one to all, and then settled on Jason. He stood hunched over as though he expected a beating, something he'd never had in all his life. What was left of his shirt dripped water on the floor, and his jeans were plastered to his legs. So too were the trousers of the ranger wet and wrinkled against his body. And standing slightly to one side was Becky, wearing only a wet blouse that only partly covered her panties.

Becky, seeing Aunt Lynn's eyes flick to her legs and remain there a moment, reached down and touched cold, wet thighs. "My God," she cried, "I forgot my jeans!"

Mrs. Ashley, brought from the kitchen by the commotion in the living room, said, "Well, go to your room and get another pair on. Change your wet clothes while you're there."

Becky obeyed without hesitation. Near the top of the stairs she met Shannon, looking wide-eyed and dewy fresh, as though she had just awakened. Becky passed her silently and went into her room, closing the door behind her.

She peeled out of her wet clothes and, shivering so hard her teeth chattered, she pulled on a long-sleeved sweater and dry, warm blue jeans.

She went back out into the silent, empty hall, and stood a moment listening. She could hear the ranger's voice, but couldn't understand what he was saying.

She went into the girls' bathroom and looked at her reflection in the mirror. She looked the same as always. There was no sign of the strange horror that lingered, chilling her skin, making goosebumps that wouldn't smooth away. Her hair was dark and damp, and she combed it away from her face. Then she went back into the hall.

Where is Barry? she wondered. For now it seemed that it was Barry she had seen in the water. Barry with a sharpened chin and cold, flat eyes. A very dangerous Barry.

She moved down the hall toward his room, chills radiating up and down her back in soundless warnings.

She stopped outside his closed door.

"Barry?" she said softly, touching his door, but not opening it, afraid of what she would see should she open it.

"Barry?"

On the other side of the door she heard footsteps, coming hesitantly, slowly. Or stealthily and malevolently. She was afraid to open the door, to face what was on the other side.

She wished she hadn't knocked.

CHAPTER 9

THE DOOR KNOB TURNED, slowly. The latch did not click. The knob began turning in the opposite direction, as if *he* on the other side did not want her to know that he was opening the door. Becky found herself taking a step backwards, her eyes helplessly mesmerized by that slowly turning knob. Then abruptly the knob began to rattle, moving up and down rather than around. And a plaintive voice called out from the other side of the door.

"Becky?"

It was her little brother calling for her. It sounded like her little brother. She started to touch the door knob and then pulled her hand back, the face in the water swimming again in front of her eyes. She saw him beyond the door, Barry grown large, Barry grown evil and deadly.

"Becky, help me. I can't get the door open."

"Barry," Becky responded on a sob half of fear as she grasped the doorknob and turned it, hearing the latch click open. He was, after all, her baby brother.

She couldn't deny the sound of his young voice needing her.

When she saw that he was the real Barry, *her* Barry, she fell to her knees in front of him. With tears in her eyes she held out her arms. He remained where he was, just beyond her reach.

"Barry, are you all right, sweet baby?"

He nodded. He took a step nearer her, then ran into her arms. His hand patted her cheek. "Don't cry, Becky," he soothed. "It's all right. It'll be all right. Jason won't hurt you anymore."

Becky pulled back and looked into his eyes. "Barry, did you think Jason was hurting me?" She paused for his answer, but he only returned her gaze in silence, his eyes round and timorous. "He wasn't hurting me," she said. "We were only playing."

Communicating with her little brother was not easy, Becky had found, especially since his bad experience at school. Before that it had been fun to talk to him, to hear him repeat every new word he heard and then arrange the new words in sentences. She and David had delighted in bringing multi-syllable words to Barry and listening to his pronunciation and the uses he put them to. Then he had been sent to the day school, and the change had started sometime during that year. On looking back, she couldn't pinpoint the time because, for one thing, she had become so busy with her own school and her friends, new and old, and all the activities her dad had allowed her to participate in. When she found out that Barry had changed, that he might never be the same again, she had felt guilty that she had almost forgotten he was there. Both she and David had stopped bringing long words to him and had stopped playing the word games. They had stopped talking to him much, or spending much time with him. Then when the shock came, when they found out Barry had been abused by a woman into whose care he had been entrusted, when their dad cautioned them on their treatment of Barry, it became painfully awkward to talk to him at all.

How far did she dare go? Suddenly he no longer was affectionate. Suddenly he was no longer the laughing, noisy little boy who didn't care if you laughed at him when he didn't pronounce every syllable clearly. He had changed, and to her sorrow, and her everlasting guilt, she hadn't realized when the change came. If their mother had lived, maybe she would have noticed and done something about it before it was too late.

Was it too late?

What had happened to her baby brother, Barry?

Had he in some way split not only personality, but physical matter too so that there were two of him now, one of which was cruel and dangerous?

"Barry," she said, "I need to talk to you about something very important."

"What?"

She searched for words, for descriptions, for question forms that would make sense. She looked into his innocent eyes, and gave up. She'd talk to Jason first. The thing in the water had fought him; for Jason to say he hadn't seen anything was ludicrous. Maybe he was afraid to say what he had seen. But later, when the others weren't around, then they could talk about it.

Becky kissed Barry's forehead. "Nothing, angel baby. We'll talk later. Want to go downstairs with me now?"

"All right."

She held his hand in hers, thinking this was the first time in months, in many months, that she had held his hand. She had been oddly afraid of him since the day their father had told them that something terrible had happened to Barry. She had felt his difference, even then. Had she been feeling the splitting of his psyche? Would her dad believe her if she told him her fears? Would Shannon? Or Mrs. Ashley? No, of course not. Being an adult meant there were things you knew were not possible. There were many other explanations for what she had seen, such as hallucination. That, her dad would tell her, Mrs. Ashley and Shannon and Aunt Lynn would tell her, was what she had seen. Her own hallucinations.

When they reached the bottom of the stairs, Barry pulled his hand out of hers, and pushed on, his back against the wall.

Jason was getting ready to go upstairs, and as she passed by him, she tried to draw his eyes to hers with sheer mind control, but she failed. He carefully kept his eyes lowered. He was not going to look at her. He acknowledged her presence only by drawing to one side, as though to touch her now would be fatal.

Aunt Lynn was talking to the ranger, her head turned toward him, but one arm out toward Jason as though to push him along ahead of her. "Thank you very much, Mr. Masters, for helping Jason. If he says he's all right, I'm sure he is. Thank you again."

She glanced at Becky as she too passed by, following Jason up the stairs. "Are you all right, dear?" she asked.

"Yes, I'm all right."

"Marvelous."

Aunt Lynn kissed Becky's cheek.

"Oh my, you're so cold," Lynn said. "Wrap yourself in the afghan, dear, on the sofa. I'm going up to put some ointment on Jason's back. He looks," she added cheerfully, "as though he's been in a bear fight, but he swears it was only a tree limb that tore his shirt and scratched his back. Whatever, I'm thankful he only got his feelings hurt."

"My feelings aren't hurt," Jason muttered as he climbed the stairs.

"If you're not more your old self tomorrow, my sweet, I'm taking you to the doctor."

"I thought you might take us home tonight," Becky heard him say. "We're not going to be here tomorrow, are we?"

"I see no reason for us to run home tonight, or even tomorrow," Lynn said. "So long as you stay away from the lake, unless you're properly supervised, you'll be all right. What on earth happened, Jason? Did you fall into the water? Surely you didn't attempt to go swimming this early in the season even in your clothes! Especially in your clothes. Sometimes I don't understand the kind of games you children play anymore. You have a scuba outfit, don't you? Did you bring it along? Isn't there something that you call a wet suit that you wear if you want to scuba dive?"

"It wasn't anything like that, Mom," Jason said, going into the boys' bathroom, his voice now distant, so that Becky had to strain to hear his next words.

"I slipped and fell, Mom, that's all. The boulder was slippery."

The door closed, and the voice of Aunt Lynn was a continuing mumble that no longer mattered to Becky.

Now she knew the story Jason was telling. And, if anyone should ask, her story would be the same. At least for now, until she could talk to Jason.

The ranger, Ken Masters, was at the front door getting ready to leave. But the way he was looking at Shannon was so obvious it practically shouted his interest in her, his reluctance to leave even though the wind was cold, the sun was going down, and his pants had only partly dried.

Shannon remained standing and holding the edge of the door, waiting to shut it should the man decide to go on out. They made a nice looking couple, Becky observed. Shannon with her long blond hair, her slender figure, and Ken Masters with hair that matched hers, though cut too short for Becky's taste, and a muscular body that was just right for Shannon's mate.

David and Freddie were standing and listening too, it seemed. Though Freddie grew restless and tapped David's shoulder.

"What'll we do now?"

David shrugged, but together they walked toward the rear of the house. Becky watched them go, wondering if David might understand, might deign to listen to her. But not in front of Freddie.

Mrs. Ashley peered into Becky's face. "Are you a little peaked, child?"

BECKY TRANSFERRED HER GAZE TO MRS. ASHLEY. "HUH?"

"You're looking a mite peaked to me, a little green around the gills. Why don't you come to the kitchen and let me make you a cup of hot chocolate. Come on now, you can count the calories later."

Becky followed behind Mrs. Ashley to the kitchen. The dark shadows of the conifers had already put the kitchen in a state of greenish twilight, that last light before the day was completely gone. Mrs. Ashley turned on all the lights.

"Can't stand that green light that this house seems to have most of the time," she said. "Sit down at the table, Becky. Do you want a shawl?"

"No thanks. I'm not really that cold."

"You're lucky you both didn't drown. I'd never trust that lake, not me, not to get that close to. Them boulders probably have moss on them, just enough to make them slick as glazed ice. It was lucky you was there with Jason, or he might've been gone now."

Becky looked behind her and took a long breath. The shadows in the corner behind the table seemed darker than usual, untouched by the overhead lights. The hot chocolate with the melting marshmallows on top didn't seem to help Becky's sense of coldness, of something terrible lurking in the corners where the shadows lay; nor did the smell of the food that Mrs. Ashley brought to the table.

THEY GATHERED FOR SUPPER, THE LIGHTS ON IN BOTH KITCHEN AND living room, the shadows lingering like creeping spies in little places, in tight places that Becky had never noticed before: under the refrigerator, behind the stove, and deeply and strongly in the pantry, whose door stood part way open. The blinds had not been drawn, and the light from the inside of the house glowed palely out upon the thick, dark trunks of the trees. Becky was reminded, in every direction she looked, of what she had seen, and of other things she might not have seen, invisible fingers reaching down from the green needles of the trees, a body dropping from one limb to the next, beings that were not delusions from her own mind.

Jason came down to eat, to her surprise, but he sat with his eyes down, and he sat at the end of the table, not by her side as he had until now. It was as though he blamed her for his afflictions. She tried to catch his eye, but he never looked up at her.

Later, she promised herself, she would talk to him.

If he gave her no other chance, she would go to his room, when all the others were asleep.

You can't avoid me, Jason, she promised him in silence. Whatever I saw, you must have seen too. *You must have.*

Shannon helped Mrs. Ashley clear away the dinner plates and bring the dessert to the table.

Jason looked up at his mother. "When are we going home?" he asked, his face reflecting the peevishness in his voice. He was reverting to the spoiled and babyish little cousin that Becky had not liked very well. She stared at him, but he looked only at his mother before he lowered his eyes again.

"I don't know when we're going home," she said.

Freddie paused in the voracious eating of his apple betty dessert. "I don't want to go home. If Jason's in such a hurry, can't he go by himself?"

Lynn looked at her youngest son. "How? Fly?"

Freddie shrugged, unsure of his stand. "Buses. There are buses, aren't there?"

Jason straightened, appearing suddenly to have a stronger back. "Yeah. Mom, I could go on the bus."

"And be unsupervised at home? No way, kid."

"Dad's there."

"Your dad is there at night, from nine o'clock on, if he's lucky. He doesn't have time to worry about you. Besides that, he's going on a business trip next week, to Europe. He'll be gone a month."

"I wouldn't run around."

"The answer is no. We'll go home in a few weeks. Meantime, why don't you rest up a couple of days and then start doing all the things you were doing before? You were having such a good time with Becky."

Still Jason didn't look Becky's way. He slumped, and gazed at his dessert. His younger brother watched him.

"Jason," he said, "if you don't want your dessert, can I have it?"

"Well for goodness sake, Freddie, give him a chance to taste it."

Jason handed his dish to Freddie. "That's okay, I don't want it. May I be accused, please?"

"What are you going to do? Go to bed?" Lynn asked.

"No."

"Would you like to play a game of Monopoly? Trivial Pursuit?"

"No."

"Oh, come on, it will keep your mind occupied." Lynn got up, her dessert untouched. "David, would you like a second dessert?"

"Sure, thanks."

Mrs. Ashley said, "I might as well not bother ever to ladle you up anything sweet, Lynn, you never touch it."

"I love it, Edna, but I can't keep a decent-sized waistline if I indulge myself."

"This here mania about waistlines is for the birds. That painter that painted all those chubby ladies back years ago didn't care about skinny waistlines. Those were good healthy women, then."

"Fat isn't healthy, Edna."

"It ain't unhealthy. Nature had a purpose for it. A little fat protects a body from starvation. From diseases, too. And from cold, come to think of it."

Lynn laughed. "I'll get the Monopoly game. Shall we play here on the kitchen table?"

The evening dragged. Becky played without interest, hoping as the hours slowly went by that Jason would tire of the game and go upstairs to bed, hoping that Aunt Lynn and Shannon and Mrs. Ashley would all decide they had had enough and the group would disperse, giving her an excuse to go to her room. Becky watched the clock, and watched Jason. He scarcely spoke a word all evening, but she saw that his eyes frequently went to the unshaded kitchen windows, looking out at the trees beyond, and at times he looked over his shoulder as though expecting to see something threateningly close.

Barry sat between Shannon and David, and one or the other of them helped him with his part of the game. At eight-thirty he yawned. Becky had been waiting for a sign of sleepiness from him.

"It's Barry's bedtime, isn't it, Shannon?" she asked.

"Yes, almost."

Becky opened her mouth to offer to help him to bed, but the words wouldn't come forth. She looked at the innocent face of her little brother and thought of the other face, the face in the water.

She didn't want to go alone into the upper part of the house with him, and yet it seemed ludicrous that she was afraid. She gave her money to Freddie, who sat on her right.

"I'll take him up to bed tonight, okay?"

Shannon looked at her with mild surprise. "Certainly, if you want to."

Becky shrugged, an attempt at casualness. "I'm kind of ready to go to bed myself," she said. "So I just thought he could go up with me, and the rest of you could continue the game."

Shannon said to Barry, "Would you like to go to bed, Barry?"

He nodded and climbed down from his chair. "Goodnight everyone," Becky said, and looked pointedly at Jason. But there was no response from him. The others said goodnight, and Becky took Barry's hand. It was small and cool in hers, boneless, like a little featherless bird, a small fist within the palm of her hand.

At the foot of the stairs in the living room, Becky looked up into darkness. She turned on the lights of the upstairs hall. Their steps on the stairs sounded loud and hollow, and she was conscious of the sound, as if somewhere above in the long length of the empty hall there were ears listening for their approach. From the game being played at the kitchen table came laughter as David conquered something desirable. The sounds of the voices there did little to subdue the dread Becky felt as she climbed the stairs with Barry's little fist in her hand.

He yawned again, using his free hand to cover his mouth.

When they were halfway down the hall, Barry twisted his hand out of hers. "I can go by myself," he said, and ran, his short little legs pumping.

Becky stood still, watching him, tempted to let him go alone to his room, and get into bed without help. Always before either David or Shannon had helped him, and at home their dad had put him to bed. Since she had offered, wasn't she obligated?

She reached his door just as he was preparing to slam it in her face.

"I'll tuck you in, Barry," she said. "Do you want me to read you a nice story?"

He hesitated. Becky pushed the door open and herded him toward the bed with her fingers lightly touching his shoulder. A cold wind swept across his bed, ruffling the spread, pushing the curtains at the window into the room like banners.

"Good Lord," she muttered, "who opened your window?"

"I did," he said.

"You couldn't have. You're too little." With effort she pulled the bottom sash down and locked it. The window frame was made of wood, she noticed, and it didn't move easily like the windows at home.

"I did some," Barry said.

"Where are your pajamas?"

"Under my pillow."

Barry lifted his pillow, and pulled forth a pair of blue knit pajamas.

"Do you need help?"

"No, I can put them on."

"Fine." Becky looked for a window blind, but there was none, and the curtains weren't the kind that could be pulled together. Though she tried, there was a six inch space in the center that was not covered. Between the curtains she could see the green needles of a tall pine tree. The limb scratched against the upper pane, making a noise like someone dragging long, pointed fingernails across a blackboard. Becky shuddered.

Barry had pulled the top of the pajamas over his head, and was pulling up the bottoms when Becky left the window. She picked up the shirt and jeans he had discarded.

"Get into bed and I'll turn out the light," she said. "Or would you like to have it left on?"

"No."

She tossed his clothes into the hamper in the corner, and folded the spread and laid it on the hamper. She kissed Barry on the forehead. At the door she looked back at him. Both hands clutched his blue blanket beneath his chin. His face was a pale ivory oval against the blue of his pillow and the blue of the blanket.

"I love you, Barry," Becky said softly.

"I love you," he replied.

"Do you want me to close your door or leave it open?"

"Close it."

Becky turned out his bedroom light and closed the door. She stood in the silent hallway and looked down its length. Still she could hear the screech of the pine bough against the window, a sound almost deadened by the closed door. Then she heard Barry's voice, murmuring, murmuring.

At first she thought he was talking to her, calling her back perhaps to read him a bedtime story after all. But as she listened, she realized he was not talking to her, he was talking to himself.

Or to someone who had been waiting in his room.

She almost opened the door again, but her hand on the knob froze. A band of fear tightened around her heart and coiled in her stomach. Her fingers withdrew from the knob with a will of their own, and she backed away, turned and hurried toward her own room.

She sat in her darkened room, on her bed, her knees hugged tightly against her chest, and stared out at the lighted hallway.

IT SEEMED AN ETERNITY BEFORE BECKY HEARD FOOTSTEPS ON THE stairs and the others began coming up to bed. Mrs. Ashley passed first, then the two boys, David and Freddie, both continuing the game by discussion. Becky heard Shannon say goodnight, then saw her pass along the hall and return after a moment. She had checked on Barry in his room. Becky wondered if Shannon had opened Barry's door and left it open.

Then at last Jason came in view and went into his room across the hall.

Becky waited, her chin resting on her knees.

The house quieted. From somewhere below there was a faint sound of voices and canned laughter, and Becky knew that Aunt Lynn was watching a sitcom on television.

Becky began to count minutes. She would allow twenty or thirty to pass, she decided, to lessen the chance that Mrs. Ashley or Shannon would come out into the hall again.

It was eleven-thirty when at last she slipped off her bed and tiptoed into the hall. All the lights had been turned off except the one on the wall above the stairs, and it was no more than a feeble night light. The rest of the hall seemed too heavily shadowed, too still and waiting.

Becky went to Jason's closed door and paused, looking carefully along the hall from one opened bedroom door to another. Shannon's door was open, and so was David's. Mrs. Ashley had closed her door, and Freddie had closed his. Barry's, at the far end of the hall, deep in shadows and distant from the light at the head of the stairs, might have been left open by Shannon. Becky couldn't see.

Her hand touched the door knob, her fingers tightened slowly, and she flinched against any sound it might make. The metal was cold, and suddenly she was reminded of death. And of the white face in the water. It had stood out in the dark water, with its chalk-white, mask-like first glimpse, in her memory, like something that might not really be alive. Yet it had moved, ferociously, fighting Jason. What had happened to him, to *it,* after that? Where was he when the ranger went down and brought Jason up? He hadn't mentioned seeing anyone. Like a fish, like the animal she had seen too, it must have swum beneath the boulders again.

The knob turned silently, and Becky checked the hall behind her once more before she pushed the door open and stepped into Jason's room.

To her surprise all the lights were on, and Jason was sitting bolt upright in his bed staring at her, his mouth hanging open as if he had lost his senses. She realized almost immediately that she had scared him. That he had been awake, and he had heard the doorknob whisper in its turning.

She swallowed a mouthful of air, and licked her suddenly dry lips. She returned his stare. She saw his eyes close briefly, as if in great relief. Then he was looking at her again, hard and angry.

"What are you doing here?" he hissed.

"Jason . . . I'm sorry if I scared you. But I have to talk to you."

"Now?"

"It's the first chance I've had, you know that."

She went without invitation to his bed and sat on the edge of it. His glare didn't soften, but beneath the firm set of his jaw she detected a faint quivering. She leaned on her hand nearer him, so that he could hear her whisper.

"Jason, I've got to talk to you about what was fighting you in the water."

"What?" He frowned.

"That—that boy."

"What boy?"

"I think something weird, really weird, is going on. I want to know what you saw. In the tree before you ran. That jumped out of the tree on you. The thing that made the scratches on your back. And the boy in the water. What did you see? Did you see his *face*?

"You're crazy. I don't know what you're talking about. I didn't see anything. My back was scratched by tree limbs. There wasn't anything in the water."

"Jason—"

He jerked his blanket up to his chin. "Go on to bed, Becky, and stop acting crazy. There wasn't anything in the water, or in the tree. Nothing chased me. I didn't see anything at all. I'm getting out of here just as soon as I can. If Mom won't take me, I'm going by myself."

Becky drew back. Jason was scared, she could see that, too scared even to talk to her.

"You're acting like you blame me for what happened," she accused.

"That's silly. Why would I blame you?"

"What did happen, Jason? What made you run to the lake?"

"Nothing. Nothing!"

He was almost in tears now, and Becky felt embarrassed for him. Of all things, she didn't want to see him cry. She turned her head away.

If he had seen the face in the water, he was too frightened of it to talk about it even to her.

"I thought maybe that you thought you were just having delusions or something," she whispered. "I wanted you to know that I saw it too. I swam into the lake to try to help you, and I saw the boy holding you, trying to drown you—"

"No!" he cried, his voice hoarse and too loud. "There was no one there. What's the matter with you?"

Later, she thought, when he wasn't so scared, maybe he would talk about it to her. Tomorrow, maybe, or the next day.

At the door she looked back at him, but again, as he had all evening, he was avoiding her eyes. He sat on his bed with his blanket pulled up, and although his legs were long, and his shoulders broad, he looked young and vulnerable.

"Good night, Jason," she said.

CHAPTER 10

JASON WANDERED from room to room of the lodge, trying to avoid Becky. Whenever he happened to be in the same room with her, whenever he happened to glance at her, she was looking at him. He could see that she wanted to talk to him, perhaps she wanted to ride bikes again and play around and have fun the way they had before—before he acted like a nut and jumped into the lake.

When he saw that Becky had sat down with a book in front of the television and was half watching an afternoon soap opera and half reading her book, he went into the kitchen.

"Are you hungry?" Mrs. Ashley asked. She was taking something that smelled really good from the oven, and for a moment he almost forgot his restlessness.

"What are you baking?"

"Gingerbread. Did you ever eat hot gingerbread with pure butter?"

"No."

"Sit down and I'll serve you a piece."

Jason sat at the end of the table that was closest to the wall. Even that didn't help much. Ever since *something*—he hadn't seen what—had seemed to jump out of the tree at him, he had felt that it was behind him. Only when his back was safe against a wall, or the head of his bed, did he get rid of the feeling that something was following him around. At times he felt like he couldn't stand it another minute, or that he would run screaming again, maybe into the lake again, or anywhere to get rid of it. He had hardly slept last night at all. He'd nod off, then wake abruptly, to see that his room was quiet and he was alone. He had watched the sun rise through his window. He was glad the night was over. He even felt a little hungry. But when he came down to watch Mrs. Ashley cook breakfast, he had found that he could hardly swallow.

He wanted to go home. Oh God, how he wanted to go home. He wanted to feel the mists of San Francisco again, and watch the fog drift away over the bay. He wanted to see his buddies, do the things he did when he was out of school. He wanted to sprawl in the cluttered safety of his own room and reread his favorite old comic books.

But he had asked his mom so often to leave that he had finally begun to whine, the way he did when he was ten years old. It made him bitter toward her, gave him a feeling of hatred around his heart. Why didn't she listen to him? All she wanted to do was lie on her bed and read those dumb books. She had brought a suitcase full with her, all paperback romances. "It's my vacation too, Jason," she had said the last time he went to her room to beg her to take him home. "Give me a few more days, at least."

A few more days. That was a promise. They wouldn't stay a month, as they had first planned, but just a few more days. He looked at the clock. It was only ten minutes after ten in the morning. It seemed like an eternity since the ranger had helped him out of the lake.

Mrs. Ashley placed on the table before him a serving of golden brown gingerbread, sliced in half and melting two pats of butter. It smelled delicious, and Jason found it tasted as good as it smelled. At least now he could swallow.

"Not feeling so good today, are you?" she asked. She poured a glass of milk and set it beside his plate.

"Not too good, I guess."

"Had a nasty experience yesterday."

He shrugged a shoulder. He didn't want to talk about it or think about it. He glanced over his shoulder, but the wall was only an arm's length away. No one stood behind him.

"Maybe if you went on and rode your bicycle with Becky again you'd feel better."

No, he thought vehemently. He didn't want to see Becky again either. When he saw her he felt like a fool, because he couldn't explain his behavior. He had heard something in that tree, after the little kid Barry had run away, something had made him look up into the tree. And he saw a shadowy form dropping from limb to limb. But its body had been as insubstantial as a part of fog. In short, there was nothing there. But after that he actually *felt* things. He felt them. The pain of invisible claws raking his back, vile breath on his cheek, hands pulling him down, down into the water. To admit these things was to admit he was losing his mind.

He had to go home. He had to get away from here.

He didn't want to see Becky any more.

"Maybe you could ride over to the village," Mrs. Ashley persisted, "and go to the ice cream shop for a malted. It's only a couple of miles or so."

"Maybe," he said, to shut her up. He got up from the table. "Thanks for the cake. It was really good."

"I always liked gingerbread," she said. "Make it for myself when I don't have anyone else to cook for. My own sons both loved gingerbread too. And so do my grandsons. But I don't get to see them but once a year or so, they live so far away. My oldest son is in Houston, Texas. He's an engineer. And my baby boy lives up in Washington. My grandchildren are growing up."

Jason wandered about the kitchen, wanting to leave, but not able to as long as Mrs. Ashley was talking. He was relieved when finally she paused long enough for him to say thanks again and slip out the back door.

He stood on the porch and looked into the trees. He yearned to lose himself among them, to walk and walk, but he was afraid to.

He sat down on the steps. To his left, leaning against the porch, was his old bicycle, and Becky's. They both were scratched and peppered with dents. His bicycle had been here at the lodge since it was new, when he was about ten or eleven years old, maybe younger. So had Becky's.

He heard the voices of Freddie and David. They were yelling at each other. They always seemed to be yelling, as if they were afraid they wouldn't be heard if they didn't raise their voices.

They came skidding around the corner of the house on their bicycles, and stopped.

"Hi," they both said.

"How're you feeling?" David asked.

"Okay."

"Want to ride with us?" Freddie asked eagerly. "We'll race you to the end of the lane."

"No, thanks." He felt a little guilty for refusing. He shrugged, changing his mind. Freddie always acted so happy when Jason joined him for a little activity of some kind, a little ball throwing, a bike ride. He didn't have anything else to do, he decided, and it would help pass some time. "Want to shoot some baskets?"

"Yeah, hey yeah!" Freddie dropped his bicycle. "Come on, David."

"Okay. Do you know where the ball is?"

"Somewhere in the shed. I'll find it."

Jason followed behind them and waited at the door of the shed while the two boys began rummaging around in the junk. The shed was dark and shadowed, the only light coming in at the door. Jason stood with one foot on the threshold looking in. Everybody's old junk had found its way into the shed it seemed. There was even an old treadle sewing machine in one corner. Shelves on the wall held such items as old dolls with half their hair gone and the rest a matted mess; games that no one played anymore; boxes of jigsaw puzzles; and large, unmarked cardboard boxes that were tied with string or taped.

Crowded slightly behind one of the dolls Jason saw the basketball.

"Hey, guys, there it is."

He watched David reach for it.

EDNA FINISHED EATING THE LAST BITE OF THE SERVING OF gingerbread on her plate. Her stomach had a contented feel, like an old cat that had curled up in front of a fire. She hated people talking about diets all the time, refusing to eat the desserts she had gone to so much trouble preparing, but, she thought as she patted her stomach, she really should try to take off a few pounds. Her incentives now, though, were small to almost nonexistent. Since her husband died there just didn't seem to be any reason to keep a waistline. Those pieces of pie or cake that added so much to her enjoyment of life were adding also to her waist. Once a two hand span, it now would take half a dozen hands to reach around her, she supposed, although she wasn't measuring. Ignorance is bliss, she told herself, eat the cake and forget the waistline.

She pushed her chair back and got up and cleared the table of all but the tray in the center that held paper napkins, sugar, pepper, salt and artificial sweetener. She put the two dirty plates in the dishwasher, and the rest of the gingerbread cake in the pantry. She came back to the sink with a head of lettuce from the refrigerator. Salad for lunch, always. Lynn would starve to death if it weren't for salads.

The window over the sink suddenly crashed into the room, throwing chunks of glass into the sink, and onto the front of her dress. At the same instant something whizzed on past Edna's head and hit the wall behind her. She had ducked instinctively, and with the shattered glass from the window still tinkling down from the window frame, she looked around at the object on the floor. She saw a rock almost as large as her head. It had made a hole in the wall.

She brushed fragments of glass from her arms. Beads of blood appeared here and there as she dislodged the glass. She picked a sliver of glass from her index finger. Her heart pounded with alarm and growing fury as she realized what had happened.

One of the boys had thrown the rock, deliberately aiming for the window. There was no other way that rock could have hit so precisely.

Edna rinsed the blood off her arms and patted the tiny wounds with the kitchen towel as she went to the door. The three boys were innocently playing basketball, fighting over the ball, tossing it into the basket that was fastened to the front of the shed. To look at them, one would think they didn't know beans about any broken window or any rock that had come through it so hard and fast that it had made a hole in the kitchen wall. And they were making so much noise the dead itself would stir, as if their noise would cover up their guilt.

"All right," Edna shouted from the porch, "Which one of you threw that rock?"

They turned toward her, looking like three innocents with the souls of lambs. They were stair-stacked in heights, with David in the middle. Edna couldn't really believe that David would do such a thing. And the rock was too large for the little boy, Freddie, to handle, at least to throw. It had to be Jason. And right after she had served him hot gingerbread with butter. That was gratitude!

"What rock?" David asked.

"The rock that broke the kitchen window right in front of me, and almost got me in the head! The rock that's lying right now on the kitchen floor. The very same rock that made a hole in the wall!"

She looked from face to face and finally let her glower settle on Jason.

"Don't you have anything better to do than throw rocks at windows?"

He motioned outward with his hands, a gesture of perplexity. He didn't know what she was talking about. He opened his mouth, but nothing came out.

Freddie cried, "I thought I heard something! Did it break the window?"

"Well of course it broke the window!"

Lynn came out onto the porch. She was wearing a caftan of large, splashy figures and bright colors, but she looked colorless without makeup. Edna was glad to see her. She could deal out the punishment that Edna hardly dared try. If Jason had been ten years younger he already would have been over her knee, no matter whose kid he was.

"What's all the shouting about?" Lynn asked. "Did I hear something break?"

"Just let me show you," Edna said huffily, leading the way back into the kitchen. She was followed by Lynn and the three boys. She showed them the window first and the glass that was scattered from sink to surrounding cabinet top to the floor. She pointed out the hole in the wall. And finally, the rock.

"My God," Lynn said. "And there's blood on your arm."

Edna took a tissue from her apron pocket and blotted up the tiny oozings of blood. "This is nothing," she said. "The thing is, the rock just missed my head. If I hadn't jumped, it'd be my head with the hole in it instead of the wall. This is the second time somebody was in the back of the yard throwing rocks. It happened the other day, but it hit the wall above the porch."

"You could have been killed," Lynn said.

Edna looked pointedly at Jason. He caught the accusation in her glance and stepped back, as if it were a physical blow.

"Hey, I didn't do it," he said. "I didn't even know about it until you told us. I was shooting baskets with Fred and Dave. And I know neither of them did it."

Both younger boys began shaking their heads, their eyes wide and wondering.

"I'll help you clean up," Jason said, and stooped to pick up the rock. He had to use both hands, it was so large.

Edna saw that it was not possible that even Jason had thrown the rock, and for the first time she felt the beginning chill of fear. It replaced her anger and left her trembling.

Becky and Shannon came into the kitchen from the front of the house asking, "What happened?"

Lynn explained to them, with the help of both Freddie and David.

Edna watched Jason go toward the back door with the rock in his hands. She held open the screen. She wanted to tell him she was sorry that she had suspected him, but she couldn't find her voice. Her mouth tasted bitter, and dry as an old shoe. She heard behind her the clink of glass and turned to see that Shannon was sweeping the broken window into a dustpan that Freddie was holding for her.

Lynn wiped the glass off the sink and the counter-top. Jason came back and got a paper bag from the pantry and took over the job of finishing the cleaning.

"The window will have to be replaced," Lynn said.

Only the lower half was broken. Edna looked at it. A cool breeze from the forest was blowing in, making different pitched whistling sounds. The heavy scent of pine was almost nauseating.

"I'll put cardboard there," Edna said. "I think I'd feel safer."

"I'll help you," Jason offered. "There are lots of old boxes in the shed. I'll cut a piece as soon as I finish getting the glass up."

"Thank you," Edna said. "I appreciate your help. I'm sorry I yelled at you."

"That's okay."

The kitchen gradually emptied. Shannon and Becky and Lynn went back into the hall and toward the other parts of the house. The younger boys followed Jason to the shed. With shaking hands, Edna began to make salad.

She thought of Barry suddenly. Where had he been during all the commotion that he hadn't also come into the kitchen? In his room, probably. And it was just as well.

Where had that rock come from?

She had read of things like that, of rocks flying through the air from no particular source. Of other things moving from their places, as if from invisible hands. She didn't believe any of it was possible, or that it had ever happened or ever could.

And she refused to believe it now.

Jason was grateful for the job. He managed to make it last through most of the afternoon. He carefully measured the window and transferred those measurements to a sheet of cardboard he had flattened from a box. With his knife he cut the cardboard, and with the boys giving suggestions he fastened it to the broken window. He used both a roll of gray tape he found in the shed, and small nails which he tacked through the cardboard into the window frame.

When at last he was finished the sun was beyond the mountaintop and the air from the forest felt cold on his arms.

The boys, bored with him and the covering of the window, had gone on their bikes again for a race down the lane.

"It's just like the other day," Becky said.

Jason whirled, startled. She stood on the porch watching him. He hadn't heard a sound of her approach.

"What?"

Her face was solemn. "The rock. Only this rock was bigger. And it almost killed Mrs. Ashley."

"No, it didn't. It missed her."

"What if it hadn't?"

"I don't see what that's got to do with anything," he cried angrily.

"Where did it come from? Who threw it?"

"I don't know. Nobody. Hell, man, I don't know!" He hoped he wouldn't cry, even though suddenly he felt like it. "It's crazy around here. I'm going home." Of course he couldn't. His mother wasn't ready to go. But Becky didn't challenge him. She sighed, long and softly. The cold wind, coming somehow through the trees to the north of the house, whistled in fine tunes around the edges of the cardboard.

To Jason, suddenly, it sounded like tiny voices, laughing, tinkling with their secrets; cruel little voices that cut the air around the bumbling, helpless humans. He shivered. An old tune he had heard went through his mind in silent notes, singing the lyrics, hauntingly:

"In the pines,
In the pines,
Where the sun never shines
And you shiver when the cold wind blows—"

CHAPTER 11

THE INCIDENT of the rock puzzled Shannon. She could see that Edna was disturbed, and the more the woman thought of it, the more disturbed she became. "I don't think rocks can travel by themselves," Edna said more than once to Shannon, "and yet I don't think any of our boys threw it." Shannon agreed. "And then again," Edna said, "what fool would be out in the back yard throwing rocks through the windows? Especially with the three boys in plain sight playing ball? If I were a superstitious soul, I'd say the rock came by itself." Edna worked feverishly in the kitchen, wasting energy as so much of the time she would look into the refrigerator then close the door without removing anything. Her steps carried her from pantry to counter to table, and most of the time she went empty-handed. She'd stop in the middle of the floor and look around as if she couldn't remember what she was going to do.

"Maybe we do have a bit of poltergeist activity," Shannon said, trying to think of something that would put Edna at ease. "Investigators of poltergeist activity claim that some people possess powers that cause objects to move by themselves."

Edna snorted. "Pshaw! Do you believe that? I don't believe that. I say when an object moves, there's something moving it, and it's usually a hand."

Shannon suggested that Edna take the station wagon and go to the village, and to the supermarket. That instead of being driven there, she might like to go alone. Edna agreed after a long pause. An afternoon away from the lodge might do her good, she admitted.

For the next two days Edna seemed to be back to normal. There were times when Shannon could even hear snatches of songs coming from the kitchen. But Edna's ease of mind did not remove the incident from Shannon's thoughts. Whereas she had encouraged Barry to play outside, she now felt safer with him indoors. And even there she was aware of the position of each window and how safe he was should another rock crash through. Then she too began to relax, and with Barry at her side, and often one or two of the older kids, she took long walks to the lake and along the road. Barry spent his time running on ahead, or running back and holding up the walk with his loitering. Shannon stood and waited for him in silence, enjoying the warm sunshine. Only along the road that ran near the edge of the lake did the sun shine faithfully. On the private lane to the lodge the conifers threw a heavy, perpetual shade.

Shannon noticed the change in Becky and Jason's relationship. Since the day the ranger had rescued him from the lake they neither rode bicycles together as they had before, nor did they even talk. When Becky walked with her and Barry, Jason did not. When Becky remained in the house, Jason usually caught up with them before they reached the end of the lane. Neither of them was much company. After a few tries at conversation, Shannon gave up.

The weather, which seemed to be unusually cold over the weekend and early part of their second week at the lodge, warmed at midweek. Once again Shannon decided that Barry could safely play in the corner by the front steps as long as she stayed on the porch nearby. Though she watched among the trees for movement of any kind, there was none. A few birds flitted into sight now and then. Squirrels came down the trunk of the tree in the center of the circle drive, head first, and looked curiously at Barry. Certainly there was no danger there.

Shannon hadn't told Ramon about the rock through the window.

She unsnapped and unzipped her jeans and clawed them off her legs. With her blouse barely covering her thin bikini underpants she dove into the water. It enveloped her icily, running a shock of coldness straight to her heart. She pressed her lips tightly against the water, held her breath and opened her eyes.

The water was murky, and her eyes stung. She closed them automatically, then opened them again. She had to find Jason. He had gone utterly crazy, and she had a fear that he might fight her when she found him and drown both of them. But she had to take that chance.

The water seemed deeper here than she had ever realized. Beneath the surface were more boulders as large as the one from which they had dived. Above she could see the water rippling in its everlasting race to the shore and back again. She turned and swam, going around one boulder and deeper into the lake.

She caught a glimpse of a shadow, moving swiftly. It disappeared into a crevice between the rocks. Her lungs began to feel as though they were bursting, and she swam to the surface and gulped fresh air, and for a moment the sun shone warmly on her face. She looked for help, a car along the road with people that might help her find Jason. But the road was empty. Not even Freddie and David were in sight. She took another deep breath and dove.

She swam between the boulders where she had glimpsed the shadow and came face to face with an animal that stared at her from eyes as hard-surfaced as ball bearings. It had a long, evil looking muzzle from which worm-like whiskers undulated in the water. He swam several feet under water and whipped by her with his thin long body sinuating like a snake's. His long tail cut the water behind him, and Becky pulled back to avoid being touched by it. In her surprise and her fear she almost gasped. Water burned in her nose for an instant. The animal was gone as quickly as it had appeared, and Becky forced herself to go forward into the dark water deep between the boulders.

She saw two figures, fighting, and recognized the shreds of Jason's shirt. The thing he was fighting had a long body that threw a humanoid shadow upon the boulder, a shadow as sinuous and undulating as that of the animal. She swam toward them, although a strange sense of doom surrounded her as completely as the cold water.

There was something about it that was too peculiar. If the cardboard in the window weren't evidence that it had happened, Shannon would think they'd all been dreaming.

She had told him about Jason's near-drowning, of course. His response to that was exactly what she expected. "You tell those kids they aren't to get close to that lake without a supervisor." When Shannon passed the word on to the kids, she got no response at all. Becky and David now looked at her in perplexed silence, as if the thought of going swimming without an adult around had never entered their minds.

Shannon was sitting on the steps while Barry played with his cars and trucks when the pickup came slowly up the lane and parked. The ranger got out, smiling. He looked as though he had just come from the laundry, his uniform was so sharply pressed. He wore it well, his build at its peak in fitness. Shannon could almost see him at his daily workout. He probably ran five miles a day, she thought with the chagrin of laziness. She enjoyed walking, dancing, swimming. But jogging? Not unless there was a bear behind her.

She got up, stretched unobtrusively, and went down the steps. A spot of sunshine had found its way through the trees where the clearing for the house had been made, and now warmly enclosed Barry and his playground like gods favoring a special child. After taking a long look at the ranger, Barry turned most of his attention back to his play.

Shannon stood with the backs of her hands against her hips, her fingers tucked into the hip pockets of her jeans, and smilingly waited for the man to approach.

"Hello," he said. "I'm Ken Masters. I met you the other day when I brought the kids up from the lake."

"Certainly, I remember you."

She recognized interest in his eyes. The way he kept looking at her, with an occasional, quick, almost embarrassed glance down at her body, gave him away. Although he was probably twenty-five years old, at this moment he might have been fifteen again and approaching a girl for the first time.

"I came to see how they are," he said.

She nodded, turned back toward the house. "I don't know exactly where they are, but I think they're both in the house. Won't you come in?"

"Oh no," he said hastily. "I just thought I'd ask. Couldn't we . . . I saw you sitting on the steps. If you don't have anything else to do, maybe we could just sit there and talk awhile?"

"Of course."

"I saw the two younger boys on bicycles halfway between here and the village."

"Oh really?" Shannon returned to her seat on the step, and Ken sat down beside her.

"There's hardly any traffic though this early in the year. I suppose they're safe enough."

"I hope so. They're allowed to ride pretty much as they please, but I didn't know they were wandering so far away."

"If you want me to I'll send them back."

"I'm sure they'll be all right. You were inquiring about Jason and Becky. They're okay too, but I think they're avoiding the lake now. The experience subdued both of them."

"I've been thinking about that, and wondering what happened. What was that kid doing in the water with all his clothes on? I didn't ask, because sometimes it doesn't seem to be important at the time of the accident, but since then I got to wondering."

"I don't know. I haven't heard either of them say much about it."

"Well, maybe he slipped and fell. He was in quite deep water at the edge of a boulder. The girl had been trying to get him out, apparently. I'm glad I came along when I did."

"Yes, we were fortunate that you did."

"I'm glad the kids are all right. Jason was luckier than some of the people who have had accidents in the lake."

They talked of impersonal things for awhile, and gradually the awkwardness began leaving. Shannon learned that he had been a forest ranger for three years, and that he lived year round in the mountains. That June was quite early for swimming in the lake anyway, and that lifeguards were on duty during July and August at some of the more populated areas around the lake. He didn't say, but she surmised that he was unmarried. As they talked, Barry played on, and David and Freddie came in view at the bend in the lane. They made a sharp turn on their bikes and rode out of sight again toward the lake road. They came in view occasionally then, bright snatches of color and movement beyond the smooth, dark columns of tree trunks.

"I noticed," Ken said, "that your name is different from the others. And I know I've never seen you around before. I remember the Frederick family and the others—the sister and her kids. I've seen them before on their vacations here. We have to make a point of knowing the names of the lodge owners. We kind of keep an eye on the properties during the off seasons. So I was wondering—I was hoping that you're—that you might be free for dinner some evening."

"Why thank you," Shannon said, feeling at that moment like a much older woman who should feel flattered by such attention, yet amused at the same time. "It's nice of you to ask. However, I'm employed by the Fredericks. Barry is my responsibility for the summer, and I can't leave him. He's the three-year old who's playing here beside the porch."

Ken's face looked hurt, as if she had thrown cold water at him. "Couldn't you go out after he goes to bed at night?"

Shannon started to answer no, but hesitated. Even if Ken Masters were a fresh-faced twenty-year old, which wasn't likely that he was so young, she still would be only eight years older. Not that it was important. But she found herself comparing him to Ramon, and the comparison did not flatter him. However, it would be nice to get away, she decided, for an evening in a different setting. And perhaps it would be advisable for her to start spending less time around Ramon on the weekends. There was no room in her life at this time for too much interest in any man. She would be returning to Los Angeles at the end of the summer, and school and work, and all that entailed. The Fredericks would fade from her life.

She felt a sudden twinge of sadness, and she knew it was already too late. She had allowed herself to become too fond of the Frederick kids, especially Barry. She had become too eager to see Ramon on the weekends. She looked forward to his phone calls too much. The best thing she could do would be to absent herself on Saturday nights when Ramon was here with his family.

"I could go out Saturday night," she said. "Barry's dad comes up every Friday night and stays until Sunday. He has offered me the weekend off, but there was no place to go. No place I wanted to go."

Ken's face had brightened. He hadn't learned yet to hide his feelings behind the mask of maturity. Shannon gave him a gentle smile. She liked him, she decided. His boyishness was charming.

BECKY STOOD AT THE LIVING ROOM WINDOW LOOKING OUT. SHE SAW Ken Masters sit down with Shannon on the steps and her first hope that he would come on into the house was dashed. Her interest waned almost immediately, and she turned away. The house was quiet. She thought of turning on the television, but at this time of day there wouldn't be much other than soap operas, and she wasn't in the mood for that.

If only Jason didn't act as if he hated her now.

She wondered where he was. Aunt Lynn was in her room with her door shut. Mrs. Ashley was in the kitchen as usual. Shannon was out on the porch talking to the ranger. Barry was playing beside the porch. The boys were riding their bikes. But where was Jason? Up in his room?

Becky went up the stairs slowly. The second floor was almost eerily silent. The hall stretched toward the back of the house like a tunnel through a mountain, the only light coming out from the bedrooms whose doors had been left open.

Becky saw that Jason's room was one whose door was open, but the room was empty. She stood for a moment on the threshold, looking in. There was little light here, for the curtains were pulled.

She wandered into his room. It was no larger than her own. The bed took up most of the space, sticking out from the center of the north wall. At each side of the bed were matching night stands, holding twin lamps. In the corner near the door was a narrow chest. Directly opposite the chest was a small dresser with attached mirror.

The single window was covered by a print drapery that matched the bedspread.

Becky idly passed the foot of the bed, sliding her hand along the knobby railing of the footboard. She parted the draperies, pushed them aside and gazed out the window into the dark green branches of a tree. It wasn't much of a view, she decided. On her side of the house the trees had been cleared away sometime long ago to make room for the unused road that went to the back of the house. At least now the limbs didn't grow against the windows.

When she turned away from the window, she saw the neat pile of paper on his bedside table. Beside it lay a pen. Jason had been writing something.

With avid curiosity she looked at it without touching. Then, seeing the subject, she forgot everything she had ever been taught and picked up the loose leaf notebook pages. She read carefully his neat handwriting:

TO UNDERSTAND AN IMPOSSIBLE OCCURRENCE:

I was not alone. Becky was there. She was unharmed. Note that. First of all, nothing like this had ever happened to me before in my life. I mean I'm not the kind of guy that goes around getting jumped on. What happened here was this:

I heard a sound in the tree above me. As I recall it now, it sounded like a deep growl. What I was afraid of was a mountain lion. I know they climb trees sometimes, and although they avoid people, so I've read, there was a chance that this one was not the normal, timid big cat. So I looked up, but I couldn't see anything except— movement of a tree branch several feet up in the tree, almost at the top. It happened fast, yet I saw it like slow motion, a tree limb moving, swinging down then letting up, as if a heavy object had dropped from it, then the limb below it doing the same thing. Something seemed to be coming down from the upper branches of the tree, yet I saw nothing but a kind of dark spot. Like the shadow of something. It reached the bottom limb, and dropped, and the limb sprang up. And suddenly something sharp raked my back. I could feel my skin tearing. I could hear it. It was like claws that started at my belt and raked upwards, and the weight of its body was on my shoulders and head, and there was something tight around my neck choking me. I started to run. I went crazy. Something was tearing me up, yet nothing was there. I ran, and I heard footsteps running behind me. They weren't Becky's steps. She was there too, but I had forgotten her. These other steps were heavier than Becky's steps and spaced farther apart, as if some guy was there, a guy my size or bigger.

I guess I thought the water would help. And it did. Whatever it was on my back disappeared, fell off, or maybe jumped off, when I hit the water. I went under, and down, down. It was deeper there than I had known. But that didn't scare me. It was the other thing that made me panic, whatever that was. Then when I began to swim, arms came wrapping around me and pulled me down. I couldn't get to the surface. Maybe they weren't arms, but that was what they felt like. It wasn't the same thing that had clawed my back and choked me. The rest is history. I don't know what would have happened if the ranger hadn't dived in. I don't remember that part. I guess I blacked out for an instant, maybe longer. The next thing I knew the ranger was hauling me out of the water. The other sensations, of arms pulling me deeper into the water, of claws and things, all that was gone.

Now:

It wasn't a tree limb that scratched my back and tore my shirt. I said that only because it was the only logical answer. But—maybe it really was the tree limb. I saw it swing down. The tree needles are sharp. They might have scratched me. And the mind can do kinky things. I found that out when I took that LSD and that angel dust that time. Maybe that's still working on me. So . . . the truth is:

No. 1. The limb tore my shirt, scratched my back.

No. 2. Seeing the little boy, Barry, kind of scared me. And it scared him too, I guess, the way he ran. And I was getting this thing for Becky, even though I knew I shouldn't, since she's my cousin and all, so when we jumped up and Barry ran, some part of my brain must have gone haywire (the part that did the other time) and my mind punished me by making me feel like I was being chased and mauled as if a real mountain lion had jumped out of the tree on me.

No. 3. If it happened once, couldn't it happen again?
No. 4. I deduce it's not likely to if I stay away from Becky.

BECKY LAID THE HANDWRITTEN PAGES BACK WHERE SHE HAD FOUND them. Her lips were beginning to form silent denials. "No, not me, Jason. And not the drugs you took once."

She heard footsteps in the hall. They were coming toward the bedroom, firm, slow, quite heavy steps. Too heavy to be Shannon or David or Freddie, or even Mrs. Ashley. It did not sound exactly like Jason's steps, but she knew it had to be him coming along the hall to his room. And in another moment he would find her here, snooping into his things, which would make him even more mad at her. She didn't blame him, she would be mad too if someone came uninvited into her room and read notes she had written to herself.

She hurried to the door, apologies ready, an anxious hope rising that they might make up and be friends again. The footsteps were almost there, loud in the hall, echoing faintly in duplicate somewhere in the length of the hall and through the wood of floor and walls and ceiling as if the wood were alive and repeating sound for sound. The footsteps stopped just outside the door.

Yet no one was there.

Instantly the words he had written about footsteps in the forest came back to her. And now, as though mocking her, they were here, the echoes fading away to silence.

She hesitated only a moment, her glance sweeping the length of the shadowed hall, and then watching cautiously over her shoulder, she hurried to the staircase and ran down. But now she knew: Jason had not seen what she had seen.

CHAPTER 12

JASON WAS SPRAWLED on his spine in the chair that matched the sofa, his long legs stretched out in front and crossed at the ankle. The television screen flickered slightly, colors speckling, as a high wind played with the antenna on top of the house. A soap opera was on, but Jason couldn't have told the name of it, nor, for that matter, what the characters had been doing. He gazed at it because it was something to do. Something safe.

He heard her come down the stairs, and he slid lower into his chair, hoping she wouldn't see him. But from the corner of his eye he saw her come into the seating area and sit down on the sofa. Although he carefully avoided looking at her, he had a full vision from the corner of his eye. He began to itch uncomfortably, as if he had suddenly come down with a rash. He squirmed and scratched his arm.

"Jason," she said.

He pretended he hadn't heard her. He would have gotten up to leave if it hadn't been too blatantly impolite.

"Jason, I want to talk to you about something."

"I'm watching the show."

She was quiet for a few minutes as the characters on television moved through their dramas. He was more aware of her than he was of anything else in the room or on the television screen. He heard her sigh. He saw her cross her legs and uncross them. Then abruptly she was talking again.

"I went into your room."

His shoulders stiffened.

"I know it's wrong, but I did it. And I read what you wrote."

That was the limit. That was all he could take. Even so, he now had an excuse, the one he had been waiting for. He got to his feet.

"That's a hell of a thing to do," he said angrily. "If I'd been you I think I'd have kept that news to myself. I'm going out."

She stood up and blocked his way. Her oval face was pale, her eyes appearing larger and darker than normal. She wasn't wearing any lipstick at all today, and this was the one time she needed that extra color.

"I just wanted to tell you, Jason, that it wasn't the drug you took. I think I saw the things you heard. Both of them. In the water. When I was trying to help you."

He looked for a way out, and finally turned back to go around the other end of the couch. He snorted out unamused laughter. "I think you must have taken something worse than I ever did. I don't want to hear anymore. I *know* what it was. And after this, don't go in my room.

HE STARTED TO GO OUT THE BACK WAY, BUT THAT WOULD MEAN passing through the kitchen, and he didn't want to bother with Mrs. Ashley. She'd probably want to talk about the dumb rock again. He reversed his direction and went to the front door. He saw the pickup out front, and almost backed up again to go upstairs to his room. Then he saw that Shannon and the ranger were strolling toward the truck, their backs to him. If he hurried, and if he were quiet, he could get around to the side of the house before they saw him.

As he went down the steps, he saw Barry, surrounded by a territory he had built, with roads circling and curling, and piles of dirt and needles making what looked like hills. He had at least a half dozen little play automobiles. For a nostalgic moment Jason wished he were little again, with no more problems than little boys of three have. Barry looked up and watched Jason go down the steps, but he didn't smile. Jason didn't feel like smiling either. He passed by in silence.

He hurried to the far side of the house, and the thick cover of the forest. An hour ago he would have been afraid to go there again, but now it seemed a sanctuary. The only one that was available to him.

BARRY SCOOPED DIRT UP IN HIS HANDS AND LOADED IT INTO THE RED dump truck. Jason had come down off the porch and gone out of sight around the house. Shannon was talking to the strange man. Suddenly Barry felt lonely.

"Reid, Juno," he said. "Come play with me."

He finished filling the dump truck with dirt. He rounded it up and patted the top. On his knees he pushed the truck along one of the roads. He looked over his shoulder at the porch, and saw Reid and Juno. They had just appeared, from out of the house maybe, or from somewhere else. Barry sat back on his heels. Reid was coming down the steps with Juno at his heels. But his face was turned away.

"Come play with me," Barry said again, watching them.

But instead of coming over the railing to Barry's playground, they went in the other direction. The way Jason had gone. With one hand on the railing, Reid leaped over, as graceful as an animal. He didn't once glance toward Barry. Juno slipped eel-like between the posts, his tail long and switching, the end curling and uncurling. His long whiskers twitched, as if he were eager to run. They were in Barry's sight one moment, and the next they were gone.

Barry stood up.

Through the banister posts on each side of the steps, he could see Reid just going around the corner of the house. Juno was already gone. Their movements were fast and silent, as if they zipped along walking on air just above the ground.

Then for a moment, in the distance between the trees, Barry caught a glimpse of someone. At first he thought it was Reid, but the hair was not bright and sunny, like Reid's. It was dark. Barry remembered Jason wore a short-sleeved striped shirt, white and red like the one he glimpsed among the trees. It was Jason that for a moment came in view again just before he went over the hill and out of sight entirely.

Suddenly Reid and Juno were for a breath's length where Jason had been, but almost instantly they were gone, following in Jason's footprints. They were running now, Juno in the lead stretched low on his belly, with his muzzle straight out, and his tail sweeping the air over his back.

A bad feeling came over Barry. He retracted his head from between the posts of the porch banister and ran, following Reid and Juno. He tried to take long steps, but his legs wouldn't reach. When he attempted to jump over a rotting tree limb that had fallen to the ground, his jump was less than he expected and his toe caught, pitching him face down into the needles on the other side of the log. He caught himself with his hands and slid forward, the heels of his hands raking through the piled needles into the soft soil underneath. He got up with his lower lip trembling, but he made no sound as he cleaned the dirt off his hands.

He began running again, searching among the trees ahead for another glimpse of Jason, of Reid and Juno. In a dip in the land he came upon a small patch of snow that was left over from last winter. The shadows of the forest were growing deeper, and the cold lingered, chilling his cheeks, and coming under his clothes to make goosebumps.

He heard a scream, hoarse and low, and drifting away on little cries to almost nothing. As Barry paused, held back for a moment by the terror that filled him, he heard grunts and moans, soft, little aborted cries. He heard sounds of fighting, of twigs snapping under prancing feet.

Fear almost turned him back. Terror of the unknown gripped his throat. The sounds he was hearing were like the sounds the dying animals had made when *she* killed them in front of him, and he was afraid to see what was happening in the forest. But he paused only a moment.

He ran on, curving to the left toward the sounds of fighting, and the sounds of dying.

He saw them among the trees. Jason had turned back and was trying to get away from them, running, stumbling, falling. Juno's long tail zipped out and wrapped tightly around Jason's ankles, dragging him back. Jason's fingers clawed the ground. His eyes bulged, and even though he looked straight at Barry, he seemed not to see him at all. Reid was on Jason's back, pushing him down onto the ground. His long, supple hands went around Jason's throat, choking off Jason's cries.

"No! No!" Barry cried. "No!"

He stopped again, a few feet away. He made fists of his hands and pressed them to the side of his head. His voice became silent, but his cry of protest went on, stifled in his throat.

They were killing Jason . . . killing Jason . . .

Barry picked up a stick and ran with it, and brought it down hard across Juno's back. The animal jerked away, and turned its face toward Barry. Its narrow muzzle lifted in a vicious snarl. With tearless weeping, Barry turned the stick upon Reid, and for an instant Reid's eyes met Barry's, and Barry saw there was nothing behind them. It was like looking into the flat and soulless button eyes of his teddy bear. He lifted the stick high over his head, but suddenly they were gone, both of them, and only Jason was there on the ground looking up at Barry with the stick poised in the air above his head. In contrast to the nothingness of Reid's eyes, Jason's were insane with fear. He threw up his hands against the stick, as if Barry were going to strike him with it. He whimpered, looking through his hands at Barry.

Barry saw that Jason's fear had centered on him, that Jason was afraid of him. He threw the stick down and turned away, running back toward the house. He fell twice, and he got up and ran again. He didn't look back for Jason. But when he reached the house, he hunkered down at the corner and watched, trembling, for Jason to appear.

JASON COWERED ON THE GROUND, HIS FACE BURIED IN HIS HANDS. He listened for the sounds, the footsteps, the snapping branches. His muscles remained tense, waiting for the next blow. The forest was silent around him.

He lifted his head. He felt dazed and confused, the last few minutes a bad dream, the details quick to slip away. The fear remained, though, making him afraid of every tree trunk, every hiding place in the forest.

It was the forest, he thought as he clawed his way to his feet. The forest itself was haunted, possessed by something deadly. And it had something to do with the little kid, too. He had been there. Hadn't he been there? Jason wasn't sure now. All of it was a nightmare. His brain felt as though it had been shattered, divided into fragments that no longer knew what was going on. He had to escape. Had to.

He stumbled along, going from tree to tree, afraid of what might be hiding behind each one, afraid too of the things that nested among the limbs and waited to jump down upon him. He clumsily waded through pockets of snow and heaps of rotting forest debris. He heard a sound of crying and looked around . . . was it the little boy? . . . but no, it was here, right beside him. And at last he realized it was coming from himself, and he tried to stop the sound.

He saw the logs of the house, logs that were no longer in tree form, but were laid horizontally one upon the other. At the corner of the house he came upon the little boy, and the sight of him was so startling that he almost ran back the way he had come. The crying started up again, and he tried to stop it, but when it silenced his chest felt as though it were swelling and would burst open like an over-ripened seed pod.

Jason gave Barry a wide berth. He came upon the driveway in front of the house, and passed by the station wagon. He saw a woman standing not far away who looked faintly familiar, but he couldn't remember her name.

She was staring at him. A heartbeat later she came hurrying toward him.

CHAPTER 13

SHANNON PUT an arm around Jason's back and helped him toward the house. His appearance had struck horror in her heart. He looked as though he had been mauled by a bear. It was the first thing that occurred to her. His hair was disheveled and falling forward over his forehead. Bloody scratches were on his cheeks, neck and arms. His clothing was twisted and covered with bits of debris and soil. But the most alarming of all was the half-mad cry that kept coming so softly from his throat. His terror-filled eyes stared at her as if he had never seen her before. At first she thought he might not let her approach him. "Jason," she said, "let me help you."

He drew a long breath, shattered gasps. Then he was silent. He allowed her to lead him into the house.

Becky, in a chair near the television, got to her feet. She stared in silence at Jason.

Shannon guided Jason toward the kitchen. She didn't know where else to take him. When they pushed through the swinging door she said to Edna, "Get his mother, Edna, and bring some washcloths and something to put on his wounds."

Edna hurried out of the kitchen.

Becky came through the door to situate herself against the wall.

Shannon arranged a chair for Jason between the table and the counter. She ran a glass of water and offered it to him. He clutched it in both hands. Their trembling spilled part of it down the front of his shirt. He lowered his head to the glass, tilted it and drank. When he had finished, Shannon took the glass away. She waited, not knowing what to do next. He seemed to be calming down a lot. He hadn't made a sound since they had entered the house.

Shannon brushed his hair back from his forehead.

Lynn burst into the kitchen, and behind her the swinging door squeaked in two keys as it swung back and forth. Edna caught it, and came through with a handful of washcloths and a can of first-aid spray.

When Lynn saw her son she cried out, hesitated briefly, then ran to him. "Jason," she cried, "What happened to you?"

He blinked, looked at the face of his mother, and blinked again. Shannon saw him come out of the trance-like state. He looked around as though surprised to find that he was here, in this particular place.

Mrs. Ashley turned on the hot water faucet and let the water run until it was steaming. She wet a washcloth and began to touch the scratches on Jason's face, carefully cleansing each one.

Lynn was almost in hysterics. "What happened to him? Where was he? Did he fall off his bike? Jason, talk to me!"

He dodged away from Mrs. Ashley's washcloth. "I'm all right," he said.

"I don't think the scratches are very deep," Edna said. "They just grazed the skin."

"They have to be cleaned," Shannon said.

"No," Jason said. "I'll wash my own face. It's okay." He was looking around, as if he expected to see someone who was not there. He saw Becky, but his eyes moved on, searching. He got to his feet.

"I'll take you to the doctor," Lynn began, but Jason interrupted her.

"No. Not here. I'm all right now. I just want to go home."

"Jason, where are you going?"

"I'm going upstairs to change my clothes. I want to go home, Mom. Now. If you won't take me, I'll hitchhike, or I'll call Dad and have him come and get me. One way or the other I'm leaving here."

"Do you want me to help you? Do you want me to go upstairs with you?"

"No."

He went through the door and his footsteps faded away toward the front of the house and the stairway.

The three women exchanged looks. Lynn's face, which had gone almost as white as her blouse when she first saw Jason, was now getting some color back. Edna stood with the damp washcloth in her hand. She reached around and put it into the sink.

Lynn moved jerkily.

"I'd better get Freddie in here and get him ready to leave. We'll have to hurry if we get started before nightfall."

Shannon said, "You're going home now?"

"Yes." Lynn started out of the room, but at the swinging door she paused. "Jason has been wanting to go home for several days. I wonder . . . do you suppose he has done these things to himself? Why otherwise won't he tell me what happened?"

Shannon made no attempt to answer.

Mrs. Ashley said, "He looks like he pitched head first off his bicycle. And he probably is too embarrassed to admit it. The way those boys ride those things I'm surprised that they don't get hurt more often. I saw Freddie standing on his bicycle seat and the thing wobbling around. And they're always trying to ride on just the rear wheel, the rest of it rared up."

"I suppose you're right," Lynn said. "We probably came too early in the season. Well come back in August, so they can enjoy swimming and boating. Would you mind helping me pack? I have to get Freddie's things packed, too. There's no use expecting him to help out. He's more trouble than he's worth when it comes to packing or unpacking."

"I'd be glad to help," Shannon said.

Edna said, "I'll do Freddie's things."

They dispersed to separate rooms. Lynn sent Becky to find the boys and tell Freddie to come on and get ready to leave before nightfall. Edna went upstairs to start his packing. Shannon went into Lynn's room and began removing from the closet the things she had hung there.

She thought of Edna's theory. She hadn't accepted it for one moment. Jason had not been near his bicycle. It was leaned against the back porch, and it hadn't been moved for several days.

She glanced out the window into the varying shadows of the conifer forest. What had happened to Jason? She had a feeling that no one would ever know.

IN LATE AFTERNOON THEY DROVE AWAY. THE OTHERS STOOD ON THE porch and waved goodbye. Jason had climbed into the back seat of the car, leaving the front passenger seat for Freddie. It was as though he tried to hide. Sunk back into the corner, he made no effort to wave goodbye. Freddie leaned out his window, his arm swinging. He hadn't wanted to go home. He had spent a good hour whining about it after Becky had brought him to the house.

David regretted seeing him go. He stood on the porch and watched the car until it turned the curve and was out of sight. Becky too stood on the porch, her face as solemn as David's.

Shannon looked for Barry, but he wasn't there. She realized suddenly that she hadn't seen him since Ken Masters left, since Jason came stumbling in from the forest. Before that he had been playing contentedly beside the steps. Anxiety pierced her, as it always did when Barry slipped away from her.

"Have any of you seen Barry lately?" she asked.

Becky shook her head, and David said. "He's probably up in his room."

Shannon went into the house calling. She was halfway up the stairs before she heard a faint answer. She went on to the top of the stairs and along the hall to Barry's room. His door stood open. He sat in the corner, his hands on drawn-up knees, the way he often did when, Shannon suspected, he was disturbed about something."

"You didn't come down to tell your cousins or Aunt Lynn goodbye."

He didn't answer her. He bowed his head.

"Would you like to come out of your room now?" He shook his head.

"I'm going down the hall to my room. Maybe you'll come and tell me when you're ready to go downstairs."

His head remained bowed. His hands clasped his knees. He seemed to shrink as she watched him. Shannon felt that this autistic-like behavior had been brought about because his aunt and cousins had left. He had acted much this way when his dad left.

Gently she said, "They plan to come again to the lodge when the weather is warmer. A few weeks from now." She paused for a response, but got none. "I'll leave you alone now, Barry. When you feel like talking, you can come to my room."

She retraced her steps down the hall and went into her room, leaving the door open. She sat down in a chair beside the window and looked out. Her view was toward the lake, but the branches of the trees were like a green blanket over her window. She could see the roof of the front porch a few feet below, and that was about all.

She didn't hear him come down the hall or enter her room. Suddenly he was there, a few feet away. He was holding something in his hands, pressed against his chest. He stared at her gravely over the top of it.

Shannon's heart, startled into a spurt of palpitations, settled back. "Barry! I didn't hear you following me. You're quiet as a little mouse sometimes. What have you got?"

He laid it on her knees, and she saw it was his personal book. She hadn't seen it since the day they arrived and she had unpacked his suitcases.

He whirled and ran, before she could say anything. She heard his door slam.

Perplexed, she looked at the book. Why had he brought it to her?

She opened it, looking again at the drawings, at the names "Reid" and "Juno" printed beneath them. For some reason of his own, Barry wanted her to look at his book again. She leafed through it, but other than the tracings of a network of lines on the third page, a spider-web creation with eyes and horns scattered randomly, it was blank.

Shannon took it downstairs. Mrs. Ashley, with Becky and David, had settled in front of the television to watch late afternoon cartoons. Mrs. Ashley had brought her needlework with her, and was doing some embroidery. Becky looked out the window as often as she looked at the television. Only David, who lay stretched on his stomach on the floor, appeared to be interested in what the Roadrunner was doing.

"David, Becky, what can you tell me about this book of Barry's?"

David turned over onto his elbow and looked up. "What book?"

Shannon sat on the sofa and opened the book to the pages with the drawings of the boy and the animal. "This one. Someone has helped him with it. He brought it to me just now and then ran back to his room."

"That's one of the books he made at school." Becky moved to the sofa to sit beside Shannon. She leaned against her, looking at the drawings. Shannon heard her gasp.

"I've seen them," she whispered. "They're real!" David made a sound of derision in his throat, half laugh, half snort. He moved over to Shannon's feet where he could see the opened pages of the book.

"Those are just pictures that Barry drew, that's all. You never saw any animal that looked like that, Becky."

"I did! In the lake. The day Jason almost drowned. And the boy—they were there."

"You probably saw an otter," David said, laughing.

Becky drew away. She had reached out to take the book, but pulled her hands away without touching it. She moved over, as if to get away, then got up and went to look out the front window. Shannon saw her glance at the stairway.

Mrs. Ashley, with rising curiosity, got up and came to look down at the book. "I never saw it before," she said.

"He kept it in his bookcase at home," Shannon said. "One other time he showed it to me, but this time it was almost as if he wanted me to keep it."

Edna said, "Isn't that awfully good drawing for a person his age?"

"That's what I thought too," Shannon said. "That's why I wondered if Becky or David had helped him."

"I didn't," Becky said. "I never saw it before either."

David scooted back to his former position on his stomach, his chin propped in his hands. He was finished with the subject. So too was

Mrs. Ashley. She went back to her chair and her embroidery. Becky stayed at the window looking out.

Shannon decided she would take the book up to Barry's room, talk to him about it, and then try to get him to come downstairs. She didn't like to see him shut himself into the isolation of his room. He had seemed to be making so much progress, coming out of his room each morning to take his bath without problems, then staying easily within sight the rest of the day.

"I think Barry's unhappy about Lynn and the boys leaving," Shannon said.

David asked, "Why would he care? None of them played with him."

"Maybe it's just the sense of loneliness that the departure of anyone makes. It seems so quiet, somehow, without them here. Don't you think so?"

"Sure, but then Fred and I did things together."

"If that's what it is," Edna said. "If that's why he's hiding in his room, he'll get over it."

Shannon went upstairs. The waning of the day had not been so noticeable in the larger, airier rooms of the first floor, but up here the hall was almost dark. She turned on the lights.

Barry's door was still closed. Shannon knocked lightly.

"May I come in, Barry?"

She heard his steps, quick and light. The doorknob turned ineffectually, back and forth. Shannon helped him open the door. He had turned on the Mickey Mouse lamp on the table beside his bed. A cone of yellow light spilled onto part of the bed and down onto the braided throw rug at the side of the bed. The rest of the room was shadowed.

"Thank you for showing me your book again, Barry. Would you like to talk about it?"

Barry stared at the book, his lips parted, a white bump raised between his eyebrows that was very close to a frown. He backed away.

"Don't you want the book, Barry?" Shannon asked, puzzled at his behavior.

Barry shook his head.

"But it's such a nice book. And it has lots of pages left. I'll tell you what, I'll just lay it here on the table beside the lamp."

She put the book down, and held out her hand to Barry. After a moment, he put his hand in hers, and together they went out into the hall and down the stairs.

"SHE'LL BE COMING ROUND THE MOUNTAIN WHEN SHE COMES," Freddie sang. "She'll be coming round the mountain when she comes."

His mother added her voice to Freddie's.

"She'll be coming round the mountain, she'll be coming round the mountain . . ."

Freddie looked out his window. The canyon dropped away just at the edge of the pavement, and not even a treetop stood between them and the rocky depths hundreds of feet below. The sun had gone down on their left, far beyond the mountain side that rose upwards toward a sky that was beginning to be peppered with stars. His mom had turned on the headlights miles back, before twilight. Now they swept outward over the canyon, almost missing the pavement entirely as the road made a sharp curve to the left. There was no other traffic. Freddie felt happy about going home, now that he was well on his way north. He wished Jason would start feeling good.

"Sing with us, Jason!" Freddie called without looking back at his brother, and continued on singing with their mother, "She'll be coming round the mountain when she comes."

Freddie turned to see why Jason did not sing along. Jason had been sitting directly behind him, but when he first looked around, he thought Jason had moved to the other side of the car. The light from the dash, and the pale, but lingering light of day, illuminated the back seat only faintly. Freddie stared at the figure in the opposite corner. As suddenly as he realized that Jason was not alone in the back seat, he recognized the other person.

"Barry!" he cried, and before the name died on his lips, he was aware of other things. Barry was much larger. And Barry wore on his face a smile that seemed frighteningly evil, and his eyes were dimly lighted, as if they reflected the light of the dash in the way of an animal's eyes.

Jason's head lifted, and Freddie knew that Jason had been asleep.

The figure with Barry's face slowly rotated its head. The evil smile turned upon Jason. An instant of silence passed. Lynn, seeing that Freddie was twisted in his seat and staring back, no longer singing with her, allowed her voice to mumble to a halt. She looked into the rear view mirror.

Jason screamed, a cry torn from the depths of his soul. He began to fight the mechanisms of his seat belt, as if he had forgotten how to release it. With his right hand he opened the door at his side.

Lynn jerked involuntarily on the wheel of the car as she reached around. She grabbed for Jason's arm, and missed. She shouted, "Jason! Freddie, stop Jason!"

The figure in the back seat with the face of Barry leaned forward and took the steering wheel from Lynn's control and gave it a sharp turn to the right. With Jason still fighting his seat belt, and Freddie on his knees reaching over to keep Jason from going out the open door, the car dropped over the edge of the canyon wall.

Freddie heard his mother cry softly, "Oh my God."

Her voice was strangely audible under Jason's continuing scream.

Even though he knew he was living his last minutes, Freddie was sharply aware of everything around him. He was able to feel surprise that he had not noticed before the animal that lay curled against the back window as calmly as if it were in its den. The downward fall of the car seemed not to affect it, as if it were beyond the laws of gravity.

Before the car struck the first ledge of boulders, Freddie saw the animal rise, yawn, and stretch. Then with the boy, he slipped through the window as if it hadn't been closed, and was gone.

Freddie felt a strange relief, even knowing that he, his mother, and his brother would die in seconds more.

The car burst into flames, and fell the rest of the way to the canyon floor like a lost comet from outer space.

CHAPTER 14

SHANNON WAS awake when Ramon arrived near midnight Friday night. She had been sitting in her room, in the dark, watching through the window for the lights of his car since she had said goodnight to the others. The house was silent, and had been for an hour. Lights were on in the upstairs hall and on the porch. In his bedroom downstairs, a soft light had been left on, and his bed turned back and ready. Clean, fluffy towels were out in the downstairs bathroom.

There had been times while she waited, her senses so alert she picked up even the pulse of the house, that it seemed something moved restlessly. At times the whispers of sound had become footsteps, quick and running, as of an animal, but after looking several times into the hall and seeing nothing, she attributed the sounds to her vigilance and barely controlled excitement.

Her feelings changed the moment she saw the headlights sweep through the trees toward the lodge.

Her vague, unformed sense of uneasiness was gone. Her hyperalertness calmed. She felt safe, realizing only then that she had not felt safe before he came. She wanted to go down and meet him at the door, the way she had when her feelings for him had been less personal; but she slipped quietly into bed instead, listening to the sounds he made entering the house.

He went first to his bedroom, and for a few minutes there was silence. A gust of wind whispered at the window, and sang multi-note through the needles of the conifers. She felt the vibration of movement before she heard his steps again. Then he came up the stairs and went first to Barry's room. She heard the door close softly a moment later as he left that room. He paused at Becky's door and again at David's. At the top of the stairs he paused again, as though listening. And she heard what he might have heard—an echo of footsteps that drifted away into the soft sighs of the walls.

When the house had silenced, he went on down the stairs.

A few minutes later she heard the shower running, water gurgling faintly in the pipes that rose through the walls to the upstairs bathrooms. By that time she was drifting into sleep.

BECKY STRUGGLED AGAINST SOMETHING THAT HAD HER ARMS AND legs pinned helplessly to her body. She rolled, spinning, as if she were in the air, or the water. Icy coldness seeped into every pore of her body, and strangled her when she opened her mouth to scream, and she knew then it was water. Deep, dark water. She was drowning. Something of the nether world had her in its grasp, and she felt the rope-like pressure biting into her arms and legs. Rough fur brushed against her cheek. Not the fur of any animal she had ever touched, but wiry, piercing fur. Its long tail tightened around her, and pulled her down, down into the blackness.

She woke with her screams dying in her throat, unuttered. As she jerked upright in her bed, aware of a weight on her legs, the weight lifted and there was a thud as something jumped from her bed. She sat terrified, her heart pounding so loudly it sounded like repetitive explosions in her ears. Whatever sound there was beyond was lost for the desperate time it took for her heart to calm down. She blinked into the darkness of her room. She had left her bedroom door open, but now it was closed.

She gulped softly for a breath to fill the void in her chest. She needed the comfort of light, but was afraid to move. For an indeterminate length of time, she stared into the darkness.

Starlight through the window gradually outlined the furniture. The knobby posts at the foot of her bed were black figures in the darkness of her room. Three posts, the center one taller and thicker . . .

No, there were only two posts, not three.

Her breath stilled. She strained into the darkness to see what stood at the foot of her bed, yet she was terrified to see. She knew she had only to reach out an arm to the lamp at the side of her bed and she would have light, and the thing at the foot of her bed would be revealed for what it was . . . nothing.

No, not nothing. But something. Something I don't want to see.

In the tension of her waiting, the starlight glowed brighter, as if the wind had swept aside the evergreen branch at her window, allowing her to see more clearly this intruder in her room; and the oval, the pale, almost luminescent oval of a face became faintly visible.

She could almost see his eyes, his small nose, the curve of his mouth. It was Barry in her room, standing silently at the foot of her bed, waiting for her to turn on the light. It was Barry . . .

Or it was the other.

A primitive need to escape the horrors of her fears caused her almost to slide down into the only protection available to her now, the darkness of her bed. Yet if her little brother needed her . . .

She reached over, through the cold, watery darkness of her room, and almost knocked the lamp off the table. Her icy fingers gripped the edge of the shade. She righted the lamp and at last turned it on.

Only then did she realize that it could not have been Barry. Barry, little, short, could not have seen over the railing that connected the two corner posts.

Soft light suffused her room, outlining the furniture, the emptiness. There was no one in her room. She was alone.

Her dad must have arrived. He was the one who had shut her door. Now that he was here they were safe. But she felt as though her head was being crushed, that something invisible was pressing on each temple. She was almost nauseated with the pain. She would have to go to the girls' bathroom and see if Mrs. Ashley had left a bottle of aspirin there. Her fear had gone, for the moment, with the realization that her dad had arrived. That he had checked on each of them in their beds and closed the doors behind him. That was for fire protection, she had heard him say a couple of times. If ever one was awakened by the smell of smoke, go directly to the window and climb out, do not open the door or try to help the rest of the family. Go instead as fast as possible to a neighbor's house and have them call the fire department. In that way, you helped your family.

Comforted, Becky got out of bed and went to her door. As she opened it, she turned slightly, and from the corner of her eye she saw the movement of something fast and low as it disappeared beneath her bed. And in the shadows at the end of the chest of drawers, fading into the wall as she watched, was the tall figure which had stood at the foot of her bed. The entity with Barry's face.

She knew in the coldness of threatened existence, that not even the presence of their dad protected them now.

Unable to sit still, yet equally unable to leave any room that her dad happened to be in, Becky wandered from window to window, from chair to door. She touched furniture, ran her fingers over it as if testing for dust. At one point, Mrs. Ashley even asked her, "What are you doing, Becky, looking to see if I've dusted?" She told her no, but said no more. She felt half removed from reality. Every time she saw a figure move, when David entered or left the room, when their dad made a motion of any kind, she found herself checking on each person in sight as if they, the boy and the animal, those non-creatures, were there too and possibly making themselves visible. She saw Barry, and she saw shadows that did not belong to Barry yet seemed attached to him at times. And she noticed that Barry was even more quiet than usual, and seemed to be clinging to their dad.

She wanted to talk to Dad alone, but there was no chance.

Finally, late in the afternoon, she found him alone in the living room. Mrs. Ashley had gone to the kitchen to prepare dinner, and Shannon had gone upstairs. David was out somewhere, she didn't know where, she just hoped he would stay for awhile. She didn't want him laughing at her, listening and not believing.

"Daddy," she said, coming to stand in front of him.

He looked up from the newspaper he had settled back to read. Then she saw that he was not alone after all. How could she have forgotten Barry? He was sitting on the floor at the end of the sofa, almost under the table there. He was playing with a toy that changed from a car into a robot, and seemed not to be listening to her. But there was no way to be sure.

"Yes?" their dad urged. Looking up, waiting.

"I need to talk to you," she said, watching Barry twist the robot into shape.

"Have at it," Ramon said, folding the paper and putting it aside.

"Alone," Becky said.

"We're alone."

"No, we're not. Barry's there."

Ramon glanced down toward the table and smiled. "Is it that personal? Barry, why don't you run into the kitchen with Mrs. Ashley for a few minutes." Barry crawled out from beneath the table. Still twisting the car into the robot, one leg down, another on the way, he went toward the short hall and the swing door into the kitchen. Ramon sat waiting, looking up at his daughter.

Now that she was alone with him, she didn't know what to say. If she told him what she knew, what she thought she knew, it would sound too preposterous to believe. In that moment of weighing information, she was able to see it from an adult's point of view, and her child's mind knew it would not be accepted. She said instead, "Daddy, take us home."

"Why, punkin, aren't you enjoying your vacation?" He leaned forward, took her hand and pulled her down to sit beside him. "You were doing fine last week. Is it because of Lynn and the boys leaving?"

"Terrible things were happening to Jason, Daddy," she said so hastily her breath was inadequate and left her feeling smothered. "And terrible things are going to happen to the rest of us if we don't leave."

He hugged her. "So Jason's accident is still worrying you. What you have is called anxiety, and time will cure it. I was sorry to hear about

Jason's accident, and surprised. He's a good swimmer. But just because he slipped and fell into the lake and had trouble getting out doesn't mean the same thing will happen to anyone else. Be careful on the rocks. They get slippery sometimes. And always remember not to go into the lake alone."

"But it wasn't an accident."

"No? What do you mean?"

She was on the verge of telling him about the boy with Barry's face, the . . . the being that could not have been human and yet was somehow Barry, an extension of Barry, like ectoplasm maybe; and the strange and vicious-looking animal that accompanied him. But suddenly there were quick, light footsteps on the stairs, and Shannon came into the living room. She was dressed in a soft and filmy turquoise dress, and she had put her hair up. She looked different—beautiful and sophisticated.

Becky saw Ramon look over his shoulder, and she saw his eyes change, and a half-smile form pleasantly on his lips. He looked at Shannon as though he had forgotten that Becky was in the room.

Becky stood up, feeling an unexpected sense of relief. There had been no adequate words for what she had to tell anyway.

Maybe though, she thought, Barry himself was not in danger. Maybe she could safely leave him here, as well as the others.

"Daddy," she said, drawing his attention back to her. "Can I go home with you when you go tomorrow?" She added quickly, before she should lose him again, "I can spend my days with Beth."

He didn't seem to hear her. Shannon came on over to the conversation center and sat down. She looked from Ramon to Becky, moved forward in her chair as if to leave again.

"I'm sorry," she said. "Did I interrupt something important?"

"No," Ramon said. "Becky's just feeling a little nervous and bored. You're looking lovely, Shannon. Ken Masters is a lucky man."

Becky looked at Shannon again. "Are you going out?"

"Yes. I thought I might while your father's here and you don't need me around."

There was a silence, then Becky said what she felt her dad wanted to say: "We need you."

Ramon squeezed Becky's wrist. "But that doesn't mean we have to monopolize her, do we? She can go out to dinner without us tagging along, or feeling guilty about leaving us."

Becky shrugged, feeling that Shannon really shouldn't go out and leave them. It seemed already that she belonged here, watching after Barry, and keeping an eye on her and David. Becky knew Shannon did watch her and David as well. In the beginning it had annoyed her, but now that she had gotten used to it, it helped against the feeling of fear that was increasingly a part of her. Not until now did she realize how much Shannon's presence helped.

"How much longer are we going to stay then?" she asked her dad. "Now that Barry's getting so much better, can't we all go home?"

Ramon gave her arm a little shake. "Punkin, your aunt Lynn told me they were coming back up in August. You'll have a great time swimming and picnicking then, and since Barry seems to be doing better, think how much better he'll be by the end of summer. Besides," he smiled at her, but Becky could see the seriousness in his eyes, "if we went home I have a feeling we'd lose Shannon. And we don't want that to happen, do we?"

Becky looked at Shannon. She had gentle eyes, something that was more important than her pretty face. For the first time since her mother had died, Becky found herself hoping that her dad would marry again. But only Shannon, no one else.

"No," Becky said. "We don't."

Shannon smiled at Becky, and a look of understanding passed between the two. Becky was struck suddenly by hope. Would Shannon also understand if Becky told her about Barry and those things that somehow came from him? Would Shannon help Becky understand? Maybe later they could talk. Later, when Shannon returned from her date.

SHANNON WAS SURPRISED WHEN KEN ARRIVED IN A FLASHY TRANS Am, then immediately wondered why she should feel surprised. The forest ranger's pickup truck had seemed an extension of his personality. In civilian clothes and driving a sleek car, he seemed like a different person, and her regrets deepened. She wished to be back in the house, having dinner with Ramon, Barry, Becky, David and Edna. But that was precisely the reason she should get out, she told herself as she settled into the bucket seat and felt her body thrust backwards into it as Ken rounded the corner out of the lane onto the lake road. He shifted, and glanced at her at the same time. The car rapidly picked up speed and held the upper edge of the speed limit.

"You're beautiful," he told her for the second time. "There's a dinner club out north, with dancing. Do you mind? I'd like to dance with you."

"It sounds like fun." She didn't add that she hadn't danced since the early years of her marriage. She looked out the window at the tree trunks flashing by, and remembered the last day she had ridden with her husband. He had been a fast driver too, but she had never felt in danger. A nervousness began edging into her. To keep her mind off the speed and the curves of the road that seemed to be undulating first one way and then the other into a solid forest of trees, Shannon turned her face toward Ken and began urging him to talk about himself.

Darkness settled over the forest. Occasionally they met another car, but the traffic remained thin. The sky changed from a turquoise blue ribbon above the road to deep navy blue highlighted with stars.

The distance to the dinner club was less than it seemed. Shannon guessed aloud that it must be twenty miles, and missed it by five. It was an attractive log building, highly varnished, with a parking lot of white gravel that was lighted with yellow electric lanterns spaced evenly along the outer edges of the driveway. A dozen or so cars were parked haphazardly.

Shannon was beginning to enjoy herself more than she had thought she would, but even as she tried to give all her attention to Ken, her thoughts kept wandering back to Ramon and his family. When dinner was finished, she hid her reluctance to stay longer and dance. The music was not overly loud, and Ken as a dancer was certainly competent. Her feelings of awkwardness soon dissipated. It was too dark to consult her watch as often as she would have liked. She found herself thinking that Ramon would be putting Barry to bed now, having allowed him to stay up later than usual for this Saturday night as he had last week, and then he would be going down to his room to . . . what? Would he wait up for her, reading, looking occasionally out the window for the lights of the car? Or would he go to sleep, right away, without a second thought?

She hoped he would stay awake, waiting.

And she scolded herself for thinking that, for wishing that he would fall in love with her. Hadn't she planned her life? Hadn't she assured herself that there would be no one else to lose? Yet . . .

Better to have loved and lost than never to have loved at all.

That was one proverb that was certainly true.

Now that she was removed from them, she knew that sometime during the past weeks she had grown to love all of them. The emptiness in her heart was gone, because it had been filled with Barry, with Ramon and Becky and David. And Edna too, for that matter. She was like a grandmother in the family.

Shannon smiled at Ken and tried to be a good sport. When she had accepted this date with him, she had not realized how completely her heart would be left at home.

The club closed at midnight, and thirty minutes later they were back at the lake, and now Ken drove slowly, the car barely moving. The moon had risen, and was rich and full over the eastern end of the lake, spilling a track of gold into the water. They came to a parking lot, separated from the water with cedar posts thirty inches tall as well as evenly sized and spaced boulders to prevent an accidental drive into the water. Tall trees rimmed the lake at this point, within walking distance of the lodge. They shadowed the car and the parking area. Ken rolled down his window.

He pointed eastward.

"It was right over there that the kid, Jason, was about to drown. The girl was standing on that boulder when I first saw her, dressed only in her shirt it looked like, and soaking wet. She came running out into the road when she saw my truck."

"And she hasn't been the same since," Shannon said. "It was a traumatic experience for her, as well as for Jason. We can't ever thank you enough for what you did."

He turned to face her. His face was a pale rectangle in the dim light reflected from the moon-touched water. His hand found her wrist in the darkness of the car, as if he were taking her pulse. She felt his fingers press into the softness of her wrist.

"I met you," he said.

She started to tell him that she had enjoyed his company, but she would not be going out with him again, trying in her thoughts to find words that would in no way wound him, when suddenly he leaned closer and pulled her face to his. The kiss was aggressive, and she was so surprised that she was limp and yielding at first. He leaned over her, pressing her toward the passenger door. She began to revolt, began to pull herself out of his grasp, but the move was never completed.

There was a sudden loud crack of metal, a thud of cushioned feet, as something leaped onto the hood of the car.

With a grunt, a swear word ending in his throat, Ken jerked back and up. Shannon's view of the hood of the car was no longer obscured, and she saw the dark and formless shape of something the approximate size of a young mountain lion. A long tail whipped back and forth, and there was a flash of white teeth just beyond the windshield as it snarled through the glass at them. Slanted eyes glowed yellow in the dark, as if they were lighted by phosphorus.

A sudden and terrible fear paralyzed Shannon's body as she looked into those strange glowing eyes. The moment seemed endless as the thing lingered on the hood of the car. She realized that both front windows of the car were down. That the animal could as easily leap into the car as it had leaped onto the hood.

It was gone then, as quickly as it had come. There was the sound of a leap into the trees at the side of the parking area, and then there was silence.

Shannon caught a glimpse of movement to her right, and for another heart-stopping moment, she saw the figure of a slim young boy, Jason's size. His face, moon-lighted, looked familiar. But before she could place him, he was gone. He disappeared as if he had not really existed. Shannon was left wondering if anyone had been there at all.

"What in the hell was that?" Ken muttered.

He turned on a spotlight that was mounted on the left side of the car and angled its light into the trees where the animal had gone. It revealed nothing but the forest floor strewn with needles, but otherwise as neat and tidy as if the rangers had used a special broom to sweep it. Here at the edge of the lake even the fallen branches were kept cleaned up.

"A mountain lion," Shannon gasped, looking into the darkness on her side of the car. She hastily rolled up her window and locked the door.

"That wasn't a mountain lion. They don't come this close to civilization. They don't have a head like that. It looked more like a—like a weasel or something, with that sharp muzzle."

"All I saw were its eyes and teeth and its tail. I thought I saw a boy standing over here. But surely not. Ken, couldn't we leave here?"

"Yes." He started the car, the spotlight still trained on the forest to the left. "I need to get you home, then I'll do some investigating. The tourists are beginning to show up on the lake and in the village. We can't have any wild animal attacks."

"Do weasels attack people?"

"No. Not that I ever heard. Not unless they're cornered. But when I said it looked more like a weasel than a mountain lion I was just using an example. Weasels are small animals. Smaller than that one was. I'm sorry to end the evening like this, Shannon."

"That's all right. It's past my bedtime anyway."

He didn't look toward her. With the spotlight feeling into the forest on the interior beyond the road, he backed out and drove slowly along, the light searching. When he neared the lodge he turned the light off.

"I don't want to be alarming your boss," he said. "A searchlight in the woods around his house might not be to his liking."

"He's probably asleep anyway."

"I'm taking you to the door," Ken said, as he stopped the car in the driveway behind Ramon's sedan and the station wagon. "Just to be on the safe side."

"You don't think it followed us, do you?"

"I hope not. I don't know why it would. It probably jumped onto the car out of curiosity. Maybe it recently came down out of the higher mountains and had never seen a car before. Whatever it was, I'm going back to look for it. I hope it's not a rabid animal. But animals don't attack for no reason. This one must be mad. I'd better track him down now." Shannon stood in the doorway of the lodge and watched him drive away. As soon as he had turned around and was headed back toward the lake, the searchlight came on again and made its bright track through the woods.

She stepped back into the house and closed the door. After a moment she locked it. With a chilled feeling playing over her body, she went toward the softly lighted stairway.

From the window in her room she looked again into the forest, but the light from Ken's spotlight was gone. The forest floor was dungeon black. But somewhere there moved an animal that Ken was searching for.

CHAPTER 15

"BARRY. BARRY."

Barry stirred restively in his sleep, throwing his arms out, tossing his head from side to side. Then he grew still, and his eyes moved under their closed lids, back and forth, back and forth as he settled into REM sleep. The voice was calling him, and it came from the end of a long, black tunnel. He walked in darkness, trembling in fear at the sound of the voice, yet compelled to obey it. The voice wasn't *hers,* but it was coming from someone close to her. He walked toward it, his legs like blocks of wood.

Barry. Barry.

The sound of the voice had changed. Instead of the sweet, clear tones of a young boy, it had taken on a guttural sound, a chortling, a growling amusement that made Barry tremble in fear. He wanted to run back, away, anywhere far away. But the tunnel behind him was blocked off, and there was no way to go but on, toward the black room at the far end of the tunnel. Barry began to cry helplessly, for he knew *she* would be waiting there, that the voice had tricked him.

"Barry, come play with us."

Barry woke abruptly, the tears on his cheeks cold in the night air, but drying. He sat up in bed, his eyes widening, his hearing sharpened.

The voice had not been only a part of a bad dream after all. It was Reid calling him. Reid, his best friend.

"Barry, come play with us."

It was fine and musical again, and far away, calling from among the trees that sang with the night wind. It was a happy sound that pushed out of Barry's mind the memory of the dream. Reid and Juno were playing a game, and they wanted him to join them. They hadn't been playing with him much lately. It was almost as if they didn't want to be his friends anymore, the way they kept going off and leaving him.

"Barry, come play . . ."

Barry threw his blanket back and rolled off the bed. The floor was cool beneath his bare feet. It made sounds in the dark, still night as he ran to the door. Splat, splat, splat. He laughed to himself as he heard, wishing that Reid could have heard that too. He opened his door and left it open, and he walked quietly on toward the stairway down to the living room.

If Shannon heard him she would make him go back to his room. He saw her door was closed, but there was a thin streak of light beneath it. He hesitated and almost turned back. The pale night light in the hallway made shadows behind him. It made shadows all the way down the stairway where the posts of the banister fell like tilted dominoes that were on their way to tumbling down, down. He hesitated and his heart pounded. For a moment he was back in his dreams, in fragments of dreams, with hands reaching, fingers in claws, grabbing at him from out of the darkness.

"Hurry, hurry, Barry."

Reid was closer, his melodious voice eager and impatient. Urging, urging, as if he had found something great that he wanted to share with Barry. He sounded as if he had come in closer to the house, perhaps indoors. Barry forgot the shadows, and the memories of bad dreams.

But he had to be quiet, or his daddy would hear him.

His daddy wouldn't want him to go outside at night.

But it was all right. Reid and Juno were there. They were his friends again now. They hadn't really meant to do the bad things they had done to Jason. They were sorry.

The living room was darker than the hallway upstairs. The light barely touched the bottom step, and the room looked cavernous, with great bulks of black things that Barry stared at, trying to understand what they were. As his eyes adjusted to the darker room, he saw it was just the furniture. The sofa, the chairs, the tables and lamps and the fireplace stretching up onto the wall. The door leading onto the porch was ahead of him, the upper part a soft, gray rectangle where the glass looked through into the moonlighted night.

Barry ran softly over the woven rug that reached from the foot of the stairs to the door. The knob was within easy reach, but it turned fruitlessly in his hands. The lock was a lever beneath the knob, but it resisted his small fingers. A whimper of protest rose softly from his throat. He jiggled the knob.

A shadow loomed suddenly on the other side of the glass. Reid's eyes glowed a faint pale green. His hand reached in through the wood of the door and released the lock. Then he was gone.

Barry opened the door and went onto the porch. He remembered to close the door behind him, so that no one would know he had gone out to play in the night.

The wind blew around the corners of the house, and through the tops of the trees, making all the sounds that stirred the imagination. It touched Barry with cold fingers, coming through his pajamas the way Reid and Juno went through the walls of the house. He shivered. He was alone in the dark night, with only slivers of moonlight like silver splinters sprinkled about on a black cloth. The music of the wind rising and falling, voices from an alien world, almost turned him around and sent him back into the familiarity of the house.

Then he saw the darting shadow of Juno, going along the driveway toward the lake. And running ahead of him, bending the slivers of moonlight, was the tall, strong figure of Reid.

Barry ran down the steps and followed along on his short, slow legs. He wished he could run like Reid and Juno. He wished he dared call out for them to wait for him.

His bare feet whispered on the pavement of the driveway, making soft splat, splats. The blacktop of the road began to feel rough and scratchy against his soles, and he paused to rub them. Reid and Juno had run on, and the night around him was filled with the unknown. He heard the sounds of the trees moving. He heard them dropping bits of themselves, small dead twigs they no longer needed. Sometimes they dropped a larger limb that clubbed to the ground and rolled. Or perhaps it was animals that could see in the dark. Maybe they were watching him, gathering close, surrounding him.

"Reid?" he called, his voice thin and spidery.

A light flashed suddenly through the trees, far off to Barry's right, hitting the tall, dark trunks and bouncing off to outline another. It came to a stop and then swept back the way it had come, moving more slowly. In its path, standing as still and as straight as one of the trees, was Reid. The light stopped, and beamed straight onto Reid. At his feet, Barry saw, Juno crouched, his long tail coiling up and uncoiling out behind him. Then, with the agility of a panther, he sprang up and to the darkness at the side. The light moved almost as swiftly, and then prodded among the trees, but Juno was not visible. The light came back and settled on Reid.

Barry started running, into the forest toward the arrow of light, and Reid. The sounds of his feet on the needles, on the small dead twigs discarded by the trees, was like only an extra gust of wind playing through the darkness.

Reid was waiting in the light. And the light remained steady, fixed on the figure who stood there so still. Then Barry heard a shout, a man's voice calling from the far end of the light. Vaguely now, in the distance, against the moonlighted water of the lake, Barry saw the outline of a car. It was sitting in the road at the edge of the lake, in the edge of the forest, a spotlight on its hood shining into the forest.

Reid didn't answer the voice, but he began to walk straight into the light.

Barry stopped, the cold wind crying through the tops of the trees, tossing the boughs, pushing the thin cloth of his pajamas against his skin and making him shiver. But the shiver moved inside of him too, and he began to feel that he was back in the bad dream again; that perhaps he had never gotten out.

Without looking toward him, Reid knew that he had stopped, and his voice came back to Barry through the notes of the wind. "*Barry. Barry. Come on, Barry. Come help us.*"

Help us? What were they doing? Barry had thought they were going to play, but instead they were going toward the car. He began to catch glimpses of Juno, running low to the ground in the darkness just on the far edge of the light. Reid was going faster now too, effortlessly, his feet no longer touching the ground. His face looked as if the light glowed within it, and it reached out, distorted, bulging out from the center, the nose reaching, quivering nostrils widening, green eyes glowing brighter than the light from the car.

Barry began running again, swerving to the left, taking a shortcut to the road and the car that was growing more visible by the moment. Now he saw the figure of the man beside the car. He stood with the door open, his face shadowed above his own spot-light, but his hair haloed by the moon.

Juno made a great bound toward the road, toward the car, and the man who stood there.

No, no, no. Barry's heart cried out against the fear that was growing in him, cried out to the man to hurry, hurry. But the man stood there, shining the light at Reid, and not seeing that Juno was leaping toward him, coming through the air like a bat in flight.

Then suddenly the man jerked back. He flung out his arm and struck at the swift, dark thing with the deadly tail. Juno went out of sight beyond the car. And the man moved swiftly and jumped into his car and slammed the door. The spotlight kept shining into the forest, over the hood of the car, and Reid rose into its beam and became a large head with a trailing body.

The man in the car cried out hoarsely, and the starter began to grind. The engine started, then died, then started again. Barry saw the moonlight glinting on the window glass as the man frantically rolled it up, but he knew it wouldn't do any good. Reid and Juno could go through glass and metal the way they could go through walls of wood and plaster.

Barry tried to scream. *NO, NO, NO . . .* but his voice drowned in his stricken throat. He stood unable to take another step, shadowed by the trees, and stared at the scene that was unrolling before him. He held his hands up to cover his eyes, for Reid and Juno were doing to the man what *she* had done to the little animals. He wanted not to see this further horror, yet his hands stayed at the side of his head, and his eyes kept staring, kept seeing, just as he had seen then, when *she* had killed the rabbit, and the duckling, and the . . .

"If you tell I'll do this to your daddy, and your sister and brother. I'll do this to you."

The car started, and the man jerked on the steering wheel, pulling the tires out of the edge of the forest and back onto the road. It jerked forward, but instead of going on along the road it headed straight toward the lake, toward the cliff that overlooked the lake and the deep water beneath the cliff.

Within the dark interior of the car, Barry could see the tumbling dark figures of more than one body. Juno. Reid. They were inside the car with the man. And the man had stopped guiding the car. He had jerked back, his head pulled by Reid's strong arm, and his foot jammed the accelerator to the floorboard. The car's tires screamed on the pavement of the road as it shot over it toward the cliff. The boulders at the edge of the parking area on the top of the cliff stopped the car only temporarily. The car ground against them, its engine racing, its spotlight creating weird designs through the forest behind it, tracking through the trees as if it were still looking for something there.

The figures in the car fought. The man struggled desperately, but Reid and Juno were only playing with him, Barry knew. When they were through playing, they would kill him. He knew that too. And in horror he stood rooted among the trees, unable to take his eyes away.

The boulders began to move. They were being pulled and pushed aside. Urged over the cliff in front of the car. Making room for the car to drive on into the water. Barry saw that one of the figures that had been in the car was out of it now, and hovering over one of the boulders that had kept the car from falling into the deep water. The other shadowy figure came through the upper part of the car window, like a ribbon unwinding. The man in the car had slumped over, and was no longer in sight, even though his foot was still wedged against the accelerator.

The boulders fell, making way for the car.

Moonlight glinted for a moment on the top of the car as it toppled over the edge of the cliff into the water.

The water splashed, far below, and swallowed the sound of the racing motor.

The night seemed silent now, in contrast.

Barry turned, facing into the black forest. He came up against the rough bark of a tree and felt his way around it. He cried as he had cried *then,* in silence, the tears and sobs held inside himself, roaring in his brain, blinding him. He sought the comfort and security of his room, but wandered lost in the darkness of the forest instead, his arms out feeling his way.

"Barry, Barry, come play with us . . ."

The voice, singing in the lake behind him, guided him away.

"We won't be your friends anymore if you won't play . . ."

He ran from the voice. Laughter joined with the wind in the tops of the pines and made the music evil. *Her* voice became part of it in his awareness.

"If you don't play with me I'll kill you."

A single sob escaped the tightness in his chest, but it was lost in the night beneath the sounds of the wind.

MOONLIGHT CAME THROUGH THE CLEARING IN THE TREES AND shone upon the top of the house. It spilled a heavenly light onto the steps beside which he had built his playground. It guided him out of the darkness of the forest and to the steps. On his hands and knees he climbed the steps. He stood up only when he came to the door. He reached up for the knob and turned it, and the door opened, and he went into the soft shadows of the house.

At the stairway he again went down on his hands and knees. He climbed them one after the other like a terminally ill person living one day at a time, one moment at a time. At the top of the stairs he rose to his feet and he took three steps toward Shannon's room. He stopped. Her room was dark now. All the rooms were dark. Only the hall light burned, lighting his way.

After several long moments in which his chest stopped heaving and his breath became calm, he turned down the hall toward his room.

He closed his door, although he knew it would do no good. If they wanted to come into his room they would come. But there was something he could do.

He found his book and a pencil, and opened the book to the page where . . . *she* had helped him draw the pictures of Reid and Juno. With the pencil held like a dagger in his hand, he put the black lead down onto the face of Reid. Soft sobs of anger and fear burst from him. His face twisted, features contorting. With both hands gripping the pencil, he marked over the face and figure of Reid, burying him beneath black markings. He jabbed through the page where Juno was drawn, making holes in the book.

Weeping, he pushed the book out of sight beneath his bed.

He crawled in beneath his covers, a small knot of pain.

He felt all alone now, the way he had felt *then,* before they had come to be his best friends.

CHAPTER 16

THE HOUSEHOLD WAS quiet when Shannon awoke, but there was a faint fragrance coming from the kitchen, of coffee brewing and something baking. A coffee cake, perhaps. Edna was not one to deprive herself, or anyone else, of what she called the frostings of life. "If a person listened to all the experts telling all the things that are bad for you, you'd not only not get up in the morning, you'd not go to bed at night." Shannon smiled, hearing the caustic voice in her mind. She was growing very fond of Edna Ashley.

Shannon pulled her robe around her and went to the window. It was raised slightly, letting in air that smelled cool and green with the fragrance of conifers. Pine, cedar, spruce, fir. She could identify the cedar, and at times the spruce. But all the rest looked much the same to her.

Through the window, beyond the heavy green of the trees, she caught a glimpse of the lake and the sky; the one a deep blue, and the other reflecting its blueness and becoming blue in turn. There was a promise of warmth in the air, of a day approaching summer.

She took a deep breath. She felt great, she realized. Ramon was downstairs, perhaps already in the kitchen where Edna would be serving him a slice of rich coffee cake with his coffee. Just knowing that he was there made the day beautiful.

She looked out into the hall. Here were the reminders of night, the pale light at the top of the stairs creating shadows at the turns in the walls. She went quietly past the rooms of David and Becky. Both of them were visible beyond the open doors, rolled into their blankets. David had pulled his blanket up so that it was wadded around his upper body and over his head, leaving only a sprig of hair showing. His legs, bare beyond his wrinkled-up pajamas, were stretched in a V from one corner of the bed to the other. Becky's covers were almost as smooth as when she had gone to bed. Her body made a feminine lump in the center of the bed, her knees drawn up to her chest. Her dark brown hair spread back over her pillow, wavy, glossy, as if it had been artistically arranged.

Shannon found Barry's door closed. She opened it, not sure she would see him there. Barry usually woke earlier than the other children. And especially this morning he might well be downstairs with his father.

His room seemed darker than it should have. The double panel curtains at the window had eased inward along the rod, leaving only a few inches open to the light. Beyond the glass heavily needled limbs pressed against the window, altering precious light, turning it an eerie green.

She saw that Barry was still in his bed. Like Becky, he was curled into a knot. His face was partly covered by his hand, as if he were trying in his sleep to shut out something . . . the light, the world.

She stood over him, looking down. Her heart had come alive again, so that it was almost like looking at her own son. She touched him lightly on the forehead, and when he didn't stir, she let her hand push back his hair. Then she bent and touched her lips to the smooth, warm skin.

He was sleeping like an angel, and she moved quietly so as not to disturb him. She pushed the curtains as far back as they would go, letting in more light. She left his door open when she left his room.

She showered and shampooed. She used the curling iron to turn up the ends of her hair, and fastened it back at the sides with curved ivory barrettes that she had kept since she was a girl. Instead of jeans, which she usually wore, she pulled on a summer cotton dress. She was dressing for Ramon, but half hoped he wouldn't notice. Edna would, for sure. She hesitated, almost went back to change to her usual costume, decided against it and went on downstairs.

Ramon, at the kitchen table with a cup of coffee in front of him, saw her the moment she entered the room. It was almost as if he had been watching for her, Shannon thought.

Edna said, "Oh my, don't you look pretty this morning. That date must have been good for you."

Shannon paused in surprise. She had almost forgotten her date with Ken.

"Did you have a good time?" Edna asked. In her unhurried way, she was pouring another cup of coffee, slicing another bit of cake, gathering flatware from the drawer. "I heard you come up the stairs. You must have stayed until the place closed, and then some." She brought the food to the table and placed it in front of Shannon, and said to Ramon, "This was the young man who pulled Jason out of the water. He's been coming over here with the excuse of seeing how the kids are. Now he won't have to use that for an excuse anymore. By the looks of Shannon, I'd guess he's coming back for breakfast."

Shannon was wishing fervently that she had not worn the dress. She could happily have strangled Edna. She hastened to change the subject. "No, not at all. Actually, I don't plan to see him again. It seemed like a nice day, that's all."

She thought that Ramon's quick glance toward her had a special light in it, but she dared not meet his eyes, not in front of Edna.

"Not planning to see him again?" Edna sat down, and idly stirred her coffee, her eyes wide open and steady, unblinkingly watching Shannon. "Why on earth not? If I were your age I wouldn't give it a second thought. He's not at all bad looking."

"No. Edna, this is delicious. As usual." She looked at Ramon. "Edna is an excellent cook, isn't she? And she never measures anything. She just knows what she wants."

"Too much trouble to measure," Edna said. She had gone on to looking out the window, and Shannon successfully managed a change in subject.

They talked, drank coffee, and ate another slice of coffee cake, for the better part of an hour. Edna opened the kitchen door and raised the windows to let in the warmth of the air.

Becky came in and sat down in silence, and a few minutes later David followed.

Shannon saw Ramon look at his watch. A short time later he interrupted David's chatter to go upstairs to see about Barry. When he reappeared, Barry was with him, freshly bathed and dressed, his pale blond hair neatly combed to one side. The little boy still looked as if he were half asleep, and when Ramon sat down he sat on his lap, his head leaning against Ramon's chest, his eyes staring off at nothing in particular. He didn't move until Ramon moved him.

They all went out onto the porch to watch Ramon drive away. He waved back at them as his car completed the circle in front of the house and headed out toward the lake road. His car became glimpses of color beyond the trunks of the trees, and finally was gone.

David tapped Becky on the shoulder with his fist. "Let's ride over to the village."

Edna said, "That's a long way off. There'll be traffic on the road. You might get hurt."

"It's only a couple of miles," David said. "I've been halfway there with Fred."

Edna said, "It seems to me like you could get plenty of riding right here on your own road. You wouldn't have to worry about traffic."

"I don't worry about it anyway."

"There's more cars now than there were when we came. The people are coming up to the lake now."

Becky settled the argument by turning away, going back into the house. "I don't want to ride."

David frowned out toward the lake, a dreamy look in his glazed eyes. Edna patted his shoulder as she went by on her way back into the house.

"Freddie will be back up here one of these days. Together the two of you can think of lots of things to do."

Shannon asked, "Would you like to take a walk down to the lake?"

David came out of his bored trance. He shrugged. "Yeah, I guess so. Come on, Barry, let's go walking with Shannon."

He took Barry's hand and helped him down the steps.

Shannon looked back at Edna. She had stopped at the door.

"Would you like to go with us?"

"I don't believe so. I've got some work to do, and I don't want to leave Becky alone in the house."

"We'll see you later then."

EDNA WATCHED THEM STROLL AWAY. SHE THOUGHT DAVID LOOKED like he had grown a couple of inches this spring. He was almost as tall as Shannon now. Beside him the little boy looked smaller than ever, slender and fragile, not far yet from babyhood. He didn't break away from the restraint of David's hand as he did when things were going well for him, but walked quietly instead, allowing himself to be led.

Edna went on toward the kitchen. She assumed Becky to be upstairs in her bedroom when she didn't see her in the living area with book or television for entertainment. It seemed to her, the more she thought of it, that this summer at the lodge was not doing what it was supposed to do. Even if it were helping Barry, which she wasn't convinced of yet, it was doing the other kids more harm than good. Neither of them seemed to be having much fun. They went around with long faces, bored faces; especially since Lynn and the boys had left. Becky's change had started before that: on the day Jason had nearly drowned, as near as Edna could tell.

Edna yawned widely, and thought about retracing her steps to the living room and going upstairs to take a nap. But she knew from past unpleasant experiences that if she stole a sleep in the daytime, she robbed herself of night sleep. She'd be sitting with owl eyes at three in the morning.

In the kitchen she checked the calendar again, as she had been doing for the past few days. There was a long summer ahead. She supposed they'd be leaving the lodge around the first of September, and that meant almost three months yet. She yawned, and topped it off with a deep sigh. Next Sunday was Father's Day. That would give the kids something extra to do this week, then, as they occupied their minds with what to buy for their dad.

She heated the coffee and poured herself a cup. She turned on the radio and sat down on the stool beside the counter. A man's voice droned softly on local news, saying something about a drowning . . . Edna turned up the volume.

". . . between midnight and three a.m. He was found by a young couple boating on the lake this morning. His car had submerged in approximately thirty feet of water off a scenic cliff. Authorities believe he was unconscious when he went into the water. Both doors were locked. Ken Masters was twenty-three years old."

There was more news, but Edna had stopped listening. A bone-deep chill had settled upon her, as if she too were feeling the cold water of the lake. She got her sweater off the hook in the pantry and buttoned it on. A long chill went down her body. Just to think, all this morning as they were sitting around the house drinking coffee, eating cake, and talking about this and that, not far away men and equipment had been at work bringing up a submerged car and its drowned driver. And that driver was the same young man who only last week had saved Jason's life, perhaps, by helping him out of the water. A body just never knew what twists of fate awaited him.

She decided to walk down to meet Shannon and the boys. Becky was probably safe here in the house alone for no longer than it would take to walk down the lane and back. There hadn't been any rock throwing for a couple of days now, nor anything else that made her feel they weren't quite alone. Although, to be honest, the feeling that something wasn't quite right stayed with her. She was often seeing things just beyond the corner of her eye, things that moved in the shadows of the corners. But then, it was probably just the darkness of the lodge, overpowered as it was by all those tall, green-needled trees.

At the foot of the stairs, she yelled up, "Becky, I'm going to walk down the lane and try to find Shannon and the boys. Do you want to go along?"

For a long moment there was no answer, then Becky's voice faintly returned, "No."

. . .

Becky heard the closing of the front door, a soft, dull sound beyond her bedroom walls. She felt more than heard Mrs. Ashley's footsteps on the boards of the porch. The house vibrated with the silence that was left behind. Becky's ears strained to separate whispers of sound. Footsteps again, or the vacant echo of footsteps. The silence was being filled with noises, rising to capture the emptiness left by the people who had gone for a walk to the lake. Becky rose to her elbow and listened hard.

She heard laughter. Half-smothered giggles, like evil children snickering over something horrid they had done. It came from down the hall, from Barry's room.

Becky slid quietly off her bed and went to close her door. She didn't want to look into the hall, down its shadowed length toward the room at the far end, but her eyes were drawn to it against her will. There was movement within the room, shadows cast upon the half-opened door moved jerkily as figures cavorted between door and window.

Fear compressed Becky's throat, and held her eyes on the moving shadows. The evil giggles amplified and diminished, like poor radio reception from a faraway station. Yet the shadows continued to play upon the door.

Becky felt as though she was drowning in fear. She longed to call Mrs. Ashley back, to ask her to wait. She was afraid to go alone into the hall, but she was afraid to close her door and go back into her room.

Finally, she moved, inching her way toward the stairs, her eyes transfixed by the wavering, formless images thrown on the wood of Barry's half-opened door. She had to go toward it in order to reach the head of the stairs, and it seemed ages before her hand touched the stairway banister. She began to back soundlessly down the stairs. Her eyes were seeing shadows everywhere now, all along the walls, on the floor, the ceiling, shadows that danced and cavorted, following her with an evil playfulness.

With a stifled cry she turned and almost fell down the remainder of the stairs.

. . .

SHANNON, DAVID AND BARRY HAD NEARLY REACHED THE END OF the lane. The sunshine, falling brightly upon the lake and the shoreline, looked inviting. As though called by it, Barry began to run on ahead of Shannon and David.

David said, "There are a lot more boats out today. I see . . . three, four. There's a sailboat way over on the other side, see it? I can't tell what make it is from here, can you?"

"No, I wouldn't know even if I were close enough to read the serial number on the engine."

"Here's a motorboat coming. It looks like a patrol boat. I wonder what they're looking for?"

Footsteps pounded heavily behind them, and Shannon turned. Edna was hurriedly coming along the drive, half running, at times breaking into a full jog. A strand of hair had fallen forward across her forehead, and her lips were parted in her gasp for more oxygen. She looked almost comically ridiculous, but the thought barely made contact with Shannon's mind before it became tinged with dread.

Ten feet away Edna slowed to a walk. She pressed a hand against her heaving chest and opened her mouth wider. "My . . . oh my," she said. "I didn't know I was so out of shape."

She reached Shannon and the two of them walked on out into the sunshine. David had gone on to the lakeshore and was standing near Barry, looking down-lake at the unusual activity of a cluster of patrol boats. They moved out of sight behind a tree-covered finger of land that protruded into the lake.

"I just heard over the news," Edna said, "that the young man you were out with last night was found this morning in the lake. He was in his car with all the windows and doors locked, in thirty feet of water."

"Ken? Ken Masters?" The sunshine that a moment ago had seemed so warm now failed to keep the rush of chills from Shannon's body. "What happened? How?"

"I don't know. All I know is the newsman said he had been found. He's dead, of course."

Shannon stared out over the lake. Her hours last night with Ken swept through her mind like a scene being rapidly rerun. "Something strange happened last night," she said. "We were parked beside the lake when an animal jumped onto the hood of the car, startling both of us. He brought me home right after, and he went back to look for it."

Becky's voice came from behind her, unexpectedly. "What did the animal look like?"

Shannon and Edna turned. Neither of them had heard Becky approach, though she looked out of breath as though she too had been running. Her fair skin was blotched pink and white.

"Well, did you decide to get out after all?" Edna asked, but Becky was looking apprehensively at Shannon, waiting for a reply to her question.

"I don't know," Shannon said. "It was dark there, and it seemed only to be a dark shape. It leaped off and disappeared. I was just telling Edna that Ken went to search for it after he left me at the lodge. And sometime later he must have driven his car into the lake. It came over the radio news that he was found drowned in his car."

There was a moment of silence. Barry had squatted by the edge of the water, and was watching it ebb and flow. David had climbed to the top of a large boulder where he could see farther down the lake. Becky said, "I wish Dad hadn't left so early." Shannon felt that Becky had expressed the feelings of all of them. The wind over the lake suddenly felt colder. She hugged her arms, her hands clasped on each shoulder. The wind whipped her cotton skirt around her legs.

"Shall we go back to the lodge?" She walked farther onto the beach where Barry had decided to watch the water flow over his hands. They were turning pink with the cold. She reached down, forgetting that she seldom touched him overtly. To her surprise he didn't jerk away, but turned instead and looked up at her. "Shall we walk back to the house, Barry?"

He got up and went ahead of them, wiping sand and water from his hands.

Edna called, "Come on, David."

"Just a minute. I think I see something. Boats and things down around that curve. Can I walk down there, Shannon?"

Shannon exchanged a surprised look with Edna. It was the first time David had asked permission of her. "I'll be careful," David promised. "Becky can come with me."

Becky looked at Shannon.

"Shall I? I think I will, if it's okay."

Shannon said, "I don't know why not."

"Why don't you come with us?"

"No thanks. We'll walk on back toward the house. But don't be long."

They separated, Becky and David walking in the grass at the side of the lake road, while Shannon and Edna went into the shady lane back toward the lodge. Barry kept ahead of them, running as needed.

At the porch, Edna went on into the house, telling Shannon, "I've got work to do that I ought to get done. I'll put some potatoes in the oven for dinner. In another hour the sun will be down behind the mountain."

She hummed from habit once she had entered the house and was alone. Her thoughts were still on the young man who had been so alive just twenty-four hours ago. Death came so quietly and unexpectedly at times. The lake hadn't seemed beautiful today the way it had yesterday. Today it had looked deceptive, a smooth, reflecting surface hiding dangers beyond human experience.

Edna pushed the sleeves of her sweater up, ran hot water into the sink, squeezed out a few drops of detergent and worked up a suds. She put the lunch dishes into the water to soak while she used the other half of the sink to scrub baking potatoes.

She heard footsteps in the hall, ambling, light steps that suggested either Becky or David. The swing door gave a soft squeak as it opened and closed, like a mouse in the wall. The footsteps came on into the kitchen. Without looking around, Edna asked, "Well, are you already back? That was a fast trip."

There was no answer.

At once Edna knew that the visitor was neither Becky nor David. They would have answered her. As suddenly as she realized that she was filled with anger. Was this the impudent brat who had thrown rocks at her through the window?

She whirled, ready to give the unwelcome guest a what-for, eager to teach him a few manners. She stopped, staring through nothing. Her open mouth drooped loosely in bewilderment. She felt as though she was staring into the impish face of a juvenile delinquent, yet there was no one in the kitchen but herself. If it hadn't been for the memory of the rock through the window, and a lingering, echoing sound of the very footsteps that had caused her to turn around, she would have thought she was losing her mind.

Her eyes flashed over the kitchen, from end to end. She realized she had not turned on the lights, and the room was growing shadows that reached out from corners, from the table and chairs. She took a couple of steps toward the light switch, and footsteps echoed hers, stepping as she stepped but with a moment's delay. Shadows lying long across the center of the floor shifted. Moved as she moved, and stopped.

Edna began to feel as though a river was rushing through her ears. Pushed and pulled by a high wind. She could hardly breathe, the fear had suddenly, abruptly grown so thick in her throat. It was like mucous gathering to choke her. Her eyes jerked helplessly, looking for something that was there, and yet was not there. She wet her lips with a raspy tongue and plunged on toward the door and the light switch. She didn't look behind her when the light came on, dispelling shadows over the length of the long room.

She pulled the door open and went out onto the porch.

Holding to the railing, facing into the dark forest to the north, Edna took several deep breaths. The rushing sound in her ears abated. Her heart slowed. Her fear of going back into the kitchen began to seem silly.

Light spilled out the kitchen door, across the boards of the porch. The voices of David and Becky came from somewhere beyond the corner of the house, too far away to understand. They were coming back from the lake now. When they reached the porch all of them would probably come in and settle down to books, games or television. Dinner should be cooking. She had to hurry and get the potatoes into the oven.

She strode boldly back toward the screen door, pulled it open and stepped over the threshold into the kitchen. As she pulled the door closed behind her, a red hot poker burned a trail down her bare arm from her rolled-up sweater sleeve to her wrist.

Edna gasped with pain, her breath trapped in her throat. She looked down at her arm and saw that it had been laid open thinly, as from a sharp knife point, and blood marked the trail of pain. As she stared at her arm, another trail of blood began to appear, a half inch away from the first. The pain drew her around it, like an animal that curled upon its punctured body. She was aware that she was not alone. Shadows danced upon the floor in front of her, and a faint, gleeful sound, as indistinct as insect buzzings, danced in the air as the shadows cavorted on the floor.

Edna screamed, her voice filling the kitchen. There were two things in her world then, the pain on her arm, and the sound of her own voice. The other, blessedly, was gone.

CHAPTER 17

SHANNON URGED Edna toward the couch in the living room. Edna cooperated stiffly, her eyes bulging and glazed, her arm held out and blood making little streaks slowly down from the long, red scratches. She moved like a robot under Shannon's urging, one foot reaching out, then the other. Her spine was as unyielding as a board.

"Becky, David, bring cold water and a cloth."

At last she got Edna to the couch, but the woman stood transfixed. Her cheeks quivered. All color had gone out of her face.

"What on earth . . ." Shannon said, mostly to herself. The room, she noticed, was growing quite dark. Both Becky and David were a few feet away, staring at Mrs. Ashley. "The water," Shannon reminded them. "One of you go to the bathroom and bring a wet washcloth. The other turn on the lights."

They started to go in the same direction, toward the lights. They collided, and silently disentangled themselves and David turned on the lights. Shannon heard water running in the downstairs bath. Becky came back with a dripping washcloth.

"Bring a pan of water, David," Shannon said, and began to sponge Edna's face with the wet washcloth. As though the water changed the composition of her body, Edna collapsed onto the couch.

Shannon arranged cushions under her head, and lifted her feet to rest level with her body. Edna had begun to groan, her eyes closed. David came with a pan of water and more cloths. Shannon washed the blood from Edna's arm. The cut looked shallow. It was long, from near her elbow to her wrist, and beside the long one another shorter one ran. They were ugly cuts, but didn't seem to justify Edna's reaction.

"How did you do this, Edna?" Shannon asked.

Edna stopped groaning abruptly and opened her eyes. She looked from face to face as if she had just awakened.

"Oh Lord, oh Lordy," she said, and pushed herself upright. She took the washcloth Shannon had been pressing to her forehead and laid it against her arm. Her eyes jerked past them, looked about the room. "It's gone, it's gone. I guess it's gone."

"What's gone?"

"But watch out! It could come back. Don't go into the kitchen."

"Edna, what are you talking about?" Shannon demanded, realizing that something more than the cuts had happened to Edna Ashley. The woman at this moment seemed demented.

"Where's Barry?" Edna cried. "Where's the little one?"

Shannon looked around. She saw him standing in the shadow of a chair, his face almost as colorless as Edna's. "He's here," Shannon said. "Right here. We're all here."

"Thank the Lord. We can't go back into the kitchen."

"Edna, please sit down, and calm down. Tell us how you cut yourself."

"Cut myself . . ." Edna looked down at her arm, and moved the washcloth to reveal the red, open cuts. "I didn't do it."

"Sit down, Edna," Shannon said gently. "Are you feeling all right?"

"I'm all right," she answered, sounding more normal. Obediently she sat down, but her eyes lifted, checking once again that all were near. "The rock," she said. "Do you remember the rock that came through the window? And the other one that hit the house? Well, it's all the same thing that's doing it. I'm convinced of that. We have to get out of here. Tonight. We can't stay here any longer."

Becky moved closer, as if she were choosing sides. Shannon looked from Edna to Becky and back again. "I don't know what you're talking about, Edna."

"I think I know what it is," Edna said. "It's like you said, a poltergeist. That's the only explanation I can think of. This cut—these cuts on my arm. It did it. The thing. The poltergeist. I think there may be more than one. It's in the kitchen."

Edna rambled on, talking about the thing in the kitchen. Shannon backed off, wondering which she should do first, call a doctor, or prove to Edna that nothing was in the kitchen. She decided to check out the kitchen, the way she used to check out the closet for Kelly, to prove to him there were no monsters hiding there.

When Edna saw where she was going she jumped to her feet. "No! Shannon! Don't go in there!"

"It's all right, Edna, just relax. Stay with her, Becky. David, come with me."

They went through the short hall and the swing door. It made its usual faint, mousey sound. The kitchen was brightly lighted, the red and gray tile floor reflecting the light as if it had just been polished. The back door stood open, although the screen door was closed. The cardboard in the window over the sink was like a bandage hiding a sore. The sink had dishes soaking in one side and half-scrubbed potatoes in the other.

"Looks okay to me," David said.

Shannon closed the door and locked it. She looked from one end of the room to the other. The table and chairs trailed shadows out from each leg. And the tabletop had beneath it a shadow that seemed, when Shannon glanced away from it, darker than it should have been, as if there were something more beneath it adding its own shadow; but when she glanced back, her first impression seemed fanciful. Caused perhaps by her nervousness, her sense of uneasiness that had been thrown into high gear when Edna screamed. She shivered involuntarily, hearing again the abrupt, unexpected sound of the scream exploding within the house. She had seen Becky and David coming up the lane, and had started out to meet them, when the scream stopped her. It had stopped David and Becky too. The three of them had stared at one another for a long moment, and then together they had run to find Edna standing in the middle of the kitchen in hysterics.

There was something cold and too polished about the kitchen now. She knew why she felt that way. It wasn't because of an alien presence, as Edna said, but because . . . because . . . She found that she could not pinpoint the reason, and realized she was more influenced by Edna that she should be. One of them had to keep her head on straight.

"Let's go," she said to David.

Becky and Edna were standing between the back of the couch and the hallway, watching for them. Barry had crawled up into the chair favored by his father. He sat pushed into the corner, hugging his knees against his chest, watching in silence the scene before him. For his sake, Shannon felt, she had to put a stop to the nonsense about the kitchen.

"Edna," she said softly, hoping that Barry couldn't hear her well enough to understand what she was saying. "David and I have seen that the kitchen is empty. Everything is normal. I'm sorry you cut yourself, but I'm afraid we'll frighten Barry too much if this isn't ended. Maybe you'd like to go to your room and lie down? We can cook our own dinner for a change."

Edna looked as though Shannon had slapped her. She began shaking her head. Still, she looked back at Barry, and kept her voice low. "You don't believe me at all, do you? Any of you."

Becky said, "I do. I believe you, Mrs. Ashley."

Edna grabbed this bit of credit. She clutched Becky's arm. "It's a poltergeist," she hissed. "And it's dangerous. We should leave here. Now. Tonight."

Becky was nodding her head. "I wanted Dad to take us home with him, and he wouldn't."

Shannon said, "And that's exactly one of the reasons we are not leaving here tonight, or tomorrow, or the next day. We're here for a purpose, remember?"

Becky looked undecided, confused, and Shannon felt a touch of anger, that Edna had added to what was already becoming a problem. Becky hadn't been happy at the lodge since Jason left. Given a few more days, she might have been fine. Edna, on the other hand, seemed simply not to like living at the mountain lodge. Shannon had seen her looking at the calendar, counting days.

Edna shook her head, as in regret, or apology. "I can't stay here, Shannon. I don't want to go off and leave you and the children, but if you won't go back to town too, then I'll have to go alone. I'm sorry. I know you think I'm hysterical. I might have been for a little while there, but I'm not now. I know what happened to me. And I didn't do it to myself. I stood there and watched this cut appear on my arm. And then the other. I heard sounds. Like voices, only not like voices. And I saw shadows jumping around on the floor where there was nothing to throw a shadow."

Shannon felt herself absorbing some of the fear in Edna's eyes. She recalled with sudden consternation the times she had been startled by a sense of something more in her presence than appeared to be there; of the times she had seen shadows that puzzled her, that aroused age-old fears she had never experienced before. She found herself looking at Becky, and the silent pleading in the girl's eyes. But to give in was to deny reality. She just couldn't believe Edna's explanation of how the cuts had happened, though it was she who had inadvertently put the idea of poltergeists into Edna's mind. She had faith in Edna, and doubted nothing she said, but in the most logical part of her mind, she believed that Edna had in some way cut herself and hadn't realized it at the time.

Shannon put her arm around Edna's shoulders. She felt the woman trembling. "Edna, listen to me. Could it be that you scratched yourself somewhere in the pantry, on a nail or two protruding from a shelf or something like that? Maybe there was no pain in the beginning, and a moment later when the blood came to the surface and it began to hurt—"

Edna looked at Becky, her only ally. "She just isn't going to believe me."

Shannon saw that no persuasion she might try would change Edna's mind. And she began to see also that Edna needed to get away, for whatever reason. Coming up to the lodge had been a mistake, for Edna.

"Well, Edna," she said gently, hugging her. "We'll miss you. When do you want to leave? I'll drive you over to the village. There should be a bus through sometime tonight. If not, would you rather stay over there than here?"

"Won't you reconsider and go with me?"

"I accepted a job staying with the children at the lodge for the summer."

"But, if we explain to Ramon why we had to leave . . ."

There was no appropriate answer, and Shannon saw that Edna knew that. Shannon drew away. "I'll help you pack."

Becky said, "I'm going upstairs with you."

To David Shannon said, "Then David, you stay here with Barry. Try to get him interested in play, or a book. If that fails, try cartoons on television. We'll eat out this evening. We'll have a kind of farewell party for Mrs. Ashley."

THEY RETURNED TO THE LODGE FOUR HOURS LATER, ALL OF THEM subdued, each to private thoughts. The evening had been quite pleasant once they had gotten away from the lodge. Even Edna had cheered up. They had gone first to the bus station and found that the last bus of the day left at ten-o-ten. That gave them a lot of time to eat, and then a few minutes to say goodbye. At the end, Edna had weepingly hugged all of them. Becky had gone to the station wagon with damp eyes, and David had made a point of staring off into the distance. Barry clung to David's hand in silence, but his small face seemed too pale, as it had all day, and his eyes larger than ever, as if he were gathering upon himself more of the fears and sorrows that were too much for his age. Shannon was afraid that the progress they had made was now destroyed.

They went quietly into the house. It seemed oddly vacant . . . and something more: it seemed as if it listened, and waited, and when they entered it closed around them, gathering them in. Shannon wondered if the kids had the same feelings that she did.

Their faces were lifted toward the top of the stairs as if they expected to see someone waiting there.

They hesitated, reluctant to go up. David looked toward the dark bulk of the television in the unlighted living room.

"Couldn't we watch a late show?"

"No, we couldn't," Shannon said. "You may not feel like you want to go to bed, but you'll go to sleep."

"The sooner you sleep," Becky said as she climbed the stairs, "The sooner you wake up. And the sooner . . ." she let her voice trail away.

"Shall we all walk with Barry to his room?" Shannon said with as much cheer as she could muster. She was dismayed that she suddenly dreaded going upstairs. Had Edna added that much security to her feelings? Or was it Edna's strong belief that something strange inhabited the house that made it now seem unfriendly and uninviting? She found that she wanted to keep the children together, but she knew if she suggested they all share the same room, it would be like admitting that none of them were really safe. The next best thing was to see to it that each of them was settled in his or her own room.

Barry went to bed willingly, but when Shannon started to turn out the light, he said, "Don't turn out the light, please."

"You have the little nightlight, Barry. Remember?"

"I want the big light."

"All right. If you want it out later, can you turn it out?"

"Yes."

He lay in the center of his bed, his blanket pulled up and pressed against both cheeks. He watched them as they went out the door, and said goodnight to each as it was spoken. Shannon closed the door because she knew that Ramon always closed the children's bedroom doors. But she wished to leave them open tonight, so that they would not seem so far apart. She could leave her own door open.

After David and Becky were in their rooms, Shannon took a quick shower. She turned off the water sooner than she otherwise would have because she wanted to be alert to any sound the children might make. But the house was quiet, and the doors were still closed, she saw when she went into the hall.

She was sitting in her bed, propped against her pillows, and trying to read. Her mind kept straying away from the printed words, and she reread paragraphs and still didn't know what she had read. She put the novel aside in exasperation, wishing that she could do as she had assured David he would: go to sleep right away. How presumptuous of her, she thought, to tell him such a thing. So here she was, all senses alert, as if she were expecting something to happen at any moment.

When she heard the soft, padding steps in the hall, her heart bounded nearly out of control. She stared at the open doorway until it blurred. The children were asleep . . . who was walking down the hall toward her room?

Becky stepped into view, and paused on the threshold. Shannon drew a long breath and settled back.

Becky said, "I saw your light on. Can I come in and talk?"

"Yes, of course." Shannon patted the empty side of the double bed. She was so relieved to see Becky that the girl was more than welcome. She didn't question why Becky was still awake at one in the morning.

Becky sat on the bed, halfway down, facing Shannon. Occasionally she glanced back at the open door. "I haven't been asleep," she said. "I've been listening. I heard you take a shower, and then come to your room. I heard David get up and go to his bathroom, and go back to bed. I heard sounds from Barry's room, but I don't think it was Barry making the sounds." She looked again at the doorway.

Shannon frowned, more worried than disapproving. "I've been awake. I didn't hear anything."

"Your room is farther away. My room is close to Barry's."

"Becky, has Mrs. Ashley frightened you?"

Becky drew a long breath. "Listen, Shannon, there are some things I want to tell you. I know you'll not want to believe me, but would you at least please listen? I've been thinking and thinking about this. I know Dad wouldn't believe me. I'm not even sure David would. Mrs. Ashley might. But you're the one I have to tell, because we—us kids—we have to depend on you. You're the only one who can help us."

"I don't understand."

"It's got something to do with Barry. I don't know what it is for sure, but I have this theory. Mrs. Ashley calls it a poltergeist, and in a way she's right. But I think I know where it's coming from."

Shannon felt as though she was facing a closed door that she didn't want to open, that should never under any circumstances be opened. She watched Becky's eyes in a kind of fascinated dread, listening to the girl's words, and growing colder with each syllable.

"It started back in town, sort of, before you came. About the time Barry was taken out of that school. I've been thinking and thinking, and I know that was when it began. I'd hear things from Barry's room. I'd hear him talking to himself—I thought he was talking to himself, and then I'd hear an answer. At first I thought it was funny. Barry was playing he was someone else, and he'd answer. But then it occurred to me, since I got here, that he couldn't have changed his voice that much. The other voice was—strange. Deeper, for one thing, sometimes, and sounding like he talked through something. It gave it a hollow sound. And there were other things. Mrs. Ashley talking about the shadows on the floor reminded me. There *are* shadows, Shannon, that have no bodies. And they were there, at home. Close to Barry, most of the time. That's why I didn't make a big deal out of going home too, because if we went, *they* would just go along. We wouldn't get away from them."

Becky looked directly into Shannon's eyes, and for a moment was silent. But Shannon had no intention of disputing her word, or interrupting her. With a slow horror seeping into her soul, she waited.

Becky finally looked away. It seemed easier for her to talk if she allowed her eyes to wander, constantly going to check on the shadowy rectangle of the open door.

"The first time I saw it was the day it attacked Jason. *They,* I mean. For there are two of them. One is an animal, of sorts. It's a mixture of animals. You saw its picture, in Barry's book. I didn't know its name, until I read it in the book. Juno. I'll never forget it now, or the way it really looks. When Jason ran into the lake, and I dived in to help him out, I saw that animal swimming there, under water. At first I just thought it was some kind of wild animal. It kind of scared me, but I just got out of its way and swam to help Jason. I didn't know what was wrong with him. He had begun to cry and act crazy in the forest, and he had run as if something were after him. I know now there was. I saw the boy in the water, Shannon. *I saw him trying to drown Jason.*" She leaned closer to Shannon, her eyes now steady and burning with a desperate light into Shannon's. "And do you know who that boy looked like, Shannon? Barry. He had Barry's face. But he was larger than Barry, a lot larger. He was at least as tall as Jason, and stronger built. I saw him, in the water."

She sat back, as if giving Shannon a chance to answer. But even though Shannon saw her eyes were bright with the beginning of tears, Shannon knew she wouldn't stop her now.

Becky blinked back the tears. She rubbed her eyes with the index fingers of each hand.

"That's the only time I *saw* them," she said, "but I know they're here. I have heard them, just like Mrs. Ashley said she did. And I have seen their shadows. In the beginning it seemed like they stayed close to Barry. Now they aren't. Not always. Shannon, do you know what I think it is? I think it's some kind of projection from Barry himself. Like ectoplasm. Materializations of some kind."

"And the animal?" Shannon said softly. "How could that be a projection from Barry? Even if the other were."

"I don't know. Well, their pictures were in Barry's book. Maybe when he drew them, he created them. Somehow."

"Or maybe they were already created and he merely drew their pictures."

"But the boy has Barry's face."

"In his book the face is blank."

They looked into each other's eyes. Shannon hoped to restore some rationality to Becky, in silence, but she could see in Becky's eyes a similar fight against herself, trying to make her believe.

Shannon finally said, whispered, "It's preposterous."

Becky began talking again, her words rapid and half-whispered. "Then maybe it's not a projection from Barry, but something else. Something terrible and cruel that has taken on Barry's looks for some reason. But—I'll tell you the rest of what I've been thinking. You can call it preposterous if you want to. I care, but it won't change things. And you'll see for yourself that things are happening faster, and more of it. And when you think back, you'll see I'm right."

Shannon nodded. "I'm listening."

"All right." Becky leaned closer, supporting herself with a hand flattened against the blanket. "That girlfriend of yours who was killed? That Barry ran from in the park? I think they killed her. And then we came up here, and Barry talked in his bedroom to someone besides himself. They came along too. I think that now. And this guy who was killed the other night? I think they killed him too."

Shannon didn't want to believe this, but she remembered the animal that leaped onto the hood of the car, and the improbable gleam of its eyes when there was no light shining against them. She remembered the shock of seeing it, and the band of irrational fear, as if she were looking into the eyes of something far beyond the eyes of a mere wild animal. *Animals don't attack for no reason. This one must be mad. I'd better track him down, now.* And the figure of the boy she had glimpsed for a moment? She had put it aside as an illusion, but what if it weren't?

"Most of the time they're invisible," Becky said. "Except they throw shadows, for some reason. Maybe they're not ever really invisible, but our eyes just can't separate them from reality, because they don't fit our perception of it. Or maybe they do have the power to make themselves visible only when they want to."

"You sincerely believe this, don't you, Becky?"

"Yes. I've lain awake a lot of nights thinking about it, and listening for them. I've been scared they would come into my room, but they never did when I was awake. I hoped they would go away while Daddy was here, and it seemed they did. But look what they did to Mrs. Ashley right afterwards. What are they going to do next? I'm afraid for us. You've got to help us, Shannon, please."

Suddenly, somewhere in the house below, there was a crash, followed by the faint tinkling of glass that drifted away into silence. Becky gave a soft scream that she tried to muffle with her hands. Shannon jerked up instinctively and was standing at the side of the bed when the sounds drifted away, leaving their throbbing silence. It seemed for a moment then that she was hearing laughter, a tinkling, glass-like giggling that was sounds made by ghostly beings. She could almost believe Becky's incredible explanation of the strange happenings of late.

"Shannon, what was it?" Becky whispered, and there was no doubt of the fear in the girl. Shannon reached toward her protectively, and tried to put reassurance in a light pat on Becky's shoulder.

"I'll see what it was. It sounded like a window breaking. We might have a burglar in the house." Becky began shaking her head. "Something was knocked over. It wasn't a window. Shannon, don't go down there."

"It's all right, Becky. I'll be careful."

Shannon went out into the hall, her bare feet creating only a whisper of sound on the uncarpeted boards of the floor. The polished pine felt cold and slightly sticky to her feet. She walked as if she were walking on ice, hesitating with each step, feeling stiff-legged and awkward. She couldn't let Becky know, but the sound had filled her with a crushing dread. But she wasn't afraid of the invisible—she really didn't believe Becky's horrors existed. She was afraid of the very real person who had caused the crash of window or door or whatever it was.

The stairway was a short distance along the hall and to her left, dropping away beyond the corner wall of her bedroom. She wished she had left lights on in the living room below so that the stairwell was not so dark. The one small wall bracket light at the top of the stairs lighted only the steps well enough to keep a person from falling. The light did not reach far into the cavern of the living room.

She went down the steps as she had walked along the hall, one hesitant move at a time. She was thankful for the wall against which the stairway was built. It afforded protection on one side at least. She was uncomfortably aware that her feet and legs came in sight of anyone watching from the living room before any part of that room was visible to her. She felt like bending down so that she could see, but knew she would find only darkness. She had to reach the foot of the stairs and the light switch there.

Half way down, she paused for a long heart-pounding moment, trying to listen for sounds beyond her own body. The house seemed almost unnaturally quiet. She began moving on, one step at a time.

She almost sobbed when her hand finally touched the switch on the wall at the foot of the stairs. The light from the ceiling bulb sufficiently illuminated the entire living room from one end to the other of its forty foot length.

She saw it immediately.

The large-screened television had been toppled forward. Shards of glass lay scattered on the woven cotton rug and reflected the light with tints of blue.

CHAPTER 18

THE ROOM WAS SILENT. The sound of the crash lingered, an isolated disturbance in a still night. Shannon looked at the television in bewilderment, the intense fear she had felt ebbing away. She could see the front door glass had not been broken, nor had the window glass. She began to feel sure that no burglar was involved after all, and she didn't want to try to identify this odd new sensation that was creeping over her. Like a person turning away from something too horrible to face, she began to look through the house, to check windows and doors.

As she progressed from room to room, including the downstairs bedrooms where personal items of both Lynn and Ramon remained, as well as the small den whose door opened into the wall at the foot of the stairs, she turned on every light available and left it on. No way was she going to come again into the dark ground floor.

She tested all the windows and found them locked. The doors too were still locked. Nothing else in the house seemed to have been disturbed the slightest. So at last she had to return to the television and the impossibility of it having fallen forward by itself.

Using a newspaper from the magazine rack, she began to clean up the glass. Bit by bit she picked it up and placed it on the newspaper. The smaller slivers had buried into the rug, and after she had stepped on one, she bent more carefully to her work. She realized she was avoiding thought. Maybe later, when she was back in her room, maybe then she could try to understand how it could have happened.

A voice hissed behind her.

"*Shannon*"

Shannon jumped and whirled. Becky stood on the bottom step, looking across the distance of the living space at her, and at the television face down on the floor. She came on past the couch and stopped at the edge of the area rug at Shannon's command.

"Be careful. Stay there, Becky. There's glass in the rug."

"I'll help you pick it up."

"Do it carefully. It's very sharp. I already have a couple of tiny cuts on my fingers, and one on my foot. I'd really rather you just sat on the sofa."

"No, I'll help you."

Becky seemed strangely calm. Her dark hair hung forward as she bent, glossy curls catching the light almost as lustrously as the slivers of glass.

When they had finished, Becky looked up and said, "I wonder why they picked on the television?"

Shannon said, "It was probably not balanced precisely. We're lucky none of us were in the room when it finally toppled forward." There, she thought triumphantly, without thinking. I came up with an explanation that is surely correct. Maybe now we can lay Edna and Becky's poltergeists to rest. She felt quite good and safe when she smiled reassuringly at Becky.

Shannon emptied the glass into the waste basket.

"Do you think you can sleep now?" she asked Becky. "It's nearly three o'clock."

Becky shrugged, and with no further word, went up the stairs ahead of Shannon. After she had gone into her room and closed the door, Shannon checked on both David and Barry. David was sleeping with his room dark, but Barry's lights were still on. Shannon turned out all but the light at the side of his bed. It had a low watt bulb, no more than twenty, and the light it gave out was soft and pale. It did create shadows in the corners, Shannon saw, but she was not going to allow her mind to dwell on all the things she had heard this night, or make more of a shadow than it deserved.

Still, when she went to her own room, she left her door open so that she could see into the hall, and then she slept fitfully half sitting up in bed. At another time in the night she heard another, less forceful crash in the house, at a point so far away it had to have been in the kitchen. It brought her awake. She sat fully up and looked at her digital clock. The time was four-twenty. She didn't sleep again. Her senses remained sharply attuned to every sound, every movement in the house, and it seemed that she could hear a continuous activity in the kitchen. But she didn't go downstairs until dawn. By that time, the house was silent, and outside the birds were singing as though all was well and normal in their part of the world.

The kitchen was still half dark when she pushed open the swinging door. She moved it slowly, hoping to avoid the squeak, but only prolonged it. She stepped into the kitchen and surveyed the mess in dismay.

The tray that had sat in the center of the table holding sugar bowl, salt and pepper shakers, and napkins, was now on the floor, its contents scattered widely. The sugar made a long, white streak from the table, in a semi-circle, as if the tray had been flung in an arc.

All the items that had been on the cabinet were now on the floor, the flour, sugar, coffee, tea from the canisters mixed together on the linoleum as if vandals had tried to create the worst mess they could. The oven door was hanging open. Cabinet drawers had also been pulled open and their contents added to the rest on the floor. Only the upper cabinets and the refrigerator had not been disturbed.

Shannon stepped gingerly through the mess and checked the door. It was still locked. So were the windows. She went out of the kitchen and checked again all the windows and doors in the first floor of the house, and found them locked. At last she had to admit there was an alien force at work. Becky and Edna's poltergeists had been well and alive during the night.

Uneasily, Shannon went back to the kitchen and went to work cleaning it up. She did it quickly, not carefully. She wanted the kitchen to look halfway natural by the time the kids came down.

But she couldn't help wondering when the next blow would come, and how increased in severity it might be. For it seemed obvious now that the happenings that were only small irritations in the beginning, unexplainable things that were easily ignored, were now becoming larger and larger. She found that she was thinking of *them,* accepting Becky's theory.

She had finished the cleaning and was setting the table for breakfast when Becky came in and sat down.

"Did you sleep?" Shannon asked.

"Yes. Did you?"

"Well enough. What would you like for breakfast?"

Becky reached into the fruit bowl Shannon had made for the table and took out an orange. "Just this," she said. "I'm not very hungry."

"Did you check on David and Barry?"

"Yes. David's up. He's helping Barry. They'll be down in a minute. Barry had to brush his teeth yet."

Shannon opened the back door. The fresh air rushed in, bringing the scent of the conifers and the sound of the birds. "I think it would be a good idea to air out the house today, don't you think?" she asked Becky, surprised at how easy it was to act as if life had not taken a turn toward the bizarre. She had to keep things as normal as possible at least until she figured out what to do.

David and Barry came into the kitchen, and Shannon served them toast and cereal. By the time they had finished eating, and she had finished her own cup of coffee, she had a glimmer of an idea how she might proceed. First, she had to get Becky and David out of the house.

Before she had decided exactly how to manage that, David went into the living room, and his shout startled her.

"Hey! What happened to the television?"

Becky and Shannon exchanged silent glances. A moment later David burst into the kitchen, the swinging door squeaking back and forth until it finally settled.

"It just fell," Shannon said. "It probably was not properly balanced."

"Well, what are we going to do?"

"Without television?" Shannon smiled. "We aren't that dependent on it, are we?" An idea struck her suddenly. "Why don't the two of you ride over to the village and see if there's a rental place there?"

"Shouldn't we call first?"

"But it's such a lovely day, it would be more fun to ride over."

David shrugged and leaned on the table near Becky. "Want to?"

Becky had been playing idly with the peelings of her orange, sticking her thumb nail in to create a series of half-moons, bringing all the little half-moons together eventually to form a face. It was a couple of minutes before she put the peeling aside and looked up.

"It might be fun," she said. "What are you and Barry going to do, Shannon?"

"Oh, we'll think of something."

Shannon hoped that Barry wouldn't object at both his sister and brother leaving, at being left alone for the first time with her. He went with her to the porch to watch them ride away, and made no comment on their leaving. To her relief, he seemed content to be alone with her.

"Shall we go up to your room, Barry, and make your bed?"

Without answering, he turned and ran ahead of her, through the kitchen and living area and up the stairs. There were a few toys scattered about on his bedroom floor, and she suggested that he help clean up his room by putting the toys away, keeping out only the ones he wanted to play with today. He obediently complied, tossing the toys into the box in the closet.

Shannon made the bed, and straightened the throw rugs. But the object she was looking for was gone. She finally had to ask him for it. "Where's your book, Barry? The one you draw in."

Immediately he scrambled underneath the bed, and brought it out and handed it up to her.

"Why did you put it there?" she asked.

"I wanted to," he said.

A streak of sunlight patterned the floor by the window, cutting in somehow through the foliage of the trees. It would last only a few moments, Shannon was sure, but it was a friendly invitation to sit. She pulled a rug into the golden spots and sat down on the floor and opened the book.

"Barry, we—" She stopped, seeing that he had almost totally obliterated the drawings of the boy and the animal. "Oh. You've destroyed them. Why did you do that?"

"Because they're not my best friends anymore."

"Oh really? Why not?"

Barry hunched his shoulders up and let them fall, in a shrug much like his older brother's. He didn't answer verbally.

Shannon turned the page of the book. His creation of the horned, spidery thing had not been marked over.

"I see your monster is still in good shape," she said, hoping to start him talking again. But he didn't answer.

Shannon closed the book and laid it on the bed. She held out her hands, an invitation for him to come into her arms. Although he stepped closer, he stopped again, still out of her reach. She was pleased that he had made the one step.

"Barry, I want to talk to you about Juno and Reid. Will you tell me about them?"

His head lowered until his chin was resting on his chest. His arms hung limp at his sides. "They're not my friends anymore."

"Why aren't they your friends?"

"Because they kill."

"They kill?"

"Yes."

"Who did they kill?"

"The man in the car."

Shannon's breath caught in her throat. She tried to remember if anything had been said in front of Barry. "What car, Barry? What man?"

She saw his lips purse tightly together. But she couldn't let him go silent on her now.

"Barry, how do you know this?"

Barry didn't answer. She could almost feel his withdrawal. In another minute he would turn away, huddle into his corner and refuse to come out. She had to change her questioning.

"Barry, when Juno and Reid first became your friends—do you remember that?"

He looked up. His eyes had an open, eager look. His lips dropped slightly apart. He nodded.

"You played together a lot then, didn't you?"

"Yes." He laughed. "Reid and Juno came through the walls."

"When did they first come through the walls?"

He frowned faintly, trying to remember, it seemed. "They always came through walls," he said softly, as if talking to himself.

"Where did they come from, Barry?"

His face took on a thoughtful look. The frown etched itself deeper into his brow.

"When you drew their pictures," Shannon urged, "did you already know what they looked like?"

"No. *She* helped me."

"She?"

Suddenly Barry whirled away. His hands flew stiffly out as if holding something away. They shook violently. He began to cry. "No, no, no."

"Barry? Barry!" She reached out for him, but at her touch he fell to the floor, his head down almost between his feet, and he huddled there in an incredibly small knot, his arms over his head, his cry going on and on.

"No. No. No."

She waited, feeling helpless, feeling also cruel that she had been the cause of this anguish. Her heart ached for him. He needed to be held by someone who loved him, and her arms reached for him instinctively, daring to go against directions from his psychiatrist. She picked him up bodily and pulled him onto her lap. She bent over and around him, holding him securely. He struggled, his body stiffening. She caught a glimpse of his eyes, and they looked glazed and terrified, like the eyes of a cornered animal. She began to croon soothingly, half in tears herself, but she held to him, her arms surrounding his struggling body.

"It's all right, Barry baby, I won't hurt you. Listen to me, Barry, let me tell you about the friends you have, the friends who won't betray you."

He grew still, relaxing gradually on her lap. It seemed to Shannon that he at last began leaning against her, but her arms were so tightly around him she realized she might be indulging in wishful thinking. But at least he was still, and he was listening.

"Your daddy is your best friend," Shannon said. "And Becky and David. They're your most faithful friends. And I'm your friend, too, Barry."

His head leaned against her shoulder. His breath was warm and soft on her neck.

"We will always be your friends, all of us. We play games with you too, sometimes, don't we?"

His head nodded. But then, as if he realized how close he was to her, he drew away. She let him go without restraint. He was calm now, and the fear was mostly gone from his eyes. They had crossed a barrier. He wouldn't panic now at her touch.

But there were things she had to know, and she wondered how she could further question him without both of them feeling it was a betrayal.

"We're going to play a game now, Barry," she said, getting up and going to a drawer in the chest. She pulled it out and got two pairs of his socks. "Would you like to play puppets? With socks? When I was a little girl, we made puppets out of our socks. Like this."

She sat down on the floor again, her legs crossed. She gave him one pair of the socks and put the other two glove-like on her hands. She curled her fingers down, wiggling them open and shut as she made a voice for the puppet.

"My name is Susie," she said in a falsetto, trying to sound like a little girl, and thinking to herself that only a very imaginative child would accept her effort, "I don't think I know you. What's your name?"

"Barry," he said, talking soberly to the make-shift puppet.

"I'm a puppet. Are you a puppet too?"

"No. I'm a boy."

"I have a puppet friend, his name is Bozo." Shannon lifted her other hand and coiled her fingers into a mouth. She lowered her voice and said huskily, "Hi. I'm Bozo."

Barry's eyes flicked to the new puppet. He began to smile. Suddenly eager to join the game, he stuffed his hands into his pair of socks, held them up, and wiggled the toes of the socks as he spoke.

"I'm Reid and I'm Juno. But Juno can't talk."

"Is Juno a boy?"

"No, Juno's an animal. A magic animal. He's got a long, long tail that's very, very strong. And he can go through walls just like Reid."

"Is Reid an animal too?"

"No, Reid's a boy. But he's a magic boy, a strong boy, and he can do anything . . . he can . . . he . . ." The pleasure had gone out of Barry's face. A terrible sadness replaced the light. Abruptly he jerked the socks off his hands and threw them down. He sat looking at the two crumpled little heaps that lay between his spread legs. They were white cotton with three blue stripes around the top.

Shannon wanted to withdraw from the game, take Barry's hand and go outside and walk down to the lake, perhaps, or turn his attention toward his playground of roads and towns down by the side of the porch. But to give up now was perhaps the worst thing she could do, for both Barry, and the family.

In her girl's voice, but softer, she said, "How long have you known Reid and Juno?"

Barry shook his head. "I don't know."

Shannon felt that would be the end of their communication about this mysterious pair, but suddenly Barry was talking again.

"They went to school with me. They were borned at school. In the black room, with black candles burning, they came up out of smoke."

Shannon frowned. Workings of the occult at his school? As well as the other hideous, destructive happenings?

"Miss Bea . . ." he said, almost as if he had become hypnotized. He stared at the white face of the puppet. "Miss Bea . . . said they would always be my best friends. And that's why Reid's face was like mine. Because . . ." He sighed, a long expelling of breath. His body bowed, slumping.

Shannon felt it was time to draw away. Just one more, question. One crucial question.

"Where are they now, Barry?"

He sighed again. There was no answer. He acted as if he were exhausted.

"Barry," Shannon said softly, lowering her hands, pulling the socks off. "Where are Reid and Juno now?"

He looked up at her as if he had forgotten she was there. Some animation returned to his face. "I don't know," he said. Then again he said, "I don't know where they are."

CHAPTER 19

THAT AFTERNOON, quite late, Shannon finally received a call from Ramon. She had tried calling on and off all day, but he had been unavailable. His secretary didn't know precisely where he was; he had left hurriedly early that morning after a phone call, saying only that he didn't know when he would be back.

At five-thirty the phone rang, and Shannon knew instantly that it was Ramon. She had been waiting within hearing distance of the phone, knowing that his secretary would give him the message that she had called as soon as she could contact him.

"Is something wrong?" he asked immediately.

"Yes there is," she said. "First, let me assure you the kids are okay. They're all outside right now. Becky and David are trying to teach Barry how to ride a bike. It looks as if Barry's having fun. And there has been some progress. Barry let me hold him for awhile today."

"That's great. It all sounds great. What could be so wrong then?"

"I hesitate to even try to tell you. You're going to think I'm crazy. But, well, I might as well get it over. The thing is, we've got something very weird going on here, Ramon. I'm pretty sure it was the main problem that Jason had, and it caused Edna to pack up and leave yesterday. It . . . I don't know how to say it and . . . but — " She paused, feeling as if she were walking a tightrope between two worlds. At that moment she had a glimpse of the difficulty Barry had in communicating what he knew to someone who would find it impossible to believe. She decided to stop her stammering and tell it, all of it, before he had a chance to interrupt her.

She told him of Becky's conversation and theories. She told him of Edna's experiences and beliefs. And at last she told him of her talk with Barry.

She added, "I think we should leave here and come home, and take Barry back to his doctor. I don't know what else to do. Also, I tried to call Lynn, and there's no answer. I think there should be some investigation there. I'm worried. More than that, Ramon, I'm terrified."

There was silence on the line. She wondered if she had lost him.

"I don't like telling you this now, Shannon," he finally said, with obvious effort, "but Lynn and the boys have been found. Their car went over the mountainside into a canyon. They're all dead. I was called this morning to identify them. Lynn's husband is on a business trip, and hasn't been located yet." He drew an audible breath and his voice strengthened. "Why don't you just hang on there, and I'll be there as soon as I can. I'll leave straight from here. I'm in San Bernardino. Get the kids in bed early so you and I can talk. If any of that is even remotely true I don't want you and the kids driving alone down those mountain roads. It . . ." he paused. "It might explain what caused Lynn's car to go over the edge. She's a good driver, and there apparently was no other traffic, no ice or slippery pavement."

When Shannon hung up the phone she felt as if she had cut off their final connection to the world that lay beyond the horror that was now gradually enclosing them. She went to the door and looked out, to assure herself the voices she heard really belonged to the children and they were still quite happily working at trying to teach Barry to ride their bicycles.

Now that she had only to wait, she wished they could replace the television. It would be something to keep their minds occupied. But the kids had come back from the village with the announcement that no rental agency existed. If they wanted a television, they would have to buy one.

Well, they weren't going to buy a new television set just for one evening's entertainment. But there was something else they could do to pass a few hours.

Shannon got her purse from the hall rack where it hung by its strap, and put it over her shoulder. She went out onto the porch. The kids were all three walking along the lane toward the back of the house. Becky and David were pushing their bikes. They were talking, their voices clear in the evening air.

"Are you putting your bikes away now?" Shannon called as she went down the steps.

"Yes," Becky answered. "The next time we come up here we'll have to bring Barry's own bicycle. He can almost ride ours."

"They're just a little too big," David said. "He's pretty good on Becky's though, because it doesn't have a cross bar."

Shannon said, "How would you like to go over to the village for dinner?"

"Hey, great!" David said.

"Okay," Becky said. "Now?"

"Yes, now."

Barry came running back, and Shannon held open the back door for him. He scrambled up and into the back seat and buckled himself in.

Shannon stood by the side of the car and waited for Becky and David. She looked up at the front of the log lodge. Her window reflected the green boughs that brushed against it. The perpetual shade had deepened, edging now toward night. The house had been quiet all day. There had been no appearances from their strange companions. Nothing had happened since the vandalism of the kitchen before dawn this morning. At this time it seemed so remote that it was almost unbelievable that it had happened at all. But she would be glad to get away.

When Becky and David were settled in the car, Shannon strapped herself in and turned the switch. Nothing happened.

There was not even the click of a dead battery. Shannon exchanged puzzled glances with David and Becky.

A sudden burst of irrational fear made Shannon almost supernaturally aware of their helplessness. The shadows under the trees had increased by several degrees in the last few moments. The wind from the lake had grown cold. It tossed the lower boughs of the trees and whistled through the tops in diverse, clashing notes. The music it made was the music of demons.

She knew what she would find when she looked under the hood, but she released the catch that held it down and got out of the car. At the front of the car, with her fingers hooked under the hood, she looked at the faces of the children. The windshield laid streaks of light and darkness across their features. Barry had stretched up, his head lifted, so that he could see her. The faces of Becky and David were twin studies in anxiety. Shannon was suddenly aware of the change in David. Since they had come back from the village, he had been subdued in spirit. His usual boisterousness was lacking. She knew that Becky had told him what she had seen and her theories about it. Now, looking through the glass at her, the fear in his face made him look young, almost as young as Barry.

Shannon released the hook with her fingers and pushed the hood up. It took her eyes another moment to adjust to the darkness. She didn't know a lot about engines, but anyone could have seen the damage. Wires were torn loose, and hoses ripped out and shredded. The air filter had been removed. The rest was a dark mass of shadows, and the odor of gas drifted up like fog.

She left the hood up.

"Come on," she said to the kids. "We have to go back into the house and make some phone calls."

They came without questions. They were all going back into the lodge, and Shannon saw now that she had forgotten to leave a light on. When they had come out of the house a few minutes ago, the house was still light. Darkness had filled it now as if it were in alliance with the demons in the trees, and together, for their masters, they were striving to trap the insignificant humans.

Shannon hesitated at the door, dreading to open it. She heard the footsteps of the children behind her, Barry last, coming up the steps and across the porch. Shannon took the key out of her purse.

She reached in and turned on the light. The first thing she saw was the television, still face down on the floor. It hadn't occurred to her before that she should put it upright again.

The children followed her into the house, quietly, staying close.

At the partial wall created by the rise of the stairs was a small telephone table. The local telephone book was in a drawer just under the top of the table. But instead of taking out the book and looking up the numbers she needed, Shannon lifted the phone to her ear.

They had done their work well, as she had intuitively known. The phone was dead. The wire from the telephone into the wall was intact. The damage was somewhere else. Perhaps in the telephone itself. She put it down and turned toward the children.

"We can't call the garage. The phone isn't in working order."

Words burst suddenly from both Becky and David.

"We can ride our bicycles—"

"Barry can ride with me, and you can ride with Becky."

"We could even walk! It's only a couple of miles."

And there were neighbors, Shannon thought, a few blocks away, their houses hidden by the trees. But were the owners there yet? And even if they were, what could they do? Would the four of them be allowed to leave the lodge? There was Ken Masters' accident as a reminder, and Jason's. And what had happened to Lynn and both boys?

There was also the falling darkness.

And Ramon.

They could leave him a note and tell him where they had gone, but the thought of him coming alone into this place terrified her.

"Your dad is coming," Shannon told them. "We'll wait here for him. And while we wait, we'll eat supper, and we'll play a game of Trivial Pursuit. And then I want the three of you to get into my bed and go to sleep. And when you wake up in the morning your daddy will be here with us."

CHAPTER 20

"Barry. Barry."

Barry woke up, the sound of his name trailing away and becoming a part of the rising and drifting music in the tall trees. He sat up, blinking in the dim light of the strange room. At first he didn't know where he was, or who was in bed with him. He was wedged warmly between two sleeping bodies, and he recognized Becky's hair on the pillow at his left. She was facing away from him, as was David. Now he remembered. They were in the big bed in Shannon's room. It was still night, and there were no sounds except the moaning of the wind.

Where was Shannon?

"Barry. Come play with us."

No. Barry inched down into bed, leaving only his eyes to peer out above the covers. "*Go away, I don't want to play with you anymore.*"

"Barry. Barry."

The voice came from downstairs. It pierced the walls as easily as ribbons unwinding, as easily as their bodies passing through.

Where was Shannon?

Were they going to hurt Shannon?

Barry eased himself up from beneath the covers until he was sitting on the pillows. Neither Becky nor David stirred. He could hear them breathing, softly, evenly. Becky's breathing was even softer than David's.

When his feet were out of the blankets, Barry crawled on his hands and knees down the middle of the bed and across the foot. He climbed out over the footboard and stood listening. There was nothing, not even the wind now. And then . . .

"Barry. Hurry Barry."

Barry went to the door, opened it, and stepped out into the hall. There was nothing here either, just the chair against the wall beyond the drop in the stairs. He closed the bedroom door.

He went silently to the head of the stairs and looked down. Lights were on in the living room, but there was no voice. Not even Reid's voice called out to him.

He went down the stairs, one step at a time, hesitating with each step, listening. Finally, he heard murmurs. And then again there was silence. He went down the remainder of the stairs faster, not hesitating. At the foot of the stairs he saw that the door to the den was open, and he stopped at the threshold, and looked in.

His dad and Shannon were standing in the middle of the room with their arms around each other. They were close, their faces together. They didn't see the danger they were in.

Juno was crouched on the desk, ready to spring. His tail coiled and uncoiled upon his back, the tip twitching like the tail of a rattlesnake. Saliva hung in red drops on his pointed chin, and glistened in his long whiskers. He was waiting for the signal from Reid.

Reid stood on the other side of the room, almost in the wall. His face had changed and had grown into the distorted face Barry had seen in the man's car. The center of his face bulged out, growing like Juno's, with his nose and teeth prominent. His eyes glittered. He had been waiting for Barry. His hands were thrust out, making daggers of his long, strong fingers. His nails had grown sharp and dangerous. He saw Barry had come to his bidding, and he began to move closer to the embracing couple.

"No!" Barry screamed, and his dad broke away from Shannon, although they were still touching, and both stunned faces looked at him.

As if they still didn't know about the others.

Suddenly Juno leaped. His weasel-like body struck the back of Ramon's head, and his tail coiled like a wire around Shannon's neck. They fell to the floor. Reid came forward, his tongue extended in excitement, his eyes reflecting the bodies on the floor. And Barry knew, they were going to kill his daddy and Shannon.

He began to fight them, his small hands pounding futilely at Juno's writhing body, at Reid's strength.

SHANNON WAS CHOKING. HER HANDS CLAWED AT THE TIGHT BAND around her neck, and felt that it was like a thin rope. She managed to loosen it, and felt it slither away. She opened her eyes and saw the animal's face, its long muzzle dripping saliva, its sharp teeth going for Ramon's throat. She cried out, and Ramon rolled away. Hands were lifting her, slamming her back again to the floor, and lifting her again. Her head roared with pain. Into her line of vision came a face that she knew was Reid's, but it was only vaguely like Barry's now. The forehead was his, and the pale hair. The mouth snarled at her, and she drew back in a paroxysm of fear.

She heard Barry's voice crying out, *"No, no, don't hurt my mommy and daddy. No, no,"* and she tried to answer, to tell him to run, run, to get his sister and brother and get out of the house. *Run.*

As if he had heard her heart screaming at him to run, Barry turned and fled. She saw him go out of the room and turn toward the staircase.

But would it do any good? Could they ever get away from this vicious, unbelievable pair? No, they couldn't. They couldn't.

She began to weep hopelessly.

Suddenly the atmosphere changed. She was no longer being held to the floor, no longer tossed and battered like a rag doll. She sat up and saw that Ramon was lying limp and unconscious, face down. There were long, bloody scratches on his cheek, and animal bites on his neck. She bent over him, calling his name. He moved, turned his face toward her, opened his eyes. And then he stared at something beyond her.

Shannon turned.

Barry stood framed in the doorway, and surrounding him was a quivering, moving, web-like entity. It oozed into the room, rising against the ceiling like warm air, endless, coiling, shadowy webs, and within it the horns and eyes became visible. Shannon recognized it. The third drawing in Barry's book. As if it had lain waiting, it now had come to life and was moving at his command into the room, filling the corners, covering the walls. Numerous small eyes, like the black, jeweled eyes of black widow spiders, glared out from the black web, moving slowly and inexorably in to fill the room. Only the center was left open, and somewhere within it Shannon heard a choked, inhuman cry. She looked around. The body of the animal, of Juno, had been caught into the web and was struggling helplessly, while the other, the tall, strong boy with the face that once had been like Barry's, was trying to get away. As Shannon watched, the eyes in the web leaped, like spiders gathering upon their prey, and surrounded him.

Their bodies began to lose substance as they became helplessly entangled in the web, where within were mouths that sucked their inner juices like insects being devoured by a huge spider. The flesh of the boy collapsed and shriveled, the arms and legs drooping like deflated balloons, the head falling sideways, flat and nearly featureless. The animal became a skin of rough fur dangling within the web. The creature moved and stirred within itself, and spun tight cocoons around the empty skin. It began drawing up into the corner of the room, a tight web pulling itself in, and disappearing into a crack in the walls.

Shannon realized she was on her hands and knees in the center of the room. She was intensely nauseated. She started to stand up, and she turned and Barry came into her vision.

He was standing just inside the room. He was totally calm now, every movement made in silent determination.

He was holding something in his hands.

His book.

He was tearing pages out, one after the other, and ripping them into small shreds. First the page on which the picture of Juno had been drawn, and then the page of Reid.

And then, as if finishing forever, he ripped out the page of his monster and calmly shredded it.

He dropped the book. And then he looked up, and Shannon saw his chin quiver and his eyes fill with tears. Suddenly he was running, hard, straight toward her, his arms out.

She almost fell backwards when Barry lunged into her arms. He clasped her around the neck, his tears warm on her cheek as he pressed against her.

Beside them Ramon sat up.

Shannon turned slightly, her eyes searching the room. The webs, the shriveled bodies, the eyes, those many, hard, round; black eyes, were gone.

As if they had never been at all, they were gone.

EPILOGUE

SHANNON AND RAMON sat at the kitchen table. The end of the night, the darkest night either of them could remember, pulsed with the memory of what they had seen in the den. They weren't talking much. They were drinking their third pot of coffee and waiting for the dawn to come. Shannon looked past Ramon as often as she looked at him, her eyes searching the east window for a suggestion of light beyond. They had thought about getting the kids into the car and getting away from the lodge in the middle of the night, but David and Becky were sleeping so soundly, and Barry had wilted, afterwards . . . after the things in the den were gone . . . as if he were exhausted. They had decided to put him back to bed between his brother and sister, and let them finish the night in peace.

"It's incredible," Ramon said, his voice low as if he were afraid of awakening more than the children. "Where did they come from? Were they materializations from Barry, or were they our own illusions?"

Shannon couldn't answer that. The cup she was holding, beginning to lift again to her lips, rattled against the saucer. She steadied her hand. Her stomach felt as though it were aquiver too, like her chin, her hands, her skin, even her scalp. Although she had watched the horrible manifestations disappear, until even the shadow in the corner had gone, she was still terrified. Not until they were out of the house would she feel that somehow that black, consuming web was not there, behind her, growing again to fill the room. And the others, Reid and Juno, could they be so entirely gone?

"It sucked the substance of them," she whispered, staring at the black window for a touch of pink light beyond the trees. "It was like a spider, reducing them to nothing, but—but skin? Whatever they were made of."

"Madness," he said. "It didn't happen. If we don't look at it that way, we'll go insane. There are some things the mind can't stand. I don't think I want to know any more about it. I just want to take you and the kids and go home. I want to marry you, Shannon. I want you to live with us. I don't want to be without you."

She saw a flash of tenderness in his eyes as he looked at her for a brief moment, then he looked over his shoulder at the east window. "It's getting light," he said. He pushed his chair away from the table. The legs, squeaking against the floor, seemed to shout and echo through the house, and Shannon thought she heard an answering sound from upstairs, a low thunder that was more felt than heard, a vibration of something moving through the walls. Ramon seemed not to be aware of it. He got up. "By the time we get everything ready to go, the sun will be up. We can get a mechanic to come over from the village to get the station wagon going. I'd rather we all went down in the same car, but I see no way around one of us taking one and the other driving the other one. I don't think I'll feel at ease until we're all back down in the valley, even though I know there's nothing to hurt anyone."

Shannon wished she could feel so sure. The window was still obstinately dark, no matter how hard she strained to see the dawn Ramon had seen. She closed her eyes briefly, and there it was when she looked again, something like a faint forest fire far, far away, the touch of the dawn coming, the liberation from this dark night of terror.

They went upstairs together, holding hands. Her fingers gripped his hard palm like a child's frozen in fear. Although every light in the house was on, she was seeing shadows again. *Imagining* shadows again, she told herself.

The children were still asleep, tangled like a pile of kittens. Ramon leaned over the bed.

"David. Becky. Wake up. Time to get up and get ready to go. We'll let Barry sleep awhile longer."

"Barr-ry."

Barry opened his eyes and looked around the strange room. He woke slowly, like coming up out of a dream. He remembered where he was, whose bed he was in. But he was alone now. David and Becky were gone. He could hear their voices below, and the slam of the screen door. From their conversation he knew they were carrying things out to the car. But who had called him? Reid and Juno were gone. Who had called him?

He climbed out of bed and went into the hall. He looked toward his old room at the end of the hall, where the light hardly came through, where even in the daytime the shadows were dark and threatening. He didn't want to go there anymore.

He heard his dad's voice downstairs.

"Did you get Barry up and get him dressed? We're ready to go."

No one answered him at first, then Becky said, "I'll go get him."

Barry started down the stairs. Becky came running up, her face pink and bright, her eyes happy. She grabbed him and swung him up into her arms.

"Hi, little brother. I've got to wash your face and brush your teeth. Your clothes are laid out in the bathroom. We're going home!"

Barry smiled. "Is Shannon going home with us?"

"Yes! And do you know what? She's going to stay with us. Forever and ever."

Becky took him into the girl's bathroom, and while she cleaned him up and dressed him he thought of Shannon in their home. Barry thought of all of them, together, and he listened to Becky's happy voice as she talked about all the things she was thinking of, about home, and family, and school, and how good it was going to be for them now.

But Barry began to wonder: *who had called his name when he* was *still sleeping?*

The station wagon was ready to go when they left the house. His suitcases were in the rack on top, and boxes of things were packed in the rear. Shannon was going to drive the station wagon.

"Where shall we ride?" Becky asked.

"Wherever you want," their dad said.

"I'll ride with Shannon," Barry said.

"And I'll go with Dad in the car."

Barry saw the front passenger seat in the station wagon was empty, and he climbed in, going across the seat beneath the steering wheel to sit by the window. Shannon leaned in smiling and pulled the seat belt down from above.

"Are you going to ride with me?"

"Yes."

Car doors slammed and motors started. Shannon drove slowly along the lane behind the other car. From his seat Barry could see only the top of the car ahead. The dark green limbs of the pine trees reached down into his view and brushed against the car windows as they passed by.

"Barry. . ."

Barry jerked against his seat belt and looked with terror at Shannon, but she only glanced a smile at him. Reid was gone, *Reid was gone . . .* yet his voice was calling. If Shannon hadn't heard him call, he was still there, after all. But Shannon was glancing at Barry again, still smiling, beginning now to look puzzled.

"Aren't you going to answer, Barry?" she asked.

Barry stared at her, unable to speak.

"Your brother is talking to you, Barry," she said.

Barry pushed his thumb against the seat belt button and it snapped away from him, freeing him in the seat. He got on his knees and looked into the back of the station wagon.

In the back seat, alone, David sat. His face was the same as it had been, except the eyes. The color hadn't changed, but something in their depths had. They glittered at Barry laughing silently.

"Barry," the voice said. "Aren't you glad we're going home?"

Barry was frozen to the back of his seat, his hands gripping the top, his eyes staring into the eyes that should belong to David, but no longer did.

"Barry, Barry," the voice said, and Shannon smiled again at Barry, because she could hear the voice and she thought it was David's.

"Turn around and fasten your seat belt, Barry," he said. "We're going home."

Barry stared into the eyes. He saw Reid there, laughing at him, because he had won after all.

Shannon said, "Listen to your brother, Barry. He wants to be sure you get home safely."

Barry turned around, slid down into the seat, and pulled the belt into place again.

Shannon's hand, cool and gentle, patted his where it rested on his thigh. "Everything is fine now, sweetheart," she said. "We're going home."

OTHER NOVELS BY RUBY JEAN JENSEN

1974 The House that Samael Built
1974 Seventh All Hallows' Eve
1974 House at River's Bend
1975 The Girl Who Didn't Die
1978 Child of Satan's House
1978 Satan's Sister
1978 Dark Angel
1982 Hear the Children Cry
(as R.J. Hendrickson)
1982 Such a Good Baby
1983 The Lake (as R.J. Jensen)
1983 MaMa
1985 Home Sweet Home
1986 Wait and See
1987 Annabelle
1987 Chain Letter
1988 Smoke
1988 House of Illusions
1988 Jump Rope

OTHER NOVELS BY RUBY JEAN JENSEN

1989 Pendulum
1989 Death Stone
1990 Vampire Child
1990 Lost and Found
1990 Victoria
1991 Celia
1991 Baby Dolly
1992 The Reckoning
1993 The Living Evil
1994 The Haunting
1995 Night Thunder
Pending Bear Hollow Charlie
Pending Cry of the Soul
Pending Pride of Bella Terra
PendingAnimal Backtalk

www.ingramcontent.com/pod-product-compliance
Lightning Source LLC
Chambersburg PA
CBHW020610310726
48979CB00008B/1420/J

* 9 7 8 1 9 5 1 5 8 0 1 9 3 *